T0247853

ONLY THE GUILTY SURVIVE

Also available by Kate Robards

The Three Deaths of Willa Stannard

ONLY THE GUILTY SURVIVE

A THRILLER

KATE ROBARDS

CROOKED LANE

NEW YORK

Published in the United States by Crooked Lane Books, an imprint of The Quick Brown Fox & Company LLC.

Crooked Lane Books and its logo are trademarks of The Quick Brown Fox & Company LLC.

Library of Congress Catalog-in-Publication data available upon request.

ISBN (hardcover): 978-1-63910-951-7
ISBN (ebook): 978-1-63910-952-4

Cover design by Aarushi Menon

Printed in the United States.

www.crookedlanebooks.com

Crooked Lane Books
34 West 27th St., 10th Floor
New York, NY 10001

First Edition: August 2024

10 9 8 7 6 5 4 3 2 1

To Darren, my best friend and
greatest supporter

PROLOGUE

Claire

Then

I HEAR THE RELENTLESS chittering of the birds first.

The robins, the chickadees, the blue jays. Their chorus hammers into my head, and I wonder why they're so loud. Then I realize: it's because everything else is silent.

But silence shouldn't exist here, and that's when I know something is wrong. The cacophony of the birds and the eerie quiet of the defunct nature sanctuary force me to sit up. I'd been savoring the solitude, slipping into a nap like a cat in a sunny alcove of the naturalist's old cottage. I don't normally sleep in the cottage, but after Lollie went missing, Dom and the others made room for me.

I peer out the window, but the mature trees obscure my view. Outside, the porch is empty of girls with long ragged hair and dirt-flecked feet. Their names would sound foreign from my mouth even though I've lived here for months, so I don't call out to them. With Lollie gone, I'm alone again. But fifteen other people still live here, and they rarely leave the Bird Haven.

My bare feet sink just slightly into the ground, which is still damp from last night's rain. We didn't need it; the lake's already too high for this time of the season.

They could be bathing in the lake. The shoreline smells of rot and decay and it's hard to feel clean after wading into the foamy water, but the old cottage's bathroom doesn't support so many people.

I don't hear any shouts or giggles, and Eden is always so loud. Closer to the road is the detached garage. I decide to check for the vans. Maybe they left the grounds without me. It's easy to imagine when you know you're easy to forget. I feel the familiar prickle of shame and loneliness in my chest as I approach the steel building.

Weedy, untamed brush tickles my ankles. The roll-up door is down. I jiggle the handle. Locked, just like the side door to the garage.

I follow the path to the lake and check there for the Flock. It's quiet, and so is the brook and the viewing deck. By late afternoon, I take one cucumber from the vegetable patch, deciding it's the least likely to be missed when the girls return, hungry and accusatory.

At dusk, I'm sweaty with nerves and the shame of abandonment as I locate the key to the garage in the kitchen. I move quickly and worry about Dom's uncanny knowingness, wondering if I'll be punished for questioning a plan I didn't know he had. I have to know if they took both vans. I need to see how much gas is left in the can, to know how far they can go without me and when they'll return.

The mosquitoes are out now, swarming my sticky, unwashed legs. Night's gathering fast in the shady nooks under the trees. I don't hurry to the garage.

A bony rabbit's foot dangles from the key ring. I try four keys, and the last one works. Before I push open the door, I notice that the sparrows and the starlings are loudest here. All the birds, it seems, talk over one another, just like the girls in the Flock.

I hear the low hum as I open the door. Both vans, idling inside. The glare from the headlights reflects off the wall. How long have they been here?

I reach for the passenger door nearest me, and it swings open easily. There's no one in the driver's seat, so I crawl in and peer into the back.

It's Eden I see first. Her corkscrew curls are caked with vomit and her eyes are open. I whisper her name, which still feels strange on my lips. She'll be mad I saw her like this.

Then I see the others. They swell and recede as my vision blurs at the edges. My fingers dig into the seat to steady me.

Lido. Sunny. Helena. Thomas. Morgan. Faith.

Ashy and bloated and foaming at the mouth. Propped up with secured seat belts.

I jolt backward and stumble from the van. My head's pounding, but I look to the other van. It's then I see a hose snaked from the exhaust pipe to the window and a strip of tape securing the opening.

They're huddled together in this van. No seat belts, just a heap of bodies. The twins. Goldie and Hunter, arms entwined. Jock's eyes are open, but Vinny's are closed. I recognize Raina's hair but not much else.

When I stumble from the garage, it's pitch-black dark and the birds have finally stopped, replaced by crickets and bullfrogs. But now I hear the idling vans too. My head swims.

The Flock is dead.

But where's Dom?

Part 1

C H A P T E R

1

Claire

Now

IT'S THE WAY he walks into the foyer, like the library owes him something, like we all do, that catches my attention. His hair is shorter, his eyes darker, even from a distance. But the uptilt of his chin and that eyebrow raised in appraisal are too familiar.

After all these years. Is it Dom?

If anyone would strut into my workplace after ten years in hiding, it's him.

But no. I catch his eye by mistake and look down quickly. He spots the opening and approaches the desk. I toy with the computer mouse and click into the last patron's checkout record, just to look busy.

"Point me to your section of content on the Flock," he says without waiting for me to look up.

My head darts to study him, up close this time. He's taller than Dom, and I can tell he thinks he's charming too. But he's too young to be Dom. I place him somewhere in his midtwenties, when Dom would be nearly forty by now.

"The Flock?"

"Yeah, the cult. Mass suicide, big news around here, I'm sure. I take it you've heard of them?"

I purse my lips and look away. "Mmm. We don't have a section about them. I'm sorry."

"What about articles from the *Daily News*? There must have been so many at the time. I looked online but couldn't find digitized copies. Where's your archive?"

I should point him to Lourdes so she can help him with the clunky microfiche machine, a relic from another century. But I don't know that I can trust even her, so I paste a smile onto my face in hopes of transforming it into something different from any photos he might find. I step out from behind the counter.

"Over here," I say, pointing the man to the machine. I inch away, ready to fade like a shadow.

"So, Iola's got the one paper, but I'll look at neighboring towns for coverage as well. Starting on September fourteenth, 2012."

I startle. Not the day the Flock died. The day Lollie went missing.

"Help me narrow it down?" He offers a smile as an afterthought.

"I should be getting back to the desk," I murmur.

He laughs, the sound softer than I expected. "If someone comes in, by all means, help them." He gestures back to the microfiche and stacks of film.

He's not wrong. It's summer, and Iola is a college town. There's no one in the library today, and I'll be lucky if one or two elderly townspeople saunter in to beat the heat this afternoon. It's dead quiet.

"I'm Arlo, by the way."

"Nice to meet you," I offer as I reach up to unfurl my coiled hair, brushing it—surreptitiously, I hope—over my name tag. I curl my shoulders inward, trying to make myself smaller.

With shaking hands, I demonstrate how to load the film and scroll through the pages. A futile need to conceal my involvement in the Flock drives me to tell him that the magnifying feature is broken and the slides may not be much help. But he clicks through the app, zooms, and scans content with a practiced ease.

"Seems to be working fine," he says, still standing. I'm uncomfortably aware he's using his height to exert dominance over me. My old therapist was always quick to point out just how easily I let myself be manipulated by men's body language.

"How long have you been a librarian here?" he asks, distracted. He's flipping through pages so fast I can't imagine how he can even see the content.

I'm not a librarian. My dad enrolled me at a backup school after my top-choice college rejected me, but I dropped out after a single semester that showed me how deeply broken I was, even before the deaths. I don't have a degree. I work part-time at the library's circulation desk and refer all the questions to Lourdes, who took the job just to get away from her twin toddlers for a few hours.

"A few years," I say vaguely, edging further from Arlo.

He stops the reader abruptly and zooms in, eyes darting as he scans the screen. Looking for Lollie.

"You must be asked about the suicide all the time. Curious college kids and reporters on the anniversary, I bet. I'm no different," he laughs. "But I'm going deeper than them. Think Susan Wade's book, but ten more years of facts than she had when she wrote about the Flock."

"You're writing a book?"

I've shelved Susan Wade's book countless times. It's one of the only books the library has reordered and replaced because the copy in circulation got too tatty. There's a black-and-white picture of me, pale haired and rangy, in the center of Susan's book. The cover is dedicated to Dom, of course.

"No, no one reads anymore. No offense," he tosses over his shoulder, sensing the blasphemy of knocking books in a library. "I'm a podcaster. It's the only way to reach an audience with a story. I have a new series coming out. The trailer's out now, and the first episode drops next week."

My thumb finds its way to my mouth on instinct. A habit from my past.

"Oh. So, like a book on tape," I say.

He turns. A hint of an inquisitive smile plays at his lips.

"Think of a true-crime writer as a historian. They're documenting what already happened. A podcaster—a good one—gets his hands dirty to tell the story. The Flock's suicide and Laurel Tai's murder, it's all unsolved. There's so much opportunity."

"Opportunity to what? Solve it?"

Arlo's trendy round glasses slide down his nose, but instead of pushing them up, he tilts his head back to keep my gaze. He drums his fingers near the computer mouse.

"Knock on doors," he says. "Talk to the teachers of the kids who joined the Flock, to the waitresses at the restaurants where Dominic Bragg might have eaten. Look at the place where Laurel was kidnapped. See how likely it was that the only surviving girl, the one who found them, didn't hear two running old-model vans in the freestanding garage." He turns back to the microfiche. "I'm going to figure out what we don't know yet, then broadcast it to my followers one episode at a time."

His arrogance is staggering, and that reminds me of Dom too. Who is he to think he can solve Laurel's murder and excise meaning behind my friends' deaths? After everything came to light, the investigations were extensive. The probe into Lollie's death was handled locally, but the FBI descended in Iola to collect evidence. Federal agents examined all twenty-two acres of the Bird Haven. There was a verified manhunt for Dom. His amber eyes lost some of their penetrating power when rendered in grayscale on the printouts that papered windows, storefronts, and lampposts all over town. Arbor State shut down campus for two days when the news broke, but co-eds returned nonplussed, ready to poke fun at their peers who were too "weak-minded" to know better than to join a cult. I was interviewed, of course, but between my significant memory gaps surrounding the trauma and my overly cautious lawyer, I didn't offer much information. I did little to unravel the chain of events and bring closure to the grieving families, but they could never make a case against me.

I excuse myself to return to the circulation desk. Without any new visitors, it's impossible to avoid the bright, questioning eyes of Lourdes as she tries to get my attention.

Across the library, she mouths something. "Who?"

I force a big-eyed shrug and turn, pretending to busy myself on the computer. I want to search on Arlo Stone, but I don't dare do it at the library.

When Susan Wade approached me for an interview all those years ago, she said she couldn't write the book without me. So I dodged her calls and drop-ins with the naïve hope of the nineteen-year-old I was. Hope that she'd drop the book if I didn't talk to her. She didn't, of course, and the book was released a few months later. Absent of any firsthand accounts, the book didn't rocket to popularity. It was a thin paperback with a sensationalist title: *Fatal Flock: The Untold Story of Cult Leader Dominic Bragg.*

Still, I've checked it in and out of the library so often I'm sure most people in Iola have read it once, if not twice. Me? I've never read it. The pain of what happened is already razor-sharp without me reading searing descriptions about my friends' deaths and what role I might have played in the downfall of what's been called a doomsday cult.

The truth is, I never thought of it as a cult. A commune, a spiritual group, a found family: for years, I used gentler terms, unwilling to admit I'd sacrificed my judgment and freedom in exchange for Dom's crumbling vision of utopia. It was, of course, a cult, and as the only survivor, I became little more than a campfire tale.

It doesn't help that I've never been able to articulate what happened in the weeks leading up to the Flock's demise. My memories are disorderly, the gaps substantial. I can't sequentially recount the events leading up to Lollie's kidnapping, the

discovery of her body, and the Flock's deaths. For a while, I saw a
therapist, and she said all this—the gaps, the jumbled memories,
and intrusive flashbacks—was to be expected. But she also said it
was dangerous to try to remember, that my mind was protecting
me. So I don't attempt to fill the gaps in my memory or recount
what happened. That means I've avoided reading *Fatal Flock* all
these years, despite its prevalence in town.

Susan Wade's book was just a symptom, really. The publicity
that came after the Flock's deaths was a sickness. The attention
was relentless, and so was the criticism.

How could I not have known they were planning a mass
suicide? they asked. Why didn't I warn anyone? If Dom was so
dangerous and conditions at the Bird Haven were so bad, why
did we stay?

They succeeded in heaping guilt on me, but they didn't ask
what I really wanted to know.

Why didn't they take me too?

*   *   *

After my shift, I circle around the tree-studded campus of the
university, past the shuttered cinema and Zink's Hardware on
Main Street. I drive down Depot Street to old 26, a road that
follows the spine of an 815-foot-high ridge between Iola and the
neighboring town of Lapeer.

It's notoriously picturesque, but I'm not here for the view. I
park at a pullout overlooking the rugged vistas. In the distance,
the lake is a deep blue basin.

It's here that I finally thumb through my phone, hoping for
a weak signal as I open my never-used podcast app and search
for Arlo Stone.

There: *Birds of a Feather*. I suck in my breath and tap the
play button. Slow, eerie piano music fills the car. Then engi-
neered static as audio clips from the news grow louder:

"Fourteen people dead after suspected instruction by charismatic cult leader Dominic Bragg . . ."

"Rumors had spread that the community at the abandoned bird sanctuary was no utopia . . ."

"Reports of a mysterious illness . . ."

"Kidnapping and murder of twenty-year-old Laurel Tai . . ."

"The Flock has flown the coop . . ."

I wince. It's just as humiliating and disrespectful as it was then.

The piano music returns and reaches a frantic crescendo.

"It didn't end with poison-laced drinks or a fiery shootout. It wasn't a violent death, but it wasn't pleasant either."

It's Arlo's voice, a vaguely southern accent flowing from the speaker.

"In 2012, fourteen members of the cult known as the Flock died in a mass suicide in northern Michigan. They died of asphyxiation from carbon monoxide poisoning at a site known as the Bird Haven, a former nature sanctuary where the cult lived in their final days."

The canned sound of birds chirping hammers into my head. I shake it off, remembering.

"The Flock's leader, Dominic Bragg, was never found despite a nationwide manhunt. It's been ten years, but there are still so many unanswered questions about what led to the Flock's demise."

"Why?" A plaintive woman's wail interrupts. "Why did they have to die? Why did he tell them to do this?"

"It's something that happened weeks before that could break this case open," Arlo says, returning to the microphone. "Three weeks before the mass suicide, longtime Flock member Laurel Tai went missing from her cabin at the Bird Haven."

Police sirens now, tinny and distant, in the background. I glance in the rearview mirror instinctually.

"Laurel, known simply as Lollie by her fellow cult members, was found dead by the river during the town's annual squirrel count. Autopsy findings pointed to strangulation as the cause of death. Beautiful but troubled, Laurel had recently gained the town's attention when she was crowned Apple Queen at the annual fall festival.

"This is *Birds of a Feather*. I'm your host, Arlo Stone, and I'm going to take a new approach to investigating what really happened to the Flock and the Apple Queen. Binge on this new limited series. New episodes will be released weekly."

The piano returns, unnervingly raising the hairs on my arms, then stops abruptly.

And I'm back in the car, not in the space I shared with Lollie at the Bird Haven. I never knew her as Laurel. Lollie, so warm and curious and free-spirited. If she hadn't been taken from our bed, the others would be still be alive. I'm sure of it. I wouldn't be teetering on the top of the world from my car listening to an intruder pick apart our choices.

My choices, a voice in my head whispers. It's my old therapist again, trying to break me of groupthink. *You're a "my," an "I" now. Not a "we," not an "our." You are your own person.*

I'm the only one left. It's me that Arlo will unravel.

CHAPTER

2

Laurel

Then

A RAINSTORM ROLLED IN overnight, driving us all together in the musty cottage. The Bird Haven, absent of clocks, enters into an endless night when the sun goes down. It's only when the driving wind and rain dampen our shared mattress in the weather-beaten shed that Claire and I emerge, dashing through craters of standing water. The summer's downpours have turned the Haven into a swampy mosquito breeding ground. While the constant, mania-inducing swarm of bugs leaves me yearning for the sanctuary of the cottage at times, I'm reluctant to spend time here.

Nearly a dozen Flock members are gathered in the living room when we enter. It must be close to two or three in the morning—it's hard to know, I never sleep anymore—but the room is filled with hushed singing and languid movements. Eden braids Faith's long hair, Lido strums a guitar, Sunny's top-less, and Hunter's hand is jammed inside a panting Goldie. I don't see Thomas, but he spends most nights in the old RV.

Dom is there, of course, sitting on the creaky wooden wheel-chair he found in the master bedroom of the cottage. A framed picture told me the ornithologist—Dom's great-uncle, I think—was confined to the turn-of-century antique later in life. Now, though the cane-backed chair dwarfs Dom's diminutive frame, he's somehow more intimidating when he creaks along in the vintage oak wheelchair.

Waving a dog-eared book, he calls Claire to his side when we enter. She settles at his feet, back hunched, wet pale hair dangling in her face, to read to him. I long to brush her hair behind her ear, but I don't dare interrupt while she's with Dom.

I settle beside Raina, who's petting a scruffy dog.

"Who's this?" I ask, reaching for its wavy coat. It reeks of more than just wet dog; I recognize the stink of an old, ailing dog from my childhood. It became infected, sick, without my dad around to care for it. I look at the unkempt dog panting in time with Goldie. Right at home, I think.

"A stray, can you believe it?" Raina burrows her face into its fur. "Way out here, and he found us. It's meant to be."

Everything is "meant to be" here. It's not just Raina who does it. We're all desperate to believe in something, so we assign significance to everything.

Morgan leans over Raina's scabby, unshaven legs.

"Lollie," she drolls. "Your aura is gold."

Raina's eyes open wide, and she nods vigorously. "Amber, it's amber! Like Dom's eyes," she says dreamily.

"Yes," Morgan says. "It's a sign." She starts singing, and the twins join in.

The girls begin swaying and the room heats up. Dom hushes Claire's monotonous reading and closes his eyes, freeing us from his impenetrable stare for a blissful moment.

From his straight-backed wheelchair, he intones, quietly at first, then gains momentum: "Look around. We're undefined, unrefined. We won't be confined. Finite and predefined, we're spinning into infinity in our coffins until the goldfinch sings his finale."

He repeats himself, louder each time. The girls sway, throwing their thin bodies into it. The damp room is pulsing as Dom chants his poetry. A roll of thunder unleashes a feverish intensity upon the Flock.

I sway too, with Dom's words caught in my mind in an endless loop. I see tiny birds and rain-drenched coffins until the chanting dies and we all fall into a tangled-limb mass of bodies on the floor.

*   *   *

I clock two, maybe three, hours of sleep, waking on the wooden floor with a tangle of Raina's hair in my face. It's cloudy today, and I know that will help me.

This week, as summer wanes and August marches toward September, students returned to Arbor State for the fall semester. Their arrival put me back to work.

Others grow vegetables or clean. Chop firewood or cook meals. Claire's job is to read. Mine is to recruit.

I arrive on campus as sleep deprived as the real college students. Parking myself on a bench outside the registrar's office, I pull a defunct cell phone from my bag and wait. I wish it were connected to a network, but it has little more functionality than a kid's toy. I hold the phone in front of my face and write texts to my little sister that'll go unsent.

I've found at least half of the girls currently in the Flock with this method. I wait outside the registrar's office, looking for the agonizing dejection and disenchantment of a perfect recruit. There are just over two thousand students at Arbor State. In this nondescript little brick building, students find out they're failing, that they don't meet graduation requirements, that they can't afford to stay in college. It's a place where dreams go to die. A place where I find new members for the Flock.

It's not long before a girl sits on the other side of the bench with a huff and the sulking shoulders of a potential recruit.

Her hair is well groomed, and she's showing a little too much cleavage. The girl releases another breathy sigh and gazes at the overcast sky.

"Of course I forgot an umbrella today," she mutters, half to herself. She glances my way and offers a self-deprecating smirk. "Story of my life."

This will be easy.

Gray days, when rain itches to burst from the sky, amplify everything that's wrong in life. And I can tell this girl's aching to tell me—anyone—the injustices plaguing her.

I look for girls who want the attention of men. Girls craving safety. Girls waiting to be rescued. Girls burning for a confidant.

I've turned to her, ready to offer her Dom's magnetism and the Flock's love and acceptance, when her gold necklace catches my eye. It's a simple cross, but it stops me as if I were a devil.

As a rule, I avoid girls with cross necklaces. People who've rejected religion are easier to recruit and isolate. You might think a religious girl is a simple mark, easy to manipulate, but they're already entrenched in "us versus them" thinking, and I'm on the wrong side.

"Tell me about it. I'll be the drowned rat in psych class for sure." I offer a smile and a wink. It helps to be a little flirty, even with the girls.

The girl laughs as if I've brightened her day. I have an opening, but I don't take it. I turn back to my pointless phone and type another message to my baby sister.

We can all be manipulated, especially when we think we can't.

With a few keystrokes, I delete it. Thunder rumbles in the distance, and the girl and I titter nervously, eyes cast to the dark sky. A few minutes later she gets up to leave, absently dropping her folded campus newspaper on the bench.

I pick it up. There's an edgy editorial about the university's new cannabis chemistry program on the front page along with an article on a professor's plea to fund freshwater research. The future politicians club is foaming at the mouth because Obama's visiting the state capitol in a few months and they're chartering a trip to see him speak.

It's an advertisement on the back page that catches my interest. The fall festival begins a few days after Labor Day weekend. Though I grew up a few towns over, there isn't a year I've missed Iola's annual event. Each September, Iola brings a traveling carnival to town and builds a week-long festival around it, complete with a grand parade with a dance team, drum line, marching band, and floats created by every bank and insurance agency in the county.

Despite the grainy print quality of the newspaper, I can make out the joy and hope of the girl in the advertisement. A crown is perched on a head of curls, and she's beaming. Her makeup is expressive but not overdone. I know her. Bethany Frasier. Last year's Apple Queen winner.

Since I was a little girl, I've seen the way everyone fawns over the Apple Queen pageant girls. They're the most beautiful, talented, well-rounded girls this town has to offer. They're the ones most likely to succeed, most likely to leave. They're worth more. Everyone knows it.

I daydreamed about being an Apple Blossom. They're the junior beauty queens, primed for the real pageant. But I didn't live in Iola growing up, so I wasn't eligible to be a Blossom. Not that my mother would have allowed it anyway.

Estivant, where I grew up, is hours from the interstate and home to dozens of churches, much like Iola. Summers are warm but rarely hot, and winters are cold and snowy. There's not much to do but fantasize about leaving.

I was born an adventurer but stuck with my loveless mom and strict stepdad in a Podunk town. I thought if I were a Blossom, and later an Apple Queen, the world would open up. I was ready to explore but tethered to a judgmental family.

After her win, I heard, Bethany Frasier moved to Chicago. I can just picture her amid glass-walled skyscrapers. I once heard there's a strip of the city along the lake called the Magnificent Mile. Sometimes I imagine bouncy-haired Bethany parading down a whimsical street and my heart fills with an ache I can't name.

I trace Bethany's face on the advertisement. This year, it's different. I no longer live in Estivant. The Bird Haven is my home, and I can use the ornithologist's cottage as my address to enter the contest.

I'd have to keep it a secret from Dom and the others, though. He'd be furious if he found out I'm trying to build a future outside the Flock. Like me, the girls are lost and separated from their pasts, but they still believe Dom can heal and save them.

But that's not me anymore. This summer I started to realize Dom wasn't living up to his promise, that the Flock is filled with more failed expectations. It's all an illusion. Dom's commune is mired in fear and dependency. I came to him alone and overwhelmed, ready to experience something new. At first, he offered a thriving community full of meaning and adventure. Now, I've started to recognize the lies he's ingrained in my mind. But it's more than that, really. There's this wild paranoia infused into Dom and everything he touches now. It feels unstable, dangerous. Like we're marching toward something dark and irreversible.

I've pocketed a little money to leave the Flock. The newspaper ad says there's a fifty-dollar entry fee to the Apple Queen pageant. I'll need a dress too. It'll take a big chunk of my savings just to enter the contest, but if I win, I'll have enough to get to Chicago or maybe even Nashville.

I could start a new life.

I stand up, newspaper in hand, feeling hopeful for the first time in months. I think of the way the gold of the girl's necklace caught my eye and told me she wasn't a good recruit for the Flock. Gold, just like my aura, according to Morgan.

A sign. No more waiting. It's time to escape the Flock.

3

Claire

Now

I KNOW HENRY WILL be waiting on the porch before I pull into the driveway and park under the portico.

My husband waits for me on the swing. The streetlights cast his face in shadow, but I can see the set of his jaw as I approach. I make my way across the weed-choked stepping stones leading to the porch.

Years ago, when we first got together, I felt alternately resentful and appreciative of his watchful eye. Someone had to keep an eye on me after what happened at the Bird Haven, everyone said so, and my father had his turn. Henry was vigilant, asked pointed questions, and provided security in a way I'd never recognized before. I melted into him.

He's worried, I can see. I add a bright note to my voice and ask him to walk with me. His eyebrow rises almost imperceptibly, and I see it flit across his face: suspicion first, but that's not what gets me. It's hope. I feel guilty, knowing I won't tell him what he wants to hear, at least not on this walk.

We walk slowly. It's dark now. I tell him one of Lourdes's stories about her mischievous twins, but he doesn't laugh, so I decide to tell him.

"Someone came into the library today. A podcaster," I hesitate. "He's going to talk about me and what happened."

"What's the scope of his project? Do you know?" Henry asks.

I shake my head and lean into him as we walk. This street is lined with historical houses, most with large wraparound wooden porches and scrubby yards like ours.

"I listened to a preview. A trailer, I think he called it. I don't know how many episodes he's planning or how long he'll be in town."

"You talked to him?"

"Yes. But no, not really. I helped him with the microfiche, but he didn't know who I am," I say. "It's going to be bad. Like the attention from the book but worse, because that was mostly about Dom. This is bigger, and everyone is going to blame me again." I talk fast, piling my words atop each other. Nervous even with my own husband.

"Claire, you can't know that yet," he says.

"He's going to talk about Lollie. Laurel," I correct. Henry hates when I use our names from the Flock. We didn't all have nicknames; only those in Dom's inner circle were rewarded with them. I used to slip into low, muttering group-speak too, mostly when I found myself alone, but Henry's broken me of the habit. We had our own language in the Flock, and on stressful days I'd subconsciously revert to the jargon-filled lingo to calm myself.

We're out of the neighborhood now. The bland, brown-brick buildings don't emit much light. The businesses, the ones that aren't permanently shuttered, are closed for the night or the summer, until the college kids return.

We pass Lundy's Wild West Pizza, closed, a VFW, a law office, and a florist, all closed. There's no traffic at this time, but the lights change, keeping an invisible rhythm on Main Street. Henry guides me down a curb as we cross an alley and end up in front of Zink's. The store's window shines brightly to display new tools that no one in this dying town will use. It's an act of optimism.

"You can't get involved in this," Henry warns. "Not now. This isn't the time to add stress to your life."

There it is: the warm hope I saw in his eyes earlier has dissolved into disappointment. I feel his unspoken blame acutely; I've had an overdose of guilt and criticism ever since the Flock died.

Henry wants a baby. He's made no secret of it. It's the only thing I can't bring myself to do for him.

I've been a pariah since I was nineteen. Henry's gentle and patient with me, but one day he'll realize he doesn't need my paranoid dependence. I was scared to commit to him and now I'm scared he'll leave me, so I never say no. I wear my hair how he likes, make dinner when I'm exhausted, and strain myself to work out every day. But still I hide my birth control pills behind a ratty hairbrush and lie to him about my desire for a baby.

"I'm not trying to get involved." I hear the whine in my voice. I shove my hands deeper into my pockets. "I just think this will be different from Susan Wade's book. This podcaster—Arlo Stone is his name—he'll try to talk to me, and he'll probably try to talk to you too."

Henry scoffs. "I don't know anything. I didn't even live here then."

It's true. I've told him the bare minimum. In the early days, when I was still seeing a therapist and a nutritionist and pounding pills to quell my panic attacks, I meant to tell him more, but every time I said Dom's name, he corrected me: "Dominic," he'd bark, like I was a bad puppy. I knew then that if he couldn't get past my familiar use of Dom's name, I could never tell him what it was really like to be a member of the Flock.

It's not so much that I've hidden the details from my husband, but my recollections of the past are irrevocably broken. After the trauma, I saw a therapist who seemed almost bored by my textbook symptoms—recurring flashbacks, nightmares, panic attacks, ruminating thoughts—and diagnosed me with posttraumatic stress disorder. She told me my lost memories

weren't retrievable and it would be healthier for me to avoid recollections and triggers. So I shuttered myself off from my past.
I felt disconnected, but that was normal for me. That's why I
joined the Flock in the first place. In a way, the isolation felt safe.
I struggled to make connections or find common ground with
others, though, truthfully, I didn't expend much effort. Henry
was different, though. He was patient, nonthreatening. He gave
me space and never pried into my past. If I could remember more
about what happened that summer, it'd be Henry I'd tell.

"Still, he'll assume I've told you what I remember. He'll
contact my father, of course. And my schoolteachers," I add
absently, thinking of what Arlo said in the library. I cringe,
imagining the way they'll squint into their memories, trying to
unearth anything remotely notable about me, a quiet, pale ghost
of a girl. I wonder how long it'll be until Arlo returns, knowing
who I am.

"There's not really that much to tell. Here," Henry says,
grasping my elbow and turning me around. A pickup with rowdy
teenagers spilling out the windows roars past us, and I stumble
slightly. Henry catches me and guides us down the dim street.

"I mean, yes, people died," he continues, "but they chose to
die. A group of vulnerable, unanchored people gave up on life,
but that's not a story that people are clamoring to hear, Claire.
So you knew them. That doesn't mean this podcaster is going to
unravel your life just to tell their story."

I listen almost passively, wondering if I should be angry
that my husband is dismissive of my friends' deaths or grateful that he considers me separate, more elite, than them. If he
loves me, I can't be as bad as everyone says, I think, not for
the first time.

If I could have told him more when we met, would he treat
me differently now? Would he have even pursued a relationship?
All I could tell him, by the time we met, was how much I didn't
know and how I couldn't recover the memories. He knows
about the panic attacks and nightmares, but I've never brought

up the intrusive flashbacks that trigger them. Sometimes I wonder if he minimizes my involvement because I speak so infrequently about it.

Across the street, the notes of a jaunty song slip outside as
a couple opens the door to Tres Caminos with a jangle. A take-
home bag dangles from the woman's wrist like a purse, and her
smile is so easy that I'm certain she doesn't have to hide her past
from her husband. Her name is Maureen; she checks out chick-
lit and magazines from the library.

"I'll have to tell my dad before Arlo contacts him, if he hasn't
already."

We're home before I realize it. I know, almost instinctively,
that I floated home. Arlo's only been in town a day, mentioned
Lollie a few times, and already I'm triggered. Dr. Diehl, my therapist, used to warn of this. Even brief moments of anxiety alert
my mind to unintentionally split off. A picture, or sometimes a
feeling, takes form and I lose touch with reality. I float.

I floated home with Henry suspended between my past and
present. Tonight it was the warm bloom of affection and attention and security—how I felt with the Flock—that stole me from
our walk. The feeling of being love-bombed.

Our shoes thud on the wooden steps leading to our Elliot
Street house. In the dark, I can't see the holes in the latticework
below our porch where animals have clawed their way in.

We step into the foyer, where the woodwork gleams and my
feet sink reassuringly into a plush red rug. I remind myself that
I'm satisfied with this life and urgently decide that I wasn't floating out of nostalgia for the Flock and our missing leader.

* * *

Pamela's smile is too wide for a Tuesday morning, and her scrubs
smell like an overdose of laundry detergent.

She's more a receptionist than anything else, but I suppose
if my line of work had the potential to put me into contact with
dead bodies, I'd wear scrubs to save my clothes too.

After submitting me to a few too-personal questions about Henry and when we're planning to add to our nest, as she puts it, Pamela leads me to the sterile exam room where my father works.

Grant Hollis is well known in Iola. As the county medical examiner, he deals with violence and justice and life and death every day. Sudden, suspicious, and unnatural deaths require his attention. He's autopsied members of the Flock, including Lollie.

This morning he wears a suit and no protective gear, so it must have been a relatively safe weekend in the county. An open-faced breakfast sandwich sits beside his computer.

"Well now, I can't remember the last time my Claire Bear visited me at work. It's been, what, years? What brings you by?" he asks, swiveling to face me.

I exhale, short and noisy, through my nose. I've asked him not to use my babyish childhood nickname anymore. But he says he can't change that easily and slips it into conversation often, even in public. Henry suspects he does it with intent: an infantilizing power trip. I don't disagree.

He gestures to a red desk chair, a twin to his own. I sit, and the chair sinks with a whoosh.

"Been meaning to get that fixed," he says with a hearty laugh as my cheeks color.

I try to shake it off. I'm past being embarrassed or intimidated when talking to him, but now he looms over me. It doesn't help that I'm dreading telling him about Arlo and the podcast.

"I have something to tell you," I start, searching for the words. "There's a man in town, and he's recording a podcast. An exposé, I guess you could call it. About Lollie and Dom and the Flock. And me."

Grant's expression doesn't change. After a moment, he gives one short nod and turns to his breakfast sandwich. He chews thoughtfully.

"What have you told him?" he asks.

"Nothing. You know I don't have anything to say about it. Any of it. But I know he's here, and I know he'll ask sooner or later. And there's a good chance he'll try to talk to you too."

He strokes his chin, which is peppered by short white whiskers. He and my mother always pushed me so hard. As an only child, I rose to their level, or tried to, instead of muddling around with other kids. Be adventurous, be independent, be an activist, they said.

And then my mother got cancer, and I couldn't bring myself to be any of those things.

Instead, I became weak-minded and vulnerable. Everything they hated. It really shouldn't have been a surprise the Flock drew me away from this man. After my mother died, he burrowed into his career, into more death.

He wanted me to be strong, but I couldn't do it, so he still treats me like a child.

After the Flock died and I didn't, he took me back. He shuttled me to appointments and picked out new clothes. He demanded I eat and reminded me to sleep. He accompanied me to interviews with the police and federal agents, and he insisted I talk to a therapist. He pushed me, just as he had when I was a kid. My mother wasn't there to temper his intensity and I didn't have any fight left in me, so I let him mold me back into a person. In my darker moments, I wondered if he wished I'd died with the rest of the Flock. I still wonder.

"I'll talk to him if he asks for an interview," he says finally. He takes another bite of his sandwich and swivels back to face his computer screen.

"Dad, no. No, that's not what I want. I—"

"I'll take care of it, Claire." He's typing now, ignoring me. "I suppose he'll want to know about the early autopsies. I'll have Pamela pull the files today so I can reacquaint myself with the cases."

The early autopsies. Before Lollie was kidnapped and the others suffocated. But those deaths were different. The people were older, for one. By the time I lived at the Bird Haven, most members of the Flock were young, like me. A few older people, mostly widowed women and unemployed men, had lived there in the early days.

"Let me jot down their names for her," he continues, reaching for a pen. He cocks an ear to me and waits. Finally, he looks at me, raising his eyebrows.

"I . . . I don't remember."

"Claire." His voice is edged with disapproval.

"It's been a long time, and they died before I even lived there. And you know my therapist said it'd be dangerous for me to try to retrieve lost memories." I try to keep the whine out of my voice.

"They were a part of the group you sought out as family when you left ours." He swivels in his chair again, pointedly turning his back to me. "Look, even if you don't intend to talk to this, oh, what did you call him, a reporter?"

"A podcaster."

He types a note, fingers clacking on the keyboard, making me wait. "Even if you don't plan to talk to this man, you should be familiar with the basics of what happened, and that includes knowing the names of the people who died while living there. You're past recovering your memories, and Dr. Diehl advised against it anyway, but that's basic information."

The typing ceases; still, he doesn't turn around. The way he makes me wait, how he refuses to meet my eyes: these are micro-aggressions he's used on me for years, long before I joined the Flock. Instinctively, I steel myself, knowing he's preparing for a low blow.

"After all that happened and everything you've done, knowing your fellow cult members' names is the least you can do."

* * *

I'm relieved to find the library is quiet when I arrive. As inconspicuously as I can, I scan the stacks for a sign of Arlo Stone. He's not here, but that doesn't mean he won't return soon. Especially once he figures out who I am.

Lourdes swans over to the desk after I clock in. Her shirt is too low and her eyeliner too thick for the afternoon shift at the library.

"Mrs. Horsnell checked out a book about coping with a gambling addiction this morning. I bet anything it's for her husband, or maybe her son. How much do you think they've lost?"

Gossiping about patrons is Lourdes's favorite hobby and the reason I'm so careful with my checkouts. She has access to the same computer system I do; I have no doubt she searches the borrow records for people she knows.

She continues her countdown until the students return to town for the fall semester—it's less than one week now—and waxes nostalgic about how different it was when she was in college. I smile politely and laugh when she wants it, but I can't relate. I spent those years shell-shocked and isolated.

When she invites Henry and me to her house for dinner on Saturday, I accept, because even though I'm edgy and unnerved less and less these days, I'm still isolated. Lonely. Lourdes is my only friend.

She returns to her post at the reference desk when Sharon enters. Director of the library, Sharon is a powerful force of a woman masquerading behind a white-blond helmet of old-lady curls and bifocals. She gives me a kindly pat on the elbow as she passes to her tiny office in the back, where she'll pore over magazines of book offerings, deciding what to purchase next. A few years ago I offered to help her order books online, but she declined with a polite finality, so I haven't mentioned it since.

I wait another thirty minutes until Sharon and Lourdes are absorbed by whatever's on their respective computer screens.

In the periodicals, I shuffle through the day's newspaper to locate the classifieds section. I tuck it under my arm and cast a glance back at the front desk. I straighten the books on a few shelves as I pass them, hoping to mask my intent. Wondering if they can tell I'm headed for the true-crime stacks.

Susan Wade's book is four books from the end on the bottom shelf. I've shelved it enough times to know without looking at the book spines. Even when I pass by, it seems to shimmer at me from the shelf. A ratty little package of my guilt and shame and exclusion, all bundled up. The pages say my name, I know. And Lollie's. And Dom's.

With the book bundled safely in the newspaper, I return to the circulation desk. I drop the bundle in the wastepaper basket. I wait through two patrons: an elderly man whose gaze keeps traveling to Lourdes's low-cut blouse and a lady with two small kids who looked unreasonably frazzled for a quiet, sunny summer day.

Finally, I remove a banana from my purse, toss the peel onto the classified section, and choke down the mushy bites. Henry keeps the house stocked with bananas; he's an avid biker and insists they help with leg cramps.

I lift the trash can and catch Sharon's eye as she exits her office an hour later.

"I'll take this out back. My banana was ripe, and I don't want to attract any fruit flies," I say.

Sharon offers a brisk nod as she passes. She frowns, distracted by Lourdes's top, and veers off to talk to her. I see my exit and hurry out the back door, trash can in hand.

Outside, I extract the book from the newspaper bundle and hurry it to my unlocked car, sliding it under the driver's seat.

When I go back inside, I straighten the shelf with the Edgar Allen Poe books, although it's already orderly, because I can't stop thinking about the beating of the telltale heart.

* * *

The next morning, I try to appear patient as Henry takes his time whisking an egg, dipping bread, and frying up French toast for us to have from breakfast. He savors his coffee while rocking gently on the porch swing. It's not too much longer he can linger in the morning like this; Henry works at the university, and the students return next week.

"Black with a touch of sugar. Just how you like it," he says as he hands me a steaming mug.

This is how he likes his coffee. Me? I don't know. Sometimes it feels like I forgot to form opinions.

I thought I had all the answers until I was rejected from the college of my choice and my mother was diagnosed with cancer, all within a few months. I spiraled. I was lost and vulnerable, I know now.

Then I met Dom. When everything was unsettling and overwhelming, he symbolized stability. Amid a paralyzing swell of choices, he guided me. He told me what music I liked and how I should wear my hair. He told me what to believe (him), how to eat (pescatarian), and how to vote (not at all).

My therapist helped me understand that I had no self when I was with the Flock. She gave me exercises to "find myself." Figure out who I am and what I like. I tried at first, but it was exhausting. And it turned out my father knew better who I should be anyway. And then came Henry, with his charming smile, lack of questions, and steady job.

We met at the annual Squirrel Scamper, a 5K that pays homage to the albino white squirrels that call Iola home. He was a runner, naturally, while I was a volunteer who tried to fade into the background. He was persistent and patient, and eventually I agreed to a date, then another, and another. When he told me it was time to get married, I agreed to that too, because he didn't mind that I was socially clueless or that I'd rather be right than be popular. He's good-natured and rarely gets ruffled. He guides me back to center when I become dazed and distant, which is less and less these days.

But this morning it's a chore. I can think only of getting him out of the house. I fuss with a plant by the door, trimming dead leaves and shaping it while I wait for him to finish his coffee. I take hurried sips from the mug he made for me and gather his mug to return to the kitchen while he still has a few drops left.

When he's finally gone, I fish Susan Wade's book from below the driver's seat of my car. I take the rear staircase to a reading nook on the second floor and settle into a chair already warmed by the morning sun.

I take a deep breath before focusing on the cover. On Dom. I can see how easy it'd be to focus on his lank, greasy hair or his impenetrable amber eyes and fail to see a domineering manipulator. So many people saw his short stature and patchy facial hair and they just didn't get it. How was he worth following, worth dying for?

At first, he was nurturing and supportive. I fan the pages of the book and wonder if Susan Wade could have captured that. I didn't talk to her for the book, but did someone else tell her how he made you feel important? How he was attractive, in his own way? How he was a showman, regaling us with fantastical stories as we sat around the firepit on those endless summer nights?

I steel myself for frustration and hurt and anger, because I know the book can't have gotten it right. Any of it. But still, I need to read, need to know what everyone else thinks happened.

My therapist used to say that detaching was my mind's way of protecting me from overwhelming emotions. She said my lost memories couldn't be retrieved and trying to recount them would only damage me psychologically. So I pushed away anything that would trigger a memory, and in the early days, that was nearly everything. I avoided the woods and lake, refused to eat any of the vegetables the girls grew in the Flock's garden, broke down if I heard group singing, and even shunned books for a while, because they reminded me of reading to Dom in the dim light of the Flock's cabin. And, of course, I avoided Susan Wade's book, with its tantalizing photo insert and sensationist flap copy, fervently.

It's not that I don't want to know. I do. But, admittedly, I'm scared. What if the book triggers my memories to return, filling in my spotty recollections of the past? What if Dr. Diehl was right all those years ago and it harms me to know the truth?

I trace the outline of Dom's face on the cover. I know that, without my input, Susan Wade can't have captured what it was like to be in the Flock within these pages. But it's time to know the details I've been avoiding for the last decade.

Because when Arlo Stone comes back, I need to know what he's going to ask me.

I open the book.

CHAPTER

4

Laurel

Then

"NO ONE LEAVES."

In baggy, sweat-addled clothes, Dom stands beside the dormer window in the upstairs bedroom. The four-poster bed is too big for the space; its size is emphasized by the way the sloping planes of the roof narrow the standing room.

"Tell me what I need to know," he demands, his voice clear and articulate. Up here, Dom doesn't talk in lyrical, folksy ramblings or with the passion of a zealot.

"I . . . I don't know what happened," I say. With a centering breath, I straighten my shoulders to avoid shrinking backward into the claustrophobic wood paneling enclosing the room. I tilt my chin up and meet Dom's gaze.

"Tell me why you'd leave," he says.

I know I can't keep the surprise from reaching my eyes. How does he know?

Dom can be charming, magnetic. That's what drew me here, to him. I lapped up his wise ideas and attractive, almost impenetrable stare. He made me feel important. Nurtured. How many hours did I spend up here, twisted up in his bedsheets?

But I don't see that infectious, perceptive man anymore. Standing before me is a wiry yet domineering person, thirsty for allegiance. His dark, curly hair dips past his shoulders, and today he wears round, wired-framed glasses.

"Lollie. Tell me why *you'd* leave. That's the only way I can understand this."

The emphasis on *you*: was it there before?

"She must not have seen the stability and spirituality we could give her," I try. "I mean, I thought she was a good recruit, but I was wrong. I think her ties to her family are more complicated than I realized."

"Did you leave her alone? Did she express bad thoughts while she was here?"

"No, I was her guide all weekend."

It's true: Jocelyn stayed by my side during her visit. I ushered her through a busy schedule of group singing, lectures, and even an honesty circle. Along with the other girls, I love-bombed her with flattery. I paid attention to her every remark, I touched her affectionately.

"Is there anything you're not telling me?"

My thoughts race. Jocelyn was intimidated by our confessional ritual. She's not as vulnerable to peer pressure as I thought she'd be. She craved solitude and a shower.

She picked up on my desperation to leave.

"No, really, Dom. I misjudged her, that's all. I'm sorry for wasting everyone's time."

"I'm beginning to question if you're the best guide for new recruits."

"But I'm the one who brings them here. They feel most comfortable with me."

"That may be so, but I'm beginning to question the loyalty of people in your peripheral. You're giving off a negative energy—subconsciously, I hope. Look at Claire. She's not as devoted as the others. I know she has that mangy stuffed animal from home hidden in your sleeping space. She can't let go of her past."

Just this morning, I hid Claire's time-worn bear below the mattress when I saw she'd left it out before going for a morning swim with the girls. We all hide something from home we cherish. For Claire, it's the bear, gray with age. For me, a photograph of my little sister.

"And let's not forget the debacle with Daisy."

My heart sinks. Daisy is my biggest regret.

At first, I regretted how I got sucked into her orbit. My closest friend at the time, Daisy tried to convince me to leave the Flock with her. I stayed, but her departure stained my loyal reputation in Dom's eyes. Betrayed, Daisy snitched to my parents, insisting I'd joined a cult, infuriating my mother and stepfather.

Now I regret that I didn't leave with her.

"I'll look for a new recruit this week," I offer.

"Try the bus depot and the town library," Dom instructs. "Do the high schoolers hang out in City Park? Try some other towns this week, but not Estivant. We don't want anyone to recognize you." Dom turns to the window, eyeing the girls lounging in the hammocks through the tree-laden view. "When you speak to them, do better to explain that a spiritual revolution is coming. I'm shepherding the Flock into a brave, enlightened new future."

He touches a finger to the windowpane, tracing the outline of the fire pit or maybe the old birdcages, which are now rusty and lopsided.

"See the paper on my desk? Drop it off with the *Iola Press* today."

I cross the room and pick up the handwritten page.

Jocelyn Gavin, 18, of Hero's Port, Michigan, passed away on September 1, 2012, from a poisoned mind. She left behind a loving family who wanted only to flock to safety and harmony together.

"What is this? An obituary?"

"A warning."

"I can't bring this to the newspaper. It's a threat."

"They'll run it. And when she sees it, she'll realize her mistake."

I feel as if I'm wading through a whirlpool of Dom's paranoia. I've been drawn into a crushing, chaotic tunnel, and I'm
not strong enough to escape it. I don't know if he's truly dangerous or if he just understands the deadliness of words.

Eyes trained out the window, he speaks, his voice quieter than
before: "And Lollie? You licked your lips before you answered me
earlier. I know you're lying. You can't hide from me."

* * *

Two summers ago, when I arrived at the Bird Haven, I reveled
in early-morning swims. Tromping through the woods with the
others—there were more people then, most of us young—we
had camaraderie, warmth.

It was still an adventure then. Giggling, splashing, teasing. I
loved living with different types of people, people who didn't judge,
who changed the way I thought, who took each day as it came.

The Flock was my family. We forged deeper bonds than I'd
ever experienced.

We all renounced our last names, but only a few of Dom's
inner circle were christened with new first names. I became
Lollie for the Lolita-like way I'd sucked on a lollipop when we
first met. Georgann became Goldie in honor of her halo of blond
curls. Caitlin was renamed Eden for the way she revered the
Bird Haven as paradise and Dom as her God. We were bound
together.

We forfeited our pasts to live a communal life in an idyllic
refuge. We were overabundantly optimistic in the promises Dom
made to us.

Just days out of high school, I was eager to explore everything: Dom's mind and body, my sexuality and freedom. Spiritually curious and middle-class obedient, I was bewitched by
Dom's talk of high vibrations.

I was a victim of the loneliness epidemic, so I didn't mind
when Dom rallied against solitude, insisting that time alone led
to selfish and capitalistic thoughts.

So, for two years, I haven't taken time for myself. I've reacted to the tide of Dom's whims, his demands. I came here to find myself, but now I have less of an identity than ever before. I'm little more than a groupie to a guru.

It's laughter that I remember from two summers ago, but today, in the same frothy, cold lake, it's birdcalls that dominate the air. The girls bathe in the water just a few feet from a reddish-brown bloom of algae, quiet and careful. Reticent. Guarded.

Morgan bobs below the surface to wash herself, while Claire turns away from the group, conscious of her nakedness. She's the newest girl to join the Flock, but the girls seem almost afraid to make a connection with her.

We speak low, or not at all, so we don't disturb the meditative silence of the Bird Haven.

Eden's long curls drip with water.

"Oh," she says. Wide-eyed, she points to the rocky shore a few dozen yards away from where we wade in the water. "A peacock!"

I follow her gaze. There are spindly trees and tall grasses leading into brown, rock-strewn shoreline. No majestic blue birds.

"Where?" Goldie asks, placing her hand on Faith's shoulder. All the girls, naked, with red-pocked skin from endless mosquito bites, search for the peacock.

"There," Eden insists. "It's fanning its feathers. I can't believe it; peacocks are my spirit animal. They symbolize beauty and good luck. They're protective." She takes a few unsteady steps forward.

"What are you *talking* about, Eden? There's nothing there," Raina says.

A few more splashing steps and Eden loses her balance, falling heavily into the water.

"It was just . . . where did it go?" She scrambles, crying out as she palms a sharp rock below the water's surface. She looks at her bloody hand as if it belongs to someone else, then dips it back in the water. It emerges pale and clean. Then a red blossom of blood spreads again. With a shake of her head, she turns back to the shoreline.

"Eden, here," I say, "come to the shore." I take her pudgy elbow and guide her back to the clearing where we enter the water. "You're hallucinating. Feel the earth beneath you. Ground yourself," I instruct.

She's rambling now. Confused. Insistent. I know she's had a hallucination, but still I scan the tree line, almost hoping to spot royal-blue-and-green feathers.

She vomits. Some gets caught in her wet curls, while the lake water pulls the rest into the algae bloom nestled at the shore.

"I think I manifested the peacock," Eden muses. "I've been working with Dom to shift my consciousness and open up my astral senses. The peacock was a symbolic interpretation of my energy flow. I deliberately created it, but then I paused the momentum and awakened from my dream. I need to surrender to this new gateway."

With an eerie clarity, I disconnect from my body. I'm up in the trees, looking down at us from above. Lake water laps at our toes. Am I hallucinating, just like Eden?

No, reality isn't altered. Instead, a calm awareness envelops me. I see us for what we are: two lost girls seduced by a mesmerizing promise of utopia, so deeply enmeshed in our insular world we're not speaking recognizable English anymore.

The girls flicker, and from my perch high up in the trees, I think of the way Dom rules with a feverish mix of affection and threat. I know one thing for sure: I can't let him think I'm disloyal or I'll never escape the Flock alive.

CHAPTER

5

Claire

Now

IT TAKES ME four hours to finish the book cover to cover.

It doesn't talk much about the people who died in the earlier days at the Bird Haven. There were five of them: a couple, two older women, and one widowed man. I don't remember them; they died before I lived there. Between my trauma-induced gaps and jumbled memories, everything is hazy. Besides, there were no clocks or calendars, television, or phones, and we rarely left the Bird Haven. I had no point of reference to the outside society that summer; only the Flock's chief recruiter, Lollie, got to leave. My lingering memories seem shimmery, paper thin.

But Susan Wade's book reminds me. Or I think it does. I remember the group singing and Dom's lectures. I remember collective work, staying busy. I remember confessionals and thinking that the outside, my past, was wrong and evil. I remember.

Mostly, she talks about Dom. How he was calculating, manipulative, and skilled at preying on weakness.

Was he?

That's not the Dom I remember. He was gentle, attentive, and playful. He had a special connection to animals; it was undeniable. Deer walked beside him in the forest and birds landed within arm's reach, content to linger near his magnetic aura.

I'm amused to find out the twins' real names were Stefani and Sabrina Ide. They were so interchangeable that summer, I'm not sure anyone called them anything but *the twins*. But I bristle when I realize Eden's real name was Caitlin. All this time, I didn't know she'd been rewarded with a nickname from Dom. She followed him around like a puppy dog, yes, but I never thought she was considered elite. Lollie and Goldie, they were Dom's top girls. I understood why they were christened with new names. I only spent a few months at the Bird Haven a decade ago, but still, finding out Eden had the privilege of being renamed by Dom sets off a juvenile jealousy in me.

As I read, it becomes clear that Susan Wade didn't know what it was like for the Flock at the Bird Haven. The book's full of sensationalist writing likening Dom to famous cult leaders and most-wanted fugitives. It's more speculative than fact based, and it touches only briefly on the extensive investigations. Parts of it reads as if the author is a teenybopper idolizing Dom for escaping without a trace.

By the time I set the book down, the sun is high, easily the hottest part of the day. I bury the book in my purse and carry my purse with me around the house, just to be safe. I have visions of Henry, my father, even an intruder riffling through my purse, finding the book, and . . . what? So I finally read the book about my life, my friends—why do I feel so guilty? It feels wrong, like I'll get in trouble for reading it.

I remember all the newspaper articles at the time. How could I miss them? Dom's face, and the faces of all my friends, were splashed across every newspaper in the state. My dad's subscribed to the *Iola Press* since before I was born, but he walked each paper to the trash can for months after I returned home. I didn't dig them out because I knew words lie anyway. By then, he was already shuttling me to Dr. Diehl's daily therapy sessions, and I overheard her recommend that he shield me from triggers to the extent possible as she debriefed him each afternoon.

My afternoon is open, so with the book safely hidden in my purse, I leave the house and drive the three blocks to my father's house. My childhood home.

It's a showy house on Marshall Street. A classic Victorian with stained-glass windows and ostentatious columns flanking the front doors. The yard is what makes it stand out, though. Every inch is covered in wildflowers and native plants. Coreopsis and wild geraniums, black-eyed Susan and aster. Everything wild and beautiful.

It may be my father's house, but it's my garden. I come here daily for plant therapy. I've selected every color, texture, and fragrance for healing in the plant-dominated space. When the garden was confined to a small strip of backyard, my mother tended it. I still remember the way she'd pluck a flower from the honeysuckle, pull out the stem, and offer a bead of sweet nectar for me to taste. After her death, I expanded the garden, letting the plants replace the grass.

I spend the afternoon working. Digging into the dirt, trimming, weeding, watering; it all grounds me. It quiets my mind. I think only of the plants, and my mind remains uncharacteristically focused on the present. Out here, I don't pick at the remnants of my past like scabs, examining the vague story I told the investigators back then, wondering if they're still building a case against me for my part in everything that happened. In the garden, I don't worry that my past ruined my chance at a future.

That is, until my phone pings with an alert. Shielding my eyes to block the sun's glare, I read the notification: "Birds of a Feather: Episode 1 now available." I subscribed to podcast alerts when I listened to the teaser trailer two days ago.

Suddenly, the sun feels too hot on my neck. The ferns tickle my ankles as I walk down the path to the front door. I don't often go inside when I'm here—everything I need is housed in a shed in the backyard—but today I use my key to let myself in.

When I returned home from the Bird Haven for the first time, fragile and frightened, I didn't expect to see a hospital bed in the living room. What's more, I didn't expect to find it empty. My mother had died while in home hospice care just days before, but I hadn't known she'd passed. The loss of my friends and my mother was almost too much for a nineteen-year-old to process; it's no surprise Dr. Diehl diagnosed me with posttraumatic stress disorder.

I spent two years in therapy until Dr. Bunny Diehl, a small lady with an expressionless, pumpkinesque face and fruity perfume so overpowering I smelled it on my clothes all day, passed away. More than anything, we spent our time repairing my relationship with the future. I felt stable enough when she passed that I didn't continue therapy. I hadn't met Henry yet, and my world was small but manageable.

I head upstairs to my old bedroom. It's painstakingly preserved as it was when I left as a teenager. I didn't have the energy to change it when I returned after the Flock died, so it's still bubblegum pink and reminds me of an achingly painful, confusing time in my life.

Sweaty and itchy from my garden work, I settle into my old favorite spot in the narrow aisle between the bed and the wall, a tight corner where I feel both secure and hidden.

I hit play and punch up the phone's volume. The opening notes of eerie piano music are back, filling the room.

"When the Apple Queen went missing, there was no way of knowing that it would lead to the suicide deaths of fourteen members of the cult known as the Flock three short weeks later. In fact, there was no way of knowing the Apple Queen was missing at all. Her bunkmate at the commune known as the Bird Haven, Claire Hollis, didn't report the kidnapping. It took three days for the police to find out Laurel Tai was missing—three crucial days that provided her killer ample time to dispose of her body."

Arlo's smooth voice fades, replaced by the sound effect of a bubbling brook. Lollie was found by the river, after all. I shudder.

"I'm your host, Arlo Stone, and today I'm going to dive into what might be the most important death of a Flock member—certainly a catalyst for everything that happened next."

*　　*　　*

It's a quiet evening at the library, just Sharon and me staffing tonight. Lourdes works only the morning or afternoon shift. I wait for Sharon to take her fifteen-minute break—she strolls down the street to Sherman's Dairy for a cup of mocha ice cream most days—and I hurry to one of the three guest computers.

It's not that I expect Henry to spy on my search history, but I don't trust the computers at our house. He works in technology; I don't know the extent of information he can gather on me, and I know he'd be furious if he found out I'm trying to learn more about the Flock. He understands my diagnosis and, like my dad, doesn't encourage me to uncover lost memories.

I open an internet browser and type in Susan Wade's name. It doesn't take me more than a minute to discover that she died three years ago. That's okay, I decide, because the crime reporter she used as a source for her book might be a better resource. I enter her name, Cecily Lofton, and find her name splattered over Arbor State University's website. Graduated from her career as a reporter for the *Iola Press*, Cecily now teaches journalism classes down the street. She might know Henry, or even my father, who teaches a handful of mortuary science classes as an adjunct professor when he's not at the medical examiner's office.

I skim Cecily's articles in online archives while keeping an eye on the library door. Despite the haziness of my memories, I know her reporting is curiously spot-on. She mentions groupspeak and even knows a few phrases. She notes how we all talked in low voices. She describes our pesco-vegetarian diet. And she writes about honesty circles as if she's been in one. I decide I need to talk to her. She could fill in the gaps, I feel. Straighten the picture, sharpen the shimmery edges of my memory. Maybe, if she can tell me enough, she can stop me from floating into dreamy bursts of fragmented emotions from that time.

After reading Susan Wade's book, I'm starting to wonder if Dr. Diehl was wrong. If I can recount what happened and finally fill in the details, maybe it'd be more helpful than harmful to me. Protective, even. If I know exactly what happened during the time between when Lollie was kidnapped and the Flock died in the twin vans, I can't be blindsided by what Arlo may uncover and broadcast to his listeners.

According to Cecily's faculty webpage, her next office hours are on Monday. She's in Bowers Hall, a redbrick building near the one where Henry's office is located on campus. The college students return next week, so I might be able to hide among the crowd and pay her a visit. I snap a photo of the room location on my phone and startle when I hear the front door chime, announcing someone's arrival. I close out of the window and whirl around, expecting to see Sharon clutching her cup of ice cream.

But, no, it's someone else. Diane Tai.

Lollie's mother.

I wish desperately I could hide in the back room until she leaves. She makes a beeline for the bank of copiers and begins feeding coins into one of the machines.

She's heavier now than she was years ago, and her hair is chemically straight and blond. Her feet spill over the sides of her sandals. The machine whirs to life and she works quickly, shuffling and straightening the copies that fly out.

I watch the door anxiously, praying for Sharon's return. I remember now that I forgot to fill the paper trays when I arrived, too distracted by returning Susan Wade's book to the shelf unseen. The copier will run out of paper soon, I know, and I'm the only staff available to help.

The door chimes again and a family of four enters, bringing their pre-bedtime exuberance into the quiet space. Two kids race through the stacks, and I return to my station at the circulation desk.

Sharon returns, but when she enters her office, she closes the door and picks up the phone. One of our teenage staffers arrives not long after, and she busies herself shelving books in the kids' section.

I hear a familiar whirring and clicking, following by Diane's frustrated sigh. Those fleshy feet stomp to the desk for assistance.

"The printer's out of paper," she calls from a distance.

I duck below the counter. Childish, I know. "I'm so sorry," I call, crouching. I pull a ream of paper off a low shelf near me and slide it onto the counter, hoping she'll take it and I won't have to stand.

After a minute, I hear nothing, so I stand again. Diane's distracted by a bulletin board of news and announcements, and the ream of paper still sits on the counter. My movement grabs her attention, and she finally turns.

"The copier—oh," she says. She squints. "You're still here."

"Mrs. Tai, hello. Here's the paper. Do you . . . I can help you, if you want," I stammer.

I see her face shutter and a steely resolve form in her eyes. She approaches the desk, sets down two stacks of paper, and rests her arms on the counter. She's short but she still has that domineering motherly presence I haven't felt for so long.

"Yes, you can help me, in fact. This flyer," she says, tapping a stack of papers adorned with a picture of Lollie, "needs to be hung in a visible spot here in the library. Somewhere where you'd see it every day. It's got information about a candlelight vigil for my daughter. It's been ten years since Laurel died, you know."

"I know," I whisper.

"Ten years since I heard my baby's laugh. Ten years since I felt her touch," she continues.

Longer than that, I think, but I stay quiet. Lollie was one of the original members of the Flock; she left home two years before I arrived at the Bird Haven. She left because of this woman in front of me.

But I remain quiet.

Diane stares at me, and I drop my eyes. Lollie's warm, free-spirited eyes twinkle, even in black and white. After a moment, Diane taps the other stack of paper.

"This is where I could really use your help. This flyer, this one requests any information about what happened to Laurel. Anyone who knows something, who saw something, needs to come forward."

"I've already said everything I know about that night, Mrs. Tai."

"You were *there*, Claire. You were in the room with her. Who was it? Was it you?"

Her voice is venomous but low. I shake my head and keep my eyes trained downward. She stands there for what must be another minute, but it feels like ages. Finally, mercifully, she gathers her papers, plucking one off the top of each pile. She slides those across the wooden counter, leaving Lollie's adventurous face smiling up at me.

"Dominic Bragg is gone. You don't have to keep covering for him, if that's what you're doing. Laurel didn't deserve to die. But you?"

She lets her words hang in the air. Shame settles heavily on my shoulders, just as she intended. The copier whirs to life again, spitting out hundreds of copies of Lollie's face.

I busy myself by scanning a stack of returned books. I glance up. The family of four is still here, all huddled together around a storybook. Picture-perfect.

I scan the room and startle when I see another person, his back to me as he sits at the microfiche machine. Arlo Stone. I didn't see him come in. He's clicking and jotting notes. A pair of headphones dangle around his neck. How much did he hear?

After another twenty minutes, Diane Tai leaves the library with weighty stacks of paper in her arms. Arlo waits another few minutes before he approaches the front desk.

"Claire Hollis," he says by way of greeting, checking the name tag I don't bother to cover this time. His voice is triumphant.

"That's not my name anymore. I'm married now," I say pointlessly. My hand finds its way to my mouth, and I begin to gnaw on my thumbnail.

"That must be why you're so hard to find. But here you are, right under my nose. Care to set up a time for an interview for my podcast? I can meet you here, if you'd like. Tomorrow, on your lunch break?"

He's so self-assured, I can tell he never wonders *if* I'll give him an interview, only *when*. I prickle with irritation.

"No. I don't have anything to say."

"Right. You've already said everything you know about that night," he says, throwing my words to Mrs. Tai back in my face. He waits for a reaction. I don't offer one.

"Look," he continues, "I'm just offering you a chance to tell your side of the story. To defend yourself."

"Defend myself?" I scoff. I take my hand from my mouth and shove it in the pocket of my cardigan.

"A lot of people blame you for a lot of things, Claire. For not reporting Laurel missing, for not telling anyone about the living conditions at the Bird Haven—"

"For the deaths, I know," I interrupt.

I sweep the two flyers Mrs. Tai left behind off the counter and fold them in half, throwing them in the wastebasket. I turn my attention to the computer, where I busy myself by clicking around the library catalog. My mind flicks to those brutal months, years, after the Flock died, when so many people accused me of inaction, with consequences akin to being a murderer myself. It was socially isolating. There have been threats, of course, ranging from the innocuous, such as toilet-papering our house on Halloween, to violent and invasive: a note taped to my door outlining the order in which my family should die, ending with "any infant you bring into this world." I've reported the most aggressive intimidations, but I fear it barely registers with the local police. It's only been ten years, and we're a small town—the officers who interviewed me then are still employed on the force. I've been questioned but never cleared, never charged.

"I'm just trying to find answers," Arlo says, throwing his hands in the air, palms up. Trying to show me he's nonthreatening.

I know better. I need to find answers before Arlo can broadcast my secrets to thousands of listeners.

*   *   *

On a clear, crisp night last year, Lourdes invited Henry and me over to her enviable wraparound porch, where she and her husband ferried blankets and hot toddies to us as we watched the northern lights. Surrounded by mature trees, their home had been inherited from Lourdes's uncle, who was a copper baron, as she puts it. At one time, Iola was a copper-mining community, and her uncle was at the forefront of it. The house is perched atop the world, or so it seems when you can see so infinitely far.

Tonight, the stars are out and Lourdes's fingers shimmer with rings under the twinkly bistro lights adorning their porch. The twins are in bed, but she keeps a video monitor at her side, checking the feed of their sleeping bodies every few minutes. Her husband, Daniel, hands Henry another beer without asking and wiggles a bottle of Pick Axe blond ale, picked up from the trendy microbrewery in town, in front of me.

I glance at Henry and clock the set of his jaw as evidence I should decline it. I see Lourdes watching the exchange. She winks when she catches my eye. She's been waiting for news of a pregnancy since she shared her own, but she'll need to keep waiting. I pretend for Henry, but the birth control pills still hide in the bathroom drawer.

"Sorry, can I have more water please?" I say to Lourdes, lifting my glass. She takes it and scoops up an empty dish she used to serve canapes before gliding to the French doors. Inside, the kitchen radiates warmth with its earthy green cabinets, quartz countertops, and gold finishes. Her tiny frame flits to the refrigerator and I watch her enviously, wondering if I'd be more confident if I were as pretty as her.

"So, listen to this one," Daniel says, taking a sip and settling into an overstuffed patio chair. "My glaucoma patient comes in for an emergency appointment with sudden blindness. Get this: turns out she mixed up her glaucoma eye drops with a bottle of adhesive. Glued her eyelids shut!"

Henry leans forward and prods him to continue. I shrink back, imagining sudden blindness.

Daniel senses my discomfort. "I separated her eyelids and was able to remove the glue. Vision restored," he says, his story anticlimactic but captivating to Henry all the same.

"Did you know you can see freighters on the lake from here?" Lourdes asks, changing the subject as she returns, setting before me a fresh glass of water adorned with a lemon slice. She gestures to Lake Superior, but it's too dark to see anything now. "The passenger ferry runs daily in the summer. The boys love when we spot it. It's a little miracle to them, you know? I love acting as surprised as they are, even though I know it'll pass by a little after eight every morning."

She checks the monitor again, and Daniel catches her.

"They're over two now. They're walking and talking and they tell each other knock-knock jokes. It's time to stop watching them sleep," he says gently. A conversation they've had countless times, I'm sure.

Lourdes sighs dramatically, and her rings glimmer under the lights again. "It's a habit, that's all. It helps with my phantom mommy awakenings."

I raise my eyebrows expectantly, as I know she wants me to do. Lourdes vibrates with energy, glows with attention. She's like Lollie in that way. Charming and warm and expressive. Addictive to someone like me. Lourdes has a practiced smoothness; maybe it comes from money. Lollie, though, was sparkling in her rawness. She'd never have settled down with toddlers and a husband in a big house by the water like Lourdes. No, she'd travel, untethered, leaving men in her wake to write love songs about her.

"I have these dreams, only I don't know I'm dreaming," Lourdes begins.

I steal a glance at Henry. He's masking his expression already, raising the beer to his lips to hide his smirk. He despises hearing about other people's dreams. It's a relief, because I don't want to tell him about spending the night with Lollie and Eden and Jock and Goldie and the others. I swallow up the residual dust of their nighttime frolics through my mind and remind myself that that world doesn't exist anymore, that they don't exist. The dreams always turn to nightmares and I wake, sweaty and panicked, wondering if they were actually flashbacks after all.

"I dream that something's happened to Marco or Javi. It could be anything, but it's always bad. I try to save them, but then I wake up and realize I'm dreaming."

"And I wake up because she's whacking me," Daniel adds.

Henry snorts. I smile cautiously, waiting for Lourdes's reaction to tell me what to think.

"Yes, it's true," she says, her eyes open wide. "I act out my dreams. I try to rescue the boys every night, but I just end up hitting poor Daniel. Sometimes I shout, sometimes I leap out of bed."

"Do you sleepwalk?" Henry asks, suddenly interested.

"No, I've never left the room. But Daniel had to take away the lamp on my bedside table. I keep the baby monitor there, though, because seeing the boys sleeping safely is the only thing that calms me down enough to go back to sleep."

She keeps talking, but her voice fades as Lollie's breaks in, low and breathy in the dark. She's there, in our shared room at the Bird Haven, sweaty and wild-eyed as she patted me awake in the night. She hadn't slept for days, and when she finally did, she saw and heard things that couldn't have been there, she said. A devil sat on her chest and held her down. She couldn't move, couldn't speak. I murmured back that she was too open-minded. A few days later she woke me up with stories of ants biting her all over, her vision so vivid I brushed wildly at my legs, imagining I felt them too. She clamped her hands over her ears and moaned that everything was echoing. She stopped choosing to sleep after that, giving in to the crushing weight of insomnia only rarely. Within a few weeks she went missing.

But it's not Lollie shaking me, it's Henry. "Claire, Claire," he says, distant and foggy. Lourdes and Daniel return to view. The warm night with a wide-open, starry sky isn't all that different from those nights at the Bird Haven that summer, but their shiny hair and scrubbed faces tell me I'm not there anymore. No, Daniel's eyeglasses are smudge-free, and that wasn't possible at the Bird Haven. Lourdes smells good. Henry has a little weight to spare. No, I'm here now.

But I can't shake the rare yet distinct memory of Lollie, sick like all the others. At first, everyone was just irritable, but that was easy to explain away. That summer, it was mostly all girls living at the Bird Haven, and bickering was inevitable. We didn't eat well, but we didn't know that then. We grew vegetables and ate fish we caught, but our diets weren't varied, and we were weak. Dom told us we were becoming pure, and we listened. The thought sounded magical. Right. We grew sick at the scent of cooked meat and continued our plant-based diets, growing weaker. Our sleep suffered and our periods stopped, and Dom praised it all.

But then we hurt. Muscle aches, limb pains, spasms. Me, I had it a little. But Lollie had it bad. She started to see things that weren't really there, and her memory became spotty. She lost some of her luster.

And I forgot. I forgot that I was sick, that she was sicker. I forgot about the sandy beach where the girls lay in lazy, lolling heaps. I forgot the way Helena started to stutter that summer, or the way Sunny, with her wheezy voice, would announce that her hands and feet were tingling. I forgot the way Faith talked about a demon sitting on her chest in the night too.

I forgot.

6

Laurel

Then

AT THE PINNACLE of the Bird Haven sits a rickety birding platform. It sits atop a sixty-foot ridge overlooking the lake. Once, early in the season, birders came here to count and take in the breathtaking view. After Dom took ownership of the Bird Haven, only the Flock breathlessly climbs the steep stairway built into the ridge. Yet the grassroots petitions to open the platform back up to the public don't stop.

Amid the cries of the warblers and blue jays, Claire and I sun ourselves on the platform.

"After my dad left, my mom became, like, really controlling. More often it was the little stuff that she did that drove me crazy. I wasn't allowed to shut my door all the way, let alone lock it. She laid out my outfits until I was a teenager. I couldn't have Barbies, and I never got an allowance for chores, so I never had any money. She was obsessed with dictating my life. It got worse when she remarried. My stepfather was ten times stricter than her, so . . ." I shake my head, remembering. "You can understand why I left."

Claire murmurs her agreement as she readjusts her dress. Her pale skin will burn up here, but she joins me whenever I suggest the hike.

"How could they not have seen that you needed more freedom?" she asks, her tone soft, barely above a whisper. At first, I thought she was simply shy around the others, that she'd find her voice once she saw me as a confidant, but she's still quiet even when we're alone.

She sees my expressive, adventurous side more than my mother ever did. Or maybe my mom saw it too and that's why she was so strict: to keep me from being a curious adventurer.

I once tried to explain what it was like to live with an overbearing mother to a friend, mentioning the coldness, lack of laughter, and unattainable expectations, but she scoffed. "At least you have a mom who cares," she said. I couldn't recognize her sternness as care, so since then I've been hesitant to open up about my childhood to anyone.

"Well, I, uh, I guess I had a different experience," Claire murmurs after a long silence. "My mom and dad, they wanted me to be independent. A risk-taker. They wanted a little activist. They were pretty traditional—a teacher and a doctor, after all—but it was like they were disappointed that I was this boring daughter. I just feel like they always thought I made the wrong decision. It was just . . . I don't know . . ." She trails off and licks her lips. They're red and chapped. I make a mental note to find her a tube of lip balm when I get to town to get makeup for the pageant.

"Well, we have that in common." I toss a wry smile over my shoulder as I roll onto my stomach. The sun is warm on my back.

"Do you ever feel like you overreacted by coming here?" I ask, my muffled voice masking my hesitation. My voice is normally loud and deep. Confident. If I falter, she'll know something's off. She's quiet for so long I glance up, my neck at an awkward angle, to see her gazing down at the lake.

"No. My dad was cruel, and my mom, well . . . it doesn't matter what she thinks anymore. I'll just always be a disappointment to them, so it's time I started living for myself," she says finally.

Maybe it's because Claire's only been here a few months while I've been in the Flock for two years, but I can't help but consider her to be a baby deer. She's achingly naïve and, in many ways, simply *wrong* about so much.

In the Flock, the last thing we do is live for ourselves. I see that now. We're a surrogate family. A commune of sorts. We're rejects of the community, captivated by Dom's bewitching promises, living in a blush-colored bubble of adoration centered around him.

Claire's wrong about her dad too.

I saw him just yesterday. We met at Arbor State's campus, in his lab in Wilkins Hall. The windowless building, situated on a stem snaking from the main path, isn't trafficked. He asked me about Claire first, of course. Is she eating enough, sleeping well, making friends? His eyes were tired yet alert, washed in kindness. He handed me an envelope of cash and made me promise I'd tell her he loves her.

But I don't say I saw him. I offer a vague platitude instead: "I'm sure your parents care about you."

I could tell her his suits look rumpled. That he smells of morning coffee and aftershave. That he misses her. But, selfishly, I bite my tongue. A part of me worries that if I tell her that her parents want her to come home, she'll leave the Bird Haven. I'd lose her as a friend, but that's not what bothers me. I need to keep meeting up with her dad for the money he feeds me, so I can save up enough for my own exit. I hate what this says about me and who I've become. I arrived to the Flock bruised, but I'm leaving broken. Dom's stripped me of my integrity and left only desperation.

A pair of American kestrels swoop overhead, calling out in a series of loud notes. I sit up and survey the view. The lake is a deep, dark blue, and the trees are lush and full. It's windier up here, but also warmer. I feel as if I could touch the September sun.

Lido's wind-ruffled, stringy hair appears as he ascends the steps to the platform.

"Hey, there you are," he calls. He squints and shields his eyes. "We're doing an honesty circle by the lake."

I fight a sigh. I'd rather spend an afternoon sunning up here than fielding biting remarks from the Flock. But Lido waits, his fingers dancing along his thighs to an inaudible tune. Claire rises first, offering a hand to help me up.

I follow Claire and Lido down the stairway built into the ridge, hiking my maxi skirt as I step. Claire's dress is a faded twin to my own. As she walks, I catch glimpses of her bare breasts. She's lost weight off her already slight frame.

My body aches as we hike. I walk slowly. I'm trying to avoid assigning significance to meaningless things, but I can't help but think Lido's arrival and my burning muscles are signs. Warnings to keep my mouth shut.

More than anything, I want to tell Claire I'm thinking of leaving the Flock. I want her to daydream about the Apple Queen pageant with me, to whisper and share secrets and understand me. I think of the concealed money from her father and know that it's in my own self-interest to keep quiet.

When the trees break, I see the Flock on the rocky shoreline. Faith tends to a bonfire. Morgan stares at it, expressionless. She doesn't look up when Goldie and Hunter splash her as they romp in the shallow water. Jock and Vinny playfully wrestle, while Eden braids flower stems in Helena's hair.

Dom stands from his perch on an overturned canoe on the shore, setting it rocking.

"Gather, everyone, gather," he says when he sees we've arrived.

I sit behind the twins, beside Thomas. Thomas is older, and Dom doesn't usually pull him into the honesty circle as intensely as the others. I hope to disappear into the trees back here.

"I understand someone took a drink of beer recently. Come forward and tell me why you did it."

Dom's eyes bore into me, and my instinct is to confess before I get into worse trouble. But Vinny stands.

"It was me. I found it in the woods. Some hunters left it behind. I'm sorry, and it won't happen again. I'll volunteer for more chores as long as needed," Vinny offers.

Dom nods. "Thank you for your honesty. Giving in to temptation means you haven't fully committed to my teachings. Does anyone have anything they'd like to tell Vinny?"

Eden's shrill voice rings out. "How dare you? Dom's helping us become pure beings so that we can become strong-minded warriors for the transcendence. You poisoned yourself and ruined Dom's work."

"Thank you, Eden." Dom bows his head in gratitude for his most vocal follower. "It's not only Vinny who was holding a secret. Others here are keeping things from me. Come forward and admit your weaknesses. You know who you are. But more importantly, I know. I know."

"I touched myself last night. I know it was wrong. I should have let someone else fulfill my sexual desires. It was selfish of me," Goldie admits. She blinks tears away from her big, sorrowful blue eyes.

"I was lazy yesterday and went down to the lake to avoid working in the garden," Faith says.

The others shake their heads, angry. Faith lowers her eyes.

I tuck my hair behind my ear and focus on keeping my face impassive and taking calm, even breaths. Dom's ability to spot secrets and lies is uncanny. I've offered myself to the group for dozens of infractions since I joined the Flock, but now that I have real secrets to hide, I'm terrified.

I have hundreds of dollars hidden in my shed.

I'm competing in the Apple Queen pageant this weekend.

If I win—when I win—I'm using the prize money to leave the Flock.

"There are no secrets here." Dom circles around us, brushing my hair as he passes. A sour smell wafts from him. "What about you, Lollie? Do you have anything you want to share?"

My heart begins to pound. I feel a sickening lurch in my stomach. Thinking quick, I realize I can use that.

"I've been feeling sick lately. My eyes get blurry, and my muscles hurt. Sometimes I hear this echoing in my ears." I look up. "And I know that's my own fault."

"Your feelings of sickness are descended from a lack of spiritual belief. You need to get out of your head and into your heart."

He begins to chant, quiet at first, then growing loud. He sways, and so do we. The air shimmers from the heat of the bonfire. I feel lightheaded, dizzy.

Dom, a peacock, struts around the fire, dripping sex appeal. The bewitching chant rises and fades. He begins one of his spellbinding lectures, vacillating between aloofness and warm bursts of affection. When his rants veer toward the topic of masculinity, he instructs Raina to stand.

"Take off your clothes," he instructs.

She hesitates. Dom's shoulders drop, squaring off. Slowly, she takes off her top and shorts, dropping them in the rocky sand. Dom raises an eyebrow, silent. She removes her underpants too.

Dom sits on an overturned stump and beckons for Raina to sit on his lap. He touches her breasts. Her dark hair hangs in her face. He lectures about masculinity, but it's clear he's abusing Raina to prove his power and control.

She holds her body very still. I can see in her face that she's mortified. He's stripping her self-respect right in front of us. I avert my eyes. It's wrong of Dom to do this, but couldn't he have chosen someone like Morgan for this demonstration of dominance? Judging from her robotic, lifeless stare, she wouldn't break like Raina. I can see Raina's spirit draining from her body with every moment.

"What the hell is going on here?"

We turn, the trance broken. Two hunters, clad in camouflage and Carhartt, emerge from the forest. They swing rifles on their shoulders.

"Damn," one of the hunters says, spitting a mouthful of chaw into the brush. "Is this one of them sex cults?"

Dom doesn't stand. He doesn't even stop fondling Raina. "This is private property," he says. "You're trespassing."

"Nah, man. This is public land here by the lake." The hunter shoves more chewing tobacco under his lip and squints at us.

"I own all twenty-two acres on this tract of land, from the lake to the brook to the mines."

"Huh. Well, we're gonna keep on huntin'. And if you got a problem wit it, call the sheriff." The taller hunter begins to laugh, while the other furrows his brow and curls his lip, unable to take his eyes off Raina's naked body.

"You're on my land," Dom repeats.

"Like I said," the hunter drawls, "call the sheriff. I'm sure he'd have something to say about whatever the hell it is you're up to out here."

He spits again. A trail of brown drools drips down his chin. He swipes at it with the back of his meaty hand.

"Y'all taking turns wit her?" the other hunter asks. He reaches down to adjust his pants.

"Vinny, get the gun."

The hunters exchange a glance. They hold their guns in front of their bellies as a shield.

"Jesus, Jesus. Don't shoot. We're leaving."

Their departure is long and loud. Even after their tromping footsteps fade, their laughter still rings out.

My cheeks warm with embarrassment while my chest pounds with fear.

"I hope you can see now that when I talk about entities attacking us, I'm not exaggerating. We're on a mission of awakening. These dark forces are threatened by our enlightenment. They can't understand my teachings."

Dom stands abruptly. Raina tumbles, naked, from his lap to the cold, gravelly sand. Stunned, she lays sprawled on the ground as Dom continues his raving warnings about evil outsiders.

I lock eyes with her. I sense her humiliation, her debasement.

And, just like Dom, I know. I know.

I have no choice but to leave.

7

Claire

Now

ANTICIPATION COLORS THE air on campus, shaking off the gauzy morning light filtering through the trees. I can almost feel the relief that bubbles from students finally free of hardworking midwestern parents who demanded they work minimum-wage summer jobs to pay for the textbooks they tote now.

It's nearly ten, and students buzz past as they look for their first-day classrooms. Nothing about their tan and smiling faces reminds me of my short stint as a student here. I lasted a single semester before dropping out. Memories of my time are marred by the proximity of my mother's diagnosis. Every day felt like a sludgy march toward her death until Lollie showed up outside the counseling center, charming and perceptive, and plucked me out of my misery and deposited me in the Flock. I didn't know then that she was Dom's chief recruiter, scouting girls. Collecting us. Lollie seemed wise beyond her years to me then, not to mention exotic and self-assured. Now that I'm ten years older, I see I was searching for anyone to give me an answer, any answer.

A boy hurries past and I turn, startled by his striking similarity to Lido. Lido looked just like him. Didn't he?

I stumble, frowning. I wonder if every stringy-haired, rangy boy looks like Lido or if that one really captured the upturned chin, half-closed eyes, and loose limbs I remember as he hurried down the path.

The trauma of finding my friends dead in the vans contributed to my gapped, disorderly memories, but that's only a piece of the puzzle. Some of my memories of the Flock are fuzzy thanks to the way we lived. Uncensored and liberated. Everything covered in a grainy veil of love. Until hunger set in, we stopped sleeping, and we got sick.

Other memories I've replayed so many times I'm not sure they're real anymore. I tweaked Lollie's words or turned Dom's manipulative touches into caresses. So I can't remember if Lido really had pudgy cheeks like that boy. He's become a specter to me through the years. They all have.

Before Arlo arrived, smug and eager to insert himself in trauma for gain and fame, I was content to ignore my painful past. The flashbacks and floating attacks: they're happening less and less these days. The social ostracization: I'm used to it. Yes, I am fearful of the threats to me and my family and the danger still lurking out there if Henry and I ever have a child, but even in my darker moments, I tell myself the risk lessens with every year that passes. I could have continued marching forward, albeit with sludgy steps, if not for Arlo's arrival. But now, with him inserting himself into the story—*my* story—I need to regain my memories and recall what really happened before he turns my trauma into clickbait and advertising revenue. Reading Susan Wade's book helped, but now I need Cecily Lofton to tell me what she knows.

The paths empty at the top of the hour, and I'm left alone on the path. Vulnerable. I didn't pretend like I blended in with the sparkly teenagers eager to make it to their classes on time so they can impress on the first day, but I liked the cover they afforded me. Now anyone could spot me out in the open. Henry. My father.

A girl in a denim bucket hat scuttles past, and I find the building I'm looking for. Singer Hall houses Cecily Lofton's office, and she has posted her office hours for the fall semester on the school's website. I know where to find her, and I suspect her office will be a slightly smaller version of Henry's.

A white squirrel scampers across the path in front of me, scurrying up a tree. I shudder. Even as a child, the albino creatures reminded me of rats, but now they positively disgust me. I think of Lollie every time I see one. Rather, I think of her body, and the poor hikers who found her by Union River during the annual squirrel count that fall, now ten years ago. A twin squirrel follows the first, darting across the path and up a tree, its leaves not yet touched by autumn's changing colors.

Inside Singer Hall, it's quiet. Closed doors and murmuring voices. Cecily's office is on the third floor. The door is open, and the late-morning light casts the room in a harsh glow.

Cecily Lofton looks nothing like Susan Wade. I don't know why I expected her to. I remember peeking through the curtains, watching Susan rap at the front door of our Victorian. She had a heavy bosom and heavier mascara.

Cecily, though, she's young. She can't be much older than me. Her hair still holds on to the shine of youth, and she's wearing hoop earrings bigger than a bracelet.

I hesitate in her doorway, but she sees me and waves me in. She has a beauty mark on her nose and wears a denim jumpsuit. I call her Miss Lofton, so it's no surprise she mistakes me for a student.

"I'm not a student. I'm—" I halt, unsure. "I lived with the Flock. I'm Claire."

It's enough. Cecily's eyes spark, and she gestures for me to come into her office. I shuffle in, closing the door with more care than necessary. Cecily's out of her chair, clearing a space for me in her untidy office.

"Claire," she breathes from her perch atop her desk. A vulture eyeing her prey. "Do you remember me?"

I break eye contact, scanning the small office for something to look at besides her greedy eyes and split ends, which are visible at this distance. A kaleidoscope of colors paints the wall. It's dotted with everything from beachy Polaroids to the bold brushstrokes of impressionist prints. I can't glean anything about her from this mix, but maybe that's the point.

"I remember your articles in the *Iola Press*," I say.

She smiles, and it's lopsided. "But do you remember me, like, me personally?"

"Should I?"

"I spent some time at the Bird Haven after Laurel Tai disappeared."

Impossible. An outsider at the Bird Haven? How could I not remember this?

"You lived there?" I ask, reeling.

"No, no. I didn't even stay overnight. Mostly I spent my time talking to the girls. Helena, Sunny, Goldie, and I think one other. I met with Dominic too," she says, squinting into the light as if conjuring the girls' tanned, dirt-streaked limbs and chatty mouths.

"Dom let you in after Lollie disappeared?" I can't hide the incredulity from my voice.

The days after Lollie's kidnapping passed with a long, hazy grayness. I didn't tell anyone that she was gone, not at first. Then, when Dom came looking for her and I confessed she had been taken, he didn't tell anyone either. I waited for her return by crying myself to sleep in the shed we shared or wandering the back trails, shoeless and rough soled, hoping to catch sight of her long black hair amid the brush. Alive, I told myself.

"Well, her disappearance wasn't public yet. I got an anonymous note to look into Laurel and the Flock. But when I got there, I couldn't find Laurel, and Dominic was guarded and suspicious. Rightfully so, I suppose. After a day of pawing for information, I reported Laurel missing, tipped off the police, and broke the news in the paper."

"Did we meet?"

Cecily raises an eyebrow into a perfectly sculpted, perfectly cynical arch. "As Laurel's bunkmate, I'd have loved to talk to you at the time. But no, we didn't get a chance. I saw you from a distance, but I don't know if you noticed me."

How could I not have noticed her? She'd have been a scrubbed, fresh-faced girl amid our late-summer grime and squalor.

"So what brings you here now?" she prompts.

"Have you listened to *Birds of a Feather*?"

She nods, her head bobbing close to mine. I lean back in the chair to put some space between us.

"The first episode dropped, what, a few days ago? It's good. Thorough and engaging so far. I've listed to some of Arlo Stone's older shows too. He tells a good story, that's for sure. But," she sighs, exhaling loudly from her nose, "he's not always the most impartial host once he gets into the thick of it."

"What do you mean?"

"Well, you found me here, so you know I teach journalism, right? Right," she answers herself. "You can still show diversity of opinion fairly and accurately as an impartial journalist. People forget that." She toys with an earring, tugging it until her earlobe stretches. "I've just found that Arlo Stone tends to become a little unbalanced as a story unfolds before him on the air."

"So I don't stand a chance," I say. I feel my shoulders drop, deflated.

"What makes you say that?"

"You listened. He's hinted that he's, well, skeptical, about my role in all this," I say, gesturing widely.

She offers a fishhook smile, or maybe it's a smirk. "Do you have something to hide?"

"I just . . . I just want to know what he's going to say."

Cecily blinks dramatically, theatrically. She leans back and scratches her head. "But you were there. You know better than anyone what happened at the Bird Haven."

"That's the thing," I say, looking away. My eye catches on an unframed print of floating lanterns drifting into a dreamy sky. "There's so much I don't remember. Like, an embarrassing amount. Like I wasn't there at all. Like I didn't live it." My voice hitches, and I turn back to her. "I need someone to fill in the gaps. You're an expert on the Flock. I read your articles. You know more than I can remember. And I need someone to tell me the truth, or to remind me of it, before I hear it on Arlo's podcast. I want to remember my story before he tells a different one."

I may have come to terms with my memory gaps, mostly, but I hate the thought of a smug outsider descending on Iola to broadcast a story about my life, my friends, to the world—a story that may or may not be true. I've actively tried not to think about the Flock for years, but with looming attention from the podcast, I know I finally need to get the answers. It's funny: Dr. Diehl urged me to avoid triggers and memories to protect myself, but now, with Arlo's arrival, digging into my past may be the *only* way to stay safe from scrutiny.

"Knew," Cecily says.

"What?"

"I knew more then. I don't know it now. Not necessarily. I'm open to talking, but I'd have to refresh myself with my notes from that time. It was a long time ago."

"Okay," I say, nodding my head vigorously. "Okay. So, you'll talk with me more? About Dom, about Lollie?"

Cecily agrees to meet me after she reacquaints herself with the case, as she calls it. I'm used to this. I've been a case before. A subject, a patient, a file of paperwork. A "secondary victim," I once heard myself called. We exchange numbers, and I leave after deflecting an offer for Cecily to tell my story with a ghost-writing collaboration.

I skitter though campus, as nervous as the white squirrels, worried that Henry will spot me through his office window or as he heads to a meeting. Cecily's phone number feels like gold in my pocket, weighty and full of promise. Arlo may be a threat, but Cecily could be my key to regaining control over the narrative.

I'm nearly to my car when my phone pings. Is it Cecily, so soon?

I read the notification on the screen: "Birds of a Feather: Episode 2 now available."

* * *

I sink into the clawfoot bathtub to listen to the new episode. It's midday, and a soak feels indulgent. I skip the bubble bath, opting for unsettlingly hot water. I turn up the volume on my phone and set it on the closed toilet seat. Submerged up to my neck, I wait as the piano notes conclude their already-familiar tune and my voice fills the tiled room.

High and girly yet unnaturally calm. Younger than I sound now, I think.

"Well, uh, the folks who live at the old bird sanctuary . . . well, I have a tip that they are dead."

I ask to remain anonymous and give an approximate address of the Bird Haven. The emergency dispatcher is skeptical of the tip; you can hear it in his bored monotone. Maybe if I'd conveyed more urgency, he would have too. But the Flock was dead in the only vehicles available, so I had to walk miles into town to get to a phone just to make the call. I didn't leave that night, though, as Arlo points out. I made the call two days after I found my friends. Sometimes shock propels you into action, and sometimes it brings everything to a standstill.

"At least she made the call this time. As you might recall from episode one, Claire Hollis never reported Laurel Tai's kidnapping, just three weeks before, to the authorities," Arlo says, his voice bitter. I think of what Cecily said. So much for impartiality.

I sink below the hot surface of the bathwater and let my hair float weightlessly while I wait out a commercial break. When I return, Arlo's reciting the names of all fourteen Flock members who died ten years ago.

"Helena Fields, eighteen, of White Pine, Michigan, enjoyed picking blueberries, riding her bike, and reading."

Reading? I never saw Helena pick up a book. Besides, reading to Dom was my job in the Flock. I wrinkle my nose.

"Georgann 'Goldie' Mills, nineteen, of Bete Grise, Michigan, liked to spend time with her family, her boyfriend, and friends from her youth church group. She sang in the choir."

At this, I snort. Goldie had a set of vocals on her, sure, but I only ever heard them when she was having sex with Hunter or, when he was busy, one of the girls.

Arlo continues, offering a rosy snapshot of each member of the Flock who died. In his recounting, Faith's an outdoorsy girl who loved her family's Great Dane and beachside bonfires. That rings true; she was often the one tending to a fire when we gathered on the lake's rocky shore that summer.

Jock's real name is untraceable, Arlo reports, so he can't wax nostalgic about him. His given name was Jacques, I remember, and he was a French Canadian runaway. I guess I never told anyone that in the aftermath. His dad was abusive, Jock told us, and he was only in Iola until he could get enough money to go to California. He'd been with the Flock just a few weeks when he died. He hadn't been anointed with a nickname, only a lazy, Americanized erasure.

Another voice enters the bathroom as Arlo welcomes a man named Simon to the show. In a gravelly voice, Simon recounts his job as a first responder—lingering over the stench in the garage, the condition of the bodies. Haranguing me for waiting so long to report it.

Before long, the piano returns, and so does Arlo. "The emotional impact of this single event is beyond imagination," he says. "It affected family and friends of those who passed away, of course, and also the people of the small town of Iola. Join me next week for a new episode of *Birds of a Feather* as I talk with one of Dominic Bragg's former followers."

I sit up, alert. A new voice slinks into the room, earthy and slow. "Dom's paranoia just grew and grew. Luckily, I got out before things got really bad and Lollie was taken. If I hadn't, I'd probably be dead too."

Who was that?

The episode ends and I drain the bathtub, racking my brain. My skin's hot to the touch as I redress. I thought I was the only survivor.

*　*　*

After a disarming visit to the grocery store, where Lollie's knowing smile on the memorial vigil flyer is pasted to the sliding glass door, I fix dinner for Henry and me.

He tells me about the first day of school, checking his phone at least three times as he lifts chunks of chicken into his mouth. When a server overheats, a landline gets ruptured, or the internet goes down, it's Henry's job to fix it. His workload balloons when the students return to campus after a quiet summer, and he's humming with energy.

He regales me with a story about a cybersecurity attack at a neighboring university, but I have no stories to offer back. I didn't have a shift at the library today, I skipped my garden therapy, and I spent the afternoon squinting into my memory to place the nameless woman who spoke on Arlo's podcast earlier today.

Most of the Flock members were young. Educated, affluent even. But unanchored. Most people believe that only stupid, weak people join cults. But we were just desperate to believe in something. Away from home for the first time. Alone, vulnerable. We thought it was a fresh start, but Dom waged a war against our pasts, then a war against our autonomy.

I couldn't see then how Dom manipulated us, so my therapist would regale me with stories about famous cult leaders and the women, if any, who survived. She explained how cult leaders capitalize on turbulent times to build and grow a following. How they charismatically gain trust, build an image of a safe haven, then begin to test loyalty. How, then, they break their followers down to the point we can't contemplate leaving or resisting death. Dr. Diehl's goal, I knew, was to show me I wasn't alone, that I wasn't weak or gullible. I was prey. But the exercise did the opposite: it shamed me to learn my mind was bent so easily, that all it had taken to brainwash me were a few tried-and-true conformity and obedience techniques.

There were more women than men in the Flock. We considered Dom to be either our lover or our guru. To me, he was a mystic, a leader. It wasn't until later he began to love-bomb me. What about the woman on the podcast? Who was she to Dom, and Dom to her?

Henry scoops me a bowl of ice cream after dinner. We sit shoulder to shoulder on the couch and settle in for a night of Netflix. Henry turns on a comedy special and laughs too loud. I crave a glass of wine, but I know Henry wouldn't like it, just in case there's a chance I'm pregnant. I know I'm not, so I sink into the ice cream and agree when he offers to get me a second helping.

Later, Henry pulls the curtains closed and we make love on the couch. After, he mutes the TV, and we sit in our underwear and talk about our weekend visit to Lourdes and Daniel's house on the bluffs.

"And Lourdes's story about the boys calling all insects bees," he says. "I couldn't stop laughing at her impressions of the people waiting for the ferry, all freaking out while the boys were just spotting ants."

I laugh, but I wish we didn't have to mention kids again. Lourdes's kids, or any kids.

"I like these nights together, just us," I try. "This is nice."

Sometimes it bothers me Henry asks so little about my past. By the time we started dating, what happened to the Flock wasn't the daily news story it had been in 2012. Media coverage had died down, and the police questioning had mostly stopped by then. But the town hadn't forgotten, and how could they? Iola is small, and so many families were affected by the deaths or knew someone who was. With no trace of Dom, I took the brunt of the blame. From slashed tires to smashed windows, the threats were sometimes violent. I explained all that to Henry when we met, but sometimes I wonder if he ever grasped the enormity of my role in the town's tragedy.

Eventually, we lapse into a comfortable silence, my head on Henry's bare shoulder. Earthquakes every time he laughs. We go upstairs and he falls asleep in minutes, but I lie awake.

Arlo's newest podcast has sparked more memories for me. Memories I didn't know I'd even lost. Tonight, as Henry's arm drapes over me, I think of the way I found Goldie and Hunter in the van. Then I picture them alive. Their voices always rang loudest during group sing. They were there during my first visits to the Bird Haven, and although I found out later they were love-bombing me like we did for all new recruits, their words, spoken in soft voices, seemed authentic in their flattery. Of course, I remember the confessions Goldie made during honesty circles and the way her hair fell out near the end. Hunter couldn't find the right words anymore, and his hands took on tremors.

I frown into the dark room. In those last weeks, it seemed everyone was sick. We sprawled lifelessly in the old ornithologist's cottage—Dom's inheritance, or so we were told—indulging our irritability and pain. We didn't look that much different than the way I'd find everyone in the vans at the end of the summer. The only difference that time was that I stood over the bodies instead of intertwining my sun-baked limbs with them.

I thought it was our unhealthy diet that left us ailing, but maybe it was something more than that. Why was the Flock so sick at the end? Did it have something to do with their deaths?

*   *   *

The morning sun warms my neck as I transplant a crop of sun-starved wildflowers. They'll grow in the pebble beaches of Lake

Superior, but they resist my care in my father's yard. The light's still delicate, and a gentle breeze tosses the scent of buttercups my way. I look up when I smell coffee.

My father stands on the porch. Smart and stiff in his black suit, he inhales from a plain white mug and watches me.

"Oh! I didn't know you were home," I call.

"I'm leaving for the office soon," he says. "Say, Claire Bear, are any of your mother's orchids still around?"

I nod and start picking my way through the wild growth, stopping when I realize he isn't following me. "They're on the west side of the house. I've propagated them. There're at least a dozen plants now."

He sips his coffee and nods his approval. A delivery truck pulls to the front of the house and a driver hops out. He hurries up the path, and I fumble with my yard tools to free a hand. The deliveryman reaches the porch steps first, where he offers a grin and a "Good morning" to my father.

Grant replies curtly and doesn't reach for the package. The man deposits it on the steps and returns to his van, gone as quickly as he arrived.

I bristle at his overt unfriendliness. It's noticeable in a town this small. He's usually more welcoming. As gracious as a dinner party host when he's in the public eye. But today he stands ramrod straight and carries a disapproving quietness. I internalize it immediately, wondering what I did to make him upset.

His exacting nature is a breeding ground for my insecurities; it's been that way for years. He remains a few steps above me on the porch, exuding dominance.

"I've agreed to participate in the podcast. I'll defend our family. I want you to say nothing to Arlo Stone. Nothing more, that is," Grant says. He sets his mug on the wooden railing and looks at me. "Is that clear?"

I'm nearly thirty, but still I cow down to my father. He must know that Arlo talked to me at the library, and maybe he even knows about that awful run-in with Diane Tai. He has an eerie awareness of my thoughts and actions. Are all parents like that with their children, or just him?

When I was twelve, my father came home from work one night and, before taking his shoes off, marched over to the family computer where I was browsing aimlessly and pulled the power cord from the wall. The desktop powered down with an abrupt woosh. "That's enough," he said, before storming off. I sat, stunned, before retreating to my pink room to cry. I've been trying—and failing—to figure out what makes him tick ever since.

Truthfully, fear of his judgment has driven a big part of my recovery, if you can call it that. In no uncertain terms, he urged me to move forward, to avoid dwelling on my past. To release any desire to fill in the gaps in my memory. He resumed his role as the undercurrent that keeps me moving, and in response, I went limp and let him guide me.

I sit on the steps and gaze into the blooming yard. "When will you talk to Arlo?"

"My interview is scheduled for tomorrow afternoon. The episode will air a few days later. It won't be the next release; that's already scheduled. I believe that one includes an interview with a woman named Daisy."

Daisy.

I couldn't place the voice, but I know the name: Daisy Shea. Lollie's enemy.

CHAPTER

8

Laurel

Then

"YOUR CRUEL FAMILIES expressed their disappointment, their embarrassment, in you. Not me, no. Tell me, how did your parents disappoint you? How did they fail you? Write it down on your paper. You'll feel a catharsis when you dig into your past pain."

The cane-backed wheelchair squeaks as Dom rises. A small grayish-brown rabbit nestles against his bare chest. The rabbit's ears are pinned back flat, its body tense, as the chair's squeal wakes it from slumber.

It's another rainy night. Dom's gathered us in the living room of the cottage to write our autobiographies. It's an exercise I've done before. I've been chastised for not having deep revelations, so I've penned sordid tales about an abusive, heartless home life.

The papers, I know, sit in Dom's drawer, ready to be used as blackmail should I ever try to leave the Flock.

Catlike, Dom slinks to Claire's side, rabbit in arm, and peers over her shoulder to the blank page.

"I'm surprised you, of all people, would struggle with this exercise," he says in a quiet, fluttery voice. "What, with your history . . ."

"What do you mean?" Claire asks.

"Just think of how your father treated you and your mother," he says. "Sometimes we can see the bruises, and sometimes we can only feel them." He places a hand on her chest, gently thumping her heart.

The rabbit nips at Dom's chin—another thing desperate for his attention—and he lowers it to the floor, where it nudges Dom's exposed ankles with its nose.

I bite my lip and doodle on the edge of my paper, watching warily from the corner of my eye.

"Let's revisit a memory, Claire. Close your eyes. You're just a child. It's summer. Your hair is white blond from days spent in the sun. It's dusk, but it's still warm. The day was warm, and the night is warm. Do you feel how the setting sun still warms your skin?" he prompts, waiting for her nod to continue.

"You're warm, but you dare not go inside. You hear the yelling. Your father is yelling at your mother. You're on the front porch. The white columns on the porch rise into the sky. It's warm," he reminds her. "You're eating a sticky popsicle. See the colors? Red, white, and blue. It's melting into a sticky purple mess on your hands. Your fingers are sticky."

Dom caresses Claire's hands. "Do you feel how sticky they are?"

Claire rubs her index finger and thumb together. "Yes! They're so sticky," she murmurs.

Beside her, I can see a tacky substance on her fingertips. Honey, maybe? Certainly not a manifested melting popsicle.

"With your sticky fingers, you stand on the porch, beside those tall white columns, on a warm, warm night," Dom guides, his voice mesmerizing in rhythmic repetition. "You hear more yelling. Yelling, yelling. You open the door with your sticky fingers and see your mother lying at the bottom of the stairs. Your father is yelling. He wants to hit you. He wants to bruise you. He wants you to be as purple as the mess on your hands. Your sticky hands."

With the back of his hand, Dom rubs Claire's pale cheeks, startling her from her reverie. "Write about your father. Explain how he abused you."

Dom moves on to Morgan, who's braiding Goldie's hair.

"Morgan, I can't imagine it's easy for you to write about all the ways your self-centered, capitalistic parents focused on making money instead of you," I hear him say.

Claire's concentrating on her paper, writing at a feverish pace.

"Wait," I whisper, eyeing Dom's back cautiously. "That didn't happen. Your father didn't abuse you or your mother."

"He did," she replies, not quiet enough. "I remember it now. I can see it in my mind, the ways he hurt us."

It's easy to picture her father as a villain when I think of his unsmiling eyes and formidable posture. I doubt he's laughed in years. He has an openly judgmental quality about him that makes me see how Claire's overly critical inner voice grew from a whisper to a shout. But he's not abusive, this I know.

"Claire . . ." I trail off when Dom catches my eye across the room.

Last year I sat in this room beside a girl named Daisy. I helped her construct filthy stories about her decent, hardworking parents. And then, when she left the Flock, I hand-delivered her paper to a mailbox tacked to the siding of her parents' modest one-story home.

Dom's always testing our loyalty. Statements full of lies are used against us as blackmail and assurance we have nothing left on the outside. He collects our fears and mistakes and uses them to humiliate us, only to reel us back into his orbit of intense love. He holds our fingers over flames, our heads underwater, just to rock us and whisper encouragingly afterward until we forget he's not the one saving us.

Outside, rain and wind beat against the windows. It smells damp, almost moldy, in the room. The stench of unwashed bodies and Dom's woodland creature give off an aroma of decay. It reminds me of that scruffy, ailing dog that wandered through our commune a few days ago. It slipped away with no fanfare in the night, breaking the hearts of all of us who couldn't help remembering our pets at home.

"There are evil things in your past. With me, you can overcome them. The outside world wants to hurt you. With me, you're protected," Dom calls over Morgan's shoulder.

The way she and Goldie gawk at him with unbridled love sends an unsettling chill down my spine.

Dom ambles to the center of the room, stepping over bare legs and papers full of rewritten personal histories. I chew on the tip of the ballpoint pen. I know what's coming next.

Once the veil started to lift, I saw Dom for what he really is: a showman. Every night, a performance. Each following a script.

First, he scrapes away what's left of our pasts. He wages a war against outsiders. He chips away at our faith until all we have left to believe in is Dominic Bragg. Then, when we're emotionally charged, he performs.

His speech becomes hyperbolic; his gait, manic. He paces, shouts, and bangs his fists for emphasis. He recites his haunting poems. Or maybe they're curses.

It's nothing new, this flair for drama, the way he fires everyone up. What wasn't there before, though, is the way he follows his show by cozying up to death.

"I see a garden of glowing, growing souls before me," Dom begins, and his lilting cadence tips me off: he's about to begin his routine.

"How could you have known you were being owned by the shallow people, the shadow people? You were lowly. Unowned, disowned. But now I'm tending to the garden, growing, grounding, engrossing." He speaks fast and loud, and he moves fast too. He's bending and jumping, touching our heads, shoulders, and hearts.

He pauses. Even the boys, Hunter and Vinny, clamor to touch him when he gets like this. The Flock reaches for him, their fingertips grazing his bare chest and pulling at the waistband of his stained pants.

That used to be me, too, when I still thought his speeches were unpolished and earnest. I thought him a poet; now I see a phony. I see his contradictions and inconsistencies. His manipulations are so obvious to me now. I used to yearn for the way his intensity would build as he painted idealistic pictures in his speeches; he gave me dreams. Then I listened to what he told the others and I realized he turns on that same conviction, like an overzealous salesman, and adopts whatever's most effective with each person. Each Flock member looks to him for something different because he adapts to what they need: religion, spirituality, self-help, or love. When we gather, he slips into another false persona, a poet talking in circles, so he doesn't disrupt each person's vision of him or their devotion.

"What's more important than this life is the life we'll lead when we transcend together, returning to dust," Dom says, raising his arms to the ceiling.

The bunny darts into the pulsing hive of bodies. Unafraid, it clambers over limbs, its ears straight and curious.

I kneel and trail my fingers from his navel to his waistband. I give him doe eyes and bite my lip. He'll take me to bed tonight. I'll do what I have to so he doesn't pick up on my disloyalty to the Flock.

Because I'm nothing if not perceptive, and I've seen enough to know I need to execute my defection perfectly, or I won't be safe on the outside. With just a few days until the Apple Queen pageant and my opportunity to win enough money to leave, I need to tread carefully.

*　*　*

I wake to the rattle of a pill bottle. Dom, naked and gaunt, tosses a handful of drugs into his mouth. His Adam's apple bobs as he dry-swallows.

My muscles ache as I pull myself to sitting. Blinking rapidly, I try to clear my eyes, but my vision is blurry. I rub my eyes with my palms and squint to see Dom lurch of out bed. His body is angular as he rifles through his wooden rolltop desk.

"Take one of the vans into town today. Pick up my medication at the pharmacy." He hands me a stack of bills and his ID card. "While you're out, drive by the bus depot and the truck stop near the highway. See if you can find any recruits. After that disaster with Jocelyn, you need to bring someone back to prove your loyalty to me and the Flock."

I want to protest; my eyes are still blurry, I can't drive. Instead, I fish my clothes from a pile on the floor and tuck the money in my pocket.

Downstairs, the girls are chopping vegetables for a dinner stew. Thomas is repairing one of the cabinet doors that's fallen off its hinge. Vinny and Hunter's voices carry through the open window. They're hauling firewood from the woods to a sunny nook near the cabin.

I find the van's keys in a drawer in the kitchen, fingering the bony rabbit's foot as I walk the dirt path to the freestanding garage. I think of Dom's pet rabbit, the way its ears pinned back against its grayish-brown body. Yesterday I heard it grunting before it lunged at Raina, covering her arms in scratches. I shudder at the thought and tuck the key chain in my back pocket.

The garage door isn't locked, so I roll it up to reveal two white vans parked side by side. I hop into one and start it up. Full tank of gas. I lift my hip and pull out the wad of cash Dom gave me for his medication. Four hundred dollars.

I tap my fingers on the steering wheel. It's less than I stand to gain if I win the Apple Queen pageant, but it's enough to get me away from the Flock. How far can I go with four hundred dollars and a full tank of gas?

My vision has cleared, mostly, enough to drive. The road out of the Bird Haven is narrow and unpaved. I bump along the path slowly, cringing as low-hanging branches claw at the sides of the van.

I pass gaping mouths of forgotten mine shafts and the old copper shipping port by the harbor. A pair of mountain bikers dart in front of me as they follow the ungroomed backcountry trails that were once paths for missionaries and fur traders. In the distance, I see the iconic clock tower that looms over Arbor State's campus.

Iola's a dying town. The locals are aging. The college keeps Iola alive, but the town's crumbling buildings deter new students, and enrollment is dropping. What will happen if it shutters its door like so many other businesses around here?

I take a right from Depot Street onto Main and pull into an open spot in front of the pharmacy. It's tucked between a fudge shop and the Laughing Loon, a kitschy gift shop better suited for a tourist town.

The keys are still in the ignition. I could follow Main Street back down the old 26 and head south. Away from Iola, the Bird Haven, Dom.

Four hundred dollars wouldn't get me more than a few hundred miles away. A few days at most. I could pocket the money and lie low until the pageant. If I win, I'll have enough for the first month's rent in a Podunk town somewhere downstate. Or enough to get to Chicago and figure out lodging later.

I think of Dom's pills rattling around the bottle this morning. What's his medication, anyway?

With a sigh, I shove the keys, rabbit's foot and all, into my back pocket and hop out of the van. Tinkling chimes announce my arrival at the drugstore. A kindly woman sets down a Stephen King book on the counter and greets me.

"How can I help you today?" She's soft-spoken, her voice feathery.

"I'm picking up a prescription for Dominic Bragg," I say. I have his ID in my pocket, but she doesn't ask to see it. She squeaks away in bright-pink Crocs and returns with a white bag.

Risperidone, the label reads.

"How much, uh . . . how much does this cost?" I ask, fingering the label with Dom's name.

"Well, we don't have insurance on file, so you're paying out of pocket. The retail price is three hundred ninety-one dollars for thirty one-milligram tablets."

"Oh. I'm not sure I have enough money to pay for this today." I tuck a strand of hair behind my ear. "What would happen if he didn't take his medication for a few days?"

The woman purses her lips. "I'm really not supposed to share medical information with anyone other than the patient, but . . . this is an antipsychotic. It treats mood and mental disorders. You'd need to withdraw gradually from this med. A sudden cessation, well, there could be a relapse of psychotic symptoms. Vomiting, nausea, delusions, or suicidal thoughts, even. Do you know if Mr. Bragg is completely out of his prescription?"

"I don't know. Just . . . just a moment, please."

I step away from the counter. Beside me, there's a shelf stocked with antiseptics, bandages, and gauze. From my pocket I retrieve Dom's money and count it again.

Turning around, I force cheer into my voice. "Good news. I do have enough after all." I hand her the stack of wrinkled bills in exchange for the paper bag.

Back in the van, tears fall freely. I can't save myself by unleashing a medically unstable Dom onto the others. Who knows what he'd do to them?

I turn the key in the ignition. The rabbit's foot tickles my bare knee. There's a year-round campground with primitive camping sites on the edge of town. It attracts transient people in the summer.

I'll look there for a new recruit.

CHAPTER

9

Claire

Now

DAISY SHEA AGREES to meet me at Johnny and June's, a smoky hole-in-the-wall too far from campus for any college students to get to.

It's only four in the afternoon, but there are more people in the bar than I expect. I anticipate a bedraggled woman already drunk on whiskey or wine, but Daisy is wearing tailored cigarette pants and a watch nicer than anything I've ever owned.

She waves me to a booth near the back. I take her in with the critical eye of Lollie's best friend, trying to find any flaw. But her eyeliner is enviously straight, and she smells like vanilla and lilies.

"Did Arlo tell you about my interview? Is that why you wanted to meet?" she says when I sit.

"Hello to you too," I mutter as I look to catch the waitress's eye for a much-needed drink. This was a bad idea.

"We're not friends, Claire. We never were. Let's dispense with pleasantries. I need to be home by dinner."

It's easy to remember everything Lollie told me about Daisy now that I've met her. She'd left the Bird Haven before I arrived. Once Lollie's closest friend in the Flock, Daisy tried to convince her to leave with her. When Lollie insisted on staying, Daisy told Lollie's mother where she was, inciting Diane Tai's fury. It further fractured their relationship, and Lollie's stepfather disowned her from the Tais. The Flock became her only family. And Daisy became her enemy.

"Fine. It's just . . . there's a lot I don't remember about being at the Bird Haven. My therapist said I have PTSD, and that affects my memory." I wince. Too vulnerable, and Daisy feels it too. She looks away.

"Until I heard your voice at the end of the last episode," I continue, "I forgot there were other survivors. People who chose to leave."

Daisy looks back as the waitress arrives. She waves off a drink, but I order a beer, thinking it's what will arrive fastest.

"I don't consider myself a survivor," she says, brushing her hair behind her shoulder. A too-big wedding ring glints on her skinny finger. "If anything, I'm a defector. But I really don't want to be associated with the Flock."

I frown. "Then why'd you agree to be interviewed for the podcast about them?"

She affects a troubled sigh, and I realize she's one of those girls who likes to stir up drama, then wonder why there's always a spectacle surrounding her.

"Arlo wanted to know more about what led up to Laurel's murder. He thinks that—oh, I don't know if I should be telling you this."

"What?" My voice is high and screechy, and the waitress raises her eyebrows at me as she deposits a Bud Light on the marred tabletop.

Daisy juts out her lower lip. Glossed, of course. "He thinks that Laurel was the linchpin of the Flock, and when she died, it set into motion the deaths of everyone else. Except you, obviously."

"And what did you tell him?" I prompt, taking a sip from the cold bottle. I feel less fidgety now that I have something to hold in my hand.

She tilts her head to the side, studying me. Narrowed eyes study me. "I told him I think you're involved in Laurel's death."

I glance around the room. There are two men in faded ball caps at the bar, but their eyes are trained on a television above the mirrored back wall of the bar. A woman sits alone at a high-top nearby, pretending to be engrossed in her phone. Listening to us, I'm sure. Daisy's not quiet, but then she doesn't think she needs to be.

"Why would you tell him that?" I whisper. I think of Henry, how upset he'll be, and my father, how he'll set his jaw in that familiar way, disappointed and furious all at once.

"Because it's what I believe. I think you were jealous of Laurel, maybe of her relationship with Dom—I don't know. But I think you were involved and tried to cover it up. Maybe the Flock helped, and maybe that's why they killed themselves. But why you're alive . . ." She shakes her head and sighs.

"You think I killed Laurel."

"A lot of people do. I mean, some hate you because you didn't report her missing, and others hate you because they think you killed her. Either way, you're involved. Like I told Arlo."

"That's absurd. You think the others killed themselves after helping me murder my best friend? Then why am I the last living member of the Flock?" I take a hearty swig of beer, trying to convey a self-assured nonchalance, only to hope Daisy has the answer. I've lived under an umbrella of suspicion for years. There were plenty of nights, especially after long, fruitless police questionings or days of fielding blame from strangers in town, when I thought the scrutiny would destroy me and I wondered why I couldn't have just departed with my friends.

"Well, you're not. You didn't die in the suicide, but you're not the only living Flock member."

I wait, annoyed she'll make me ask her to explain. "What do you mean?" I say finally when she checks her showy watch.

"There were Flock members who didn't live at the Bird Haven. Others 'anointed' themselves after the suicide. They follow Dominic's teachings, whatever that means, and wish they'd have been there too. Pathetic." She rolls her eyes. "But yeah, there are still loyal followers who think Dom's alive somewhere. They've got all these theories and search for him and stuff."

Daisy tosses her shoulder bag on her arm. She's done here. "You really didn't know?"

I lift the bottle to my lips again, hoping to hide my expression. Shame and embarrassment fall into their familiar positions as my cheeks flame.

"Look," she says as she stands. "We're not 'birds of a feather.' We don't flock together. I don't want to hear from you again. I told Arlo everything I have to say. It's too bad you've got memory loss or whatever, but it's probably for the best. No one wants to remember killing their best friend."

Daisy leaves, and before the door bangs shut, the woman from the high-top empties her pint glass in my lap.

"Murderer."

*   *   *

On old 26, on the outskirts of Iola, I spot Arlo Stone on the side of the road.

I hesitate for a moment, then park at a pullout that offers a view of a lighthouse in the distance.

Arlo looks surprised to see me. He's positioning a tripod in the rocky terrain, aiming it at a low billboard that sits off to the side of the road. FIND MY KILLER, it reads in giant red letters. Even the offer of a $25,000 cash reward can't distract from Lollie's dreamy smile.

"My family pays for this sign," I call to him as I stand behind my open car door, conscious of my beer-soaked pants.

"Does the reward money come from your family too?" Arlo asks as he squints into the camera's lens.

"We want to know what happened to Lollie just as much as anyone."

"That's why I'm here," Arlo says.

I wait for a car to pass. "Why do you think you can solve this when the police haven't been able to?"

I think of the extensive investigation, the years of police inquiries, the open case file, of being pulled into the station when the case was punted to an idealistic new officer. A person of interest was never named in Lollie's death. At the same time, I was never cleared of suspicion. The autopsy pointed to strangulation, but the original officers on the case couldn't agree on much more than that. Did she leave with someone willingly, or was she forced? There was no contact DNA left behind, and the bruising patterns didn't conclusively point to a man's or woman's hands. They couldn't agree on the height or the weight of the perpetrator. By butting heads so early on, they bungled the investigation, though it hardly ended there. Investigators have tried to resurrect it for years. I can't decide if their inability to solve it is good or bad for me.

"Because I'll talk to anyone who might have a lead. Because every time I share the story, I wonder, what if this is it? What if this is the interview that someone hears that prompts them to give the right information to the police? What if they finally catch her killer?"

His words settle into the vast vista beside the road. I watch him fiddle with the camera again before I speak.

"Fine. I'll talk to you."

Arlo turns and pushes his round glasses up his nose. There are bags under his eyes and his pants are too skinny, his hair too groomed, for this part of the state.

"Next Tuesday, two o'clock?" he says.

I agree.

"Good." He gazes out at sweeping views of surrounding forests flanked by Lake Superior. Below the short cobblestone guardrail, a hawk flies by on an air current below us. "I'm going to talk about you no matter what, so it'll be good to hear your perspective. You're at the center of this story."

"I thought Lollie was the linchpin of this case," I say, echoing Daisy's words.

He shakes his head, but his hair doesn't fall out of place. "I think Laurel's a catalyst, but I think you're at the epicenter of it. I think you know more than you're letting on, about everything."

I feel scrutinized. I point to his camera to change the subject. "Why are you filming? A podcast doesn't need visual content, does it?"

"It helps to have supplemental content for marketing, social media posts, that sort of thing. But, just based on the first few episodes of *Birds of a Feather*, I've gotten a few offers for a documentary about the Flock. Cults are pretty hot these days. So I'm taking some preliminary footage in case the ink dries on one of the deals."

Arlo turns and repositions the camera to face the vista.

From the lookout, I can see Lake Superior and, thanks to the clear skies, the remote island archipelago of Isle Royale some fifty miles away. Soon, when the trees stun with changing autumn leaves, this peak will become a must-see on travelers' bucket lists.

I wonder if I'll see this view much longer. Strangely, I don't want to leave Iola, despite my notoriety. The stigma is haunting, but I don't want to rebuild again. Now, though, the weight of Arlo's podcast and a possible film feel crushing.

What if the scrutiny returns to what it was after the deaths? Can I withstand that?

* * *

I wait until Labor Day, when Henry's about to go on a day-long mountain bike ride along the ungroomed backcountry trails with his coworkers, to tell him I agreed to an interview for Arlo's podcast.

It's a sunny morning, and the temperature hovers in the low sixties. Henry is checking the tire pressure on his bike on the porch when I approach with two mugs of coffee. I'm still in my bathrobe, but he's in skintight bike shorts and a shirt that accentuates the stomach pooch that's developed in his thirties despite his best efforts.

I offer him a mug, but he declines.

"It makes me too jittery on a long ride. You know that." He's irritated. His bike pump is rattling and one of his coworkers just texted that he's bringing his wife, a novice mountain biker.

"I agreed to an interview with Arlo Stone. It's next week," I blurt.

I've never been good at small talk, and I'm often too single-minded, but even I know I've picked a bad time to tell Henry. I rub at a scuff on the old porch with the toe of my slipper and avoid looking at him.

He's silent for a long time. The clicking of his wrench is the only sound. I stand, frozen, afraid to move and break the spell.

"Do you care at all about our future?" he says finally.

My shoulders sag with both relief and despondence. "Of course I do."

"You turned down countless offers for paid interviews from major networks. Why would you agree to a free interview with a nobody now? When we're trying to have a baby, of all times. The stress alone should have made you turn down this interview, but if you really wanted to talk now, you might as well sell your story and get us some financial security. It's not like your job at the library is enough to sustain a family."

"You make enough to support us," I say.

"Do you have any idea how much money a baby costs, Claire? As it is, we've been trying for months. Soon we'll have to talk about fertility treatments. And those cost an arm and a leg."

Henry sighs and turns his attention back to his bike, pressing down on the tires to check their pressure. I think of the birth control pills hidden in the bathroom. Guilt bubbles in my chest. Too familiar a feeling.

I used to think his unwavering focus on the future was a good thing, but it still frustrated me that he didn't grasp the weight of my past. Now I see that we're just on two ends of the same continuum. My depression keeps me rooted in the past the same way his anxiety fuels his concern about the future.

He leaves not long after. I sit on the porch swing and worry that I'll need to talk to him about the interview again when he gets home. Our conversation became about a baby so fast that we barely talked about the podcast. I wonder if that's how all conversations will start to go: "What's for dinner?" will become "How many days till you ovulate?" until I get pregnant or he leaves me, disillusioned and aching for a child.

I try to imagine a child clambering over the shaky boards on the wraparound porch. The Queen Anne, built for the owner of a now-shuttered department store downtown in the late 1800s, undoubtedly housed countless kids over the years. I picture a toddler hiding in the butler's pantry, tossing food off her plate in the breakfast nook, and playing with dolls on the sun porch. It's not a bad thought.

Then I think of Lollie's killer, still roaming around Iola or Lapeer or somewhere along the peninsula. I think of him coming back, targeting me, and leaving her motherless. Worse, I imagine him coming for her.

For years, I've felt followed. Watched. In my darker moments, I'm sure it's Lollie's killer. Other times I'm almost wistful imagining it's Dom, keeping an eye on me. I know now that both are equally dangerous to me and any children I might have. I've come to terms with my memory gaps, I've accepted I'll be a social pariah as long as I remain in Iola, but still I remain fearful that something—someone—will return for me.

Henry wouldn't understand how I fear for a child's safety. Would a baby be safe from me, with my history of depression? What if I have a floating episode while giving a newborn a bath and she drowns? Would a baby be safe from the outside world, from the killers and cults lurking in my past?

For some, though, the Flock isn't in the past. I think of what Daisy said at Johnny and June's. There are people who think

Dom's alive somewhere, who fell for his charisma and charm from afar.

If the Flock hadn't died, and Dom had stayed, would I still be at the Bird Haven with them?

I fish my phone out of the pocket of my bathrobe and begin to search the internet. It's not hard to find. There's a private Facebook group dedicated to the Flock, but there are open Reddit discussion threads too.

I skim the threads quickly, worried that I'll start to float if I sink too deep into the comments. Dozens of people wax nostalgic about Dominic Bragg and the Flock for pages and pages. There are some—women, I can tell from the writing style—who idolize Dom as a romantic figure. But more worship him as a mystical guru now.

They agree that Dom offered stability in an unstable world. They talk about his spirituality and his path to simplicity. They pine for the Flock's family-like sense of security. They stir my desperation.

He was a prophet of false promises, my therapist shouts in my head. *He played on your dissatisfactions.*

I rub my eyes. It's dangerous, reading these discussion threads. These people behind their screens, they crave what I lived through. They yearn to have been a part of the Flock, to have roamed the Bird Haven's twenty-two acres. To have splashed in the brook with Eden and Faith, to have been scouted by Lollie and presented to Dom.

I remember standing outside Arbor State's counseling center so long ago. Lollie approached, her black hair gleaming in the sunlight. She didn't waste time confiding in me. On a bench, while the white squirrels scampered around campus and a report of my failing grades burned in my backpack, Lollie told me how she could pick up on unspoken feelings. We bumped elbows as she told me she knew what it's like to feel lost in the tide of everyday life.

"I want to live in a world where I have the freedom to live as I want and others can too," she said. "Don't you?"

She was pretty and open and warm. Free-spirited. Everything I wanted to be.

I said yes, and she took me back to the Bird Haven with her.

If only for a short time, I had what the Flock dreamers on the internet want so bad: I had something to believe in. I had Lollie.

CHAPTER

10

Laurel

Then

EDEN AND GOLDIE flank Dom's wooden wheelchair as he sits, shirtless with a sherpa-collared denim jacket thrown over his bony shoulders, at the fire pit. A dim glow from the cottage halos around his head, giving his hair a greasy shine.

"Look at me here, tonight. I sit before my enemy with extraordinary resilience. When I was a young boy, a house fire claimed the lives of me and my family," Dom says, his voice low and quiet. He pauses, looking each Flock member in the eye. "Yes, it claimed me. Yet here I sit before you. A miracle. A deity, perhaps."

"What happened, Dom?" comes the breathy voice of Helena.

I look away and poke at the fire with the charred tip of a broken branch. I've heard the story before.

"It was Christmastime. We didn't have much, but we had a tree with a few presents. A faulty string of lights caught fire, and the dry tree went up in flames. The speed, the destruction . . . it was unimaginable. The fire killed my mother, father, brother, grandmother, and even me. I was legally dead for nearly twenty minutes before a paramedic revived me. It was that near-death experience that opened up my psyche. My consciousness, and maybe even my soul, cracked open that day. It's the reason I know what I do."

The fire: it's a myth.

The last time he regaled the group with his fantastical story of death and resurrection, the fire's cause was an unattended frying pan on the stove. Before that, still-hot ashes from his grandmother's cigarettes ignited the trash can and overtook the kitchen in minutes. Candles, a lightning fire, an errant spark, and a small gas leak.

In the two years I've lived here, I've heard countless origin stories for the legendary fire that claimed his family and gifted him his abilities.

It wasn't until this summer, though, that I went to Iola's local library to look up the story myself.

As the Flock's recruiter, I'm the only one who gets to leave the Bird Haven regularly. After a morning looking for recruits outside the town's counseling center, I went to the dead-quiet library and asked a kind old woman to help me use the microfiche machine. When she went in the back to take a call, I abandoned the machine and opened a browser on an unlocked computer.

Searching for articles about Dominic Bragg's tragic past only showed me that he's a liar and a fraud. At twenty-nine, he's older than he claims. His parents, Tracy and Philip Bragg, are alive and well, living in Forest Hills, one of the richest cities in Michigan. He has a younger brother and sister, both studying at Michigan State. Even his grandmother is alive. She organizes an annual winter coat drive for the less fortunate.

Still simmering with anger when I returned to the Bird Haven, I thought about confronting Dom with what I'd learned at the library.

Then I remembered how it felt to feel the burn of the Flock's suspicion. A few weeks before, at Dom's showy faith healing, my pains weren't cured when he laid his hands on me, and he told the others it was because I wasn't a sincere believer. For days they'd serve the last helping of food just before they got to me. Eden led the group in shunning me, and by the third day, even Claire began to distance herself.

At our next faith healing, I spoke in tongues. Dom's amber eyes lit up with approval, and the girls' stony distance lifted.

I didn't confront Dom then, and I don't challenge his story now.

Hunter drops a log in the fire, and sparks fly from the pit. I itch my ankle where the scrubby grass tickles it.

"Lollie?"

It's Raina whose voice breaks through my thoughts. The group is quiet, waiting. Dom is looking at the fire, not me. The flames brighten his amber eyes to a fiery orange.

"Dom said you invited someone to stay with us," Raina prompts.

I nod. "Yeah, Jock. His real name is Jacques," I say with a French flair, "but he's Americanized it. He's from Canada. He's away from home for the first time."

A runaway, Jock collided with me at a campground on the edge of Iola. He was looking for a ride; I offered him a family. He was vulnerable, desperate, and escaping a destructive family.

An easy target.

I might be questioning Dom and life in the Flock, but as Jock settled into my borrowed vehicle clutching all his possessions in a floppy backpack, I knew I was saving him from certain violence. He wouldn't be missed—anyone hunting for a victim on the road could see it—so I rescued him.

"He's in the RV with Thomas right now. Getting some rest, warming up. You'll meet him tomorrow."

"Jock is looking for an identity. A path. Open your hearts and welcome him, family," Dom says, spreading his arms wide, ever a showman.

A breeze rattles the doors of the rusty birdcages just beyond the fire pit. Across the campfire, Dom's face shimmers as refracted light passes through the hot air.

The distortion shakes, setting loose a thought.

Bringing Jock here, to this isolated commune in the woods . . . am I an accomplice?

*   *   *

We all take care to touch Jock when he emerges from the RV in the morning. His back, his arms, his hair. It's part of love-bombing a new recruit.

Once, in the early days, when I was inseparable from Dom, he confided in me that most Flock members are bonded in that we have a history of failing to achieve intimacy.

So we stroke, graze, and embrace him.

It's easy; he's handsome and, at nineteen, the age of most of the girls. Faith won't stop running her hands through his hair, and I can tell it pleases Dom to see how easy Jock's conversion will be.

We shower him with flattery and attention. We hover over him constantly while we wait for him to reveal what he needs most: A place to stay? Companionship? Peace of mind? A sexual offering?

This isn't how we normally recruit.

Most recruits are young girls I find on campus at the registrar's office or the counseling center, or sometimes at the bus station. I invite her to the Bird Haven for a weekend, then a week.

But Jock, he doesn't have a home, so we've accelerated his introduction to the Flock.

We spend the day as a group, hiking en masse to the water's edge to swim naked together, bumping shoulders while we harvest the vegetables and bustle around the kitchen to make a stew. We scrub and boil copious amounts of shellfish, preparing a feast to impress Jock.

Faith is assigned to have sex with Jock after dinner, and when they stumble from the cottage bedroom with matted hair and shiny cheeks, Dom begins his lecture.

He preaches into the night.

It's another night I won't get to spend in the little shed out back with Claire. I won't sleep—I never do anymore—but I like the inky darkness and all-encompassing quiet after Claire succumbs to sleep.

Dom's lecture veers between praising the Bird Haven as an idyllic refuge to painting a frightening picture of the selfish, capitalistic outsiders determined to threaten our safety and destroy the utopia he's built.

When I feel my head jerking backward, I bite my tongue to stay awake. *Look alert*, I tell myself, biting harder. Fighting sleep, sleep that never comes when I want it to. It's dangerous to be inattentive when Dom's lecturing.

There's a rattle at the window, then a rap. Dom quiets. He walks to the window, and we watch him. The window breaks with a loud crash, sending shards of glass showering toward Dom's chest.

"We're under attack!" he yells.

Hunter leaps up, groping for his boots near the sideboard. Eden stands, frantic, and bolts for the door. Raina clambers over my legs and crawls to Dom's side.

"There are people who don't want us here. They want to attack us." Dom looks wired. In the dim light of the room, I see a splinter of glass sticking out of his forearm. "Will we let them?"

A chorus of *no*s, feeble at first, grows stronger as Dom's intensity increases.

He hisses directions: Thomas, secure the doors; Sunny, pack some essentials, enough for a few days in the woods; Lido and Hunter, patrol the grounds and use force if necessary.

The rest of us huddle in a pack in the center of the room, chilled as the cool night air seeps through the broken window. Dom drones on endlessly, insisting he prophesied this attack.

I bite my lips, my tongue, to stay awake. Exhaustion fights the adrenaline coursing through my body. I feel myself losing consciousness. Dom's pacing the room. He stops and kneels beside Jock.

"Brother, you must be under great stress." Dom speaks kindly, calmly. "We're building a perfect community here, away from the violence and volatility of the outside world. Here, we know the truth. We can transcend our imperfect, overwhelming pasts. But there are people who don't understand, who are jealous, scared. They outnumber us."

Jock looks panicky, disoriented.

"What can we do?" he asks, alarmed.

"We affirm our commitment to each other and to the future we're building," Dom says, his voice consoling, almost sweet. "We're the Flock. We sing of freedom, and we trust in our wings to help us fly."

Jock considers this. I see the muscles in his forearms tighten as he squeezes Dom's hand. Acceptance.

I watch as Dom, satisfied his crisis has secured Jock's loyalty, confers with the men. He announces that the intruder has receded: "We're safe. For now." In his voice, a warning. A warning to them, or to us?

"Return to your beds," he instructs. "Get some rest. Morgan, will you make us a treat later? Brownies, perhaps."

Mentally exhausted and weak, we disentangle ourselves from the floor. I reach for Claire's hand.

"My nerves are frayed," Dom says. "Claire, stay here and read to me."

Dom and I lock eyes until I drop Claire's hand. Not for the first time, I wonder if he really can read my disloyal thoughts.

*   *   *

The shed's lone window tells me dawn is approaching. For hours, I've stared at the birdhouses dangling from the ceiling of the shed. Their chains creak when the wind blows hard, and a slammed door sends leftover birdseed raining down on our mattress. This morning a draft works its way in, and the wooden and metal houses clank together clumsily. I gaze at them as I gnaw on a balled-up sock to keep from itching the mosquito bites dotting my arms and ankles.

Bleary-eyed, I fish the flip phone from my tote bag. Though it doesn't have service, it has a calendar—the only one at the

Bird Haven. It's Saturday. The Apple Queen pageant begins this afternoon.

I use the phone screen's meager light to illuminate a heavy bucket of rock salt in the corner of the shed. With a tip of the bucket, I check that the envelope of money I've funneled from Claire's dad is still there.

I listen. Outside, barred owls make their presence known and deer amble through the brush. The Flock is quiet after tonight's intruder drill, but I don't want to risk being spotted counting my money.

Gently, I replace the bucket of ice-melting salt and return to the mattress, which is indented from years of bearing weight. Beside me, Claire sleeps, unaware.

Two years ago, I was an idealist, and that made me vulnerable to Dom's smoke-and-mirrors act. Sick of feeling alone, looking for adventure and a family, I wanted to believe in his miracles. At first, I stayed for my friends, silently hoping it'd get better, like it was at the start. Then lack of money kept me here. Now? I fear revenge.

I can almost hear a clock ticking in my mind. The pageant starts at four o'clock, but entrants must line up by three. I'll need time to do my hair and makeup somewhere away from the Bird Haven—a gas station, or maybe the library. I'll get the makeup at a drugstore first. And, of course, there's the matter of a dress. I've been eyeing one at a boutique in downtown Iola for weeks; I visit it whenever I'm on campus to recruit. The shop doesn't open until noon on Saturdays, and there's no guarantee it'll still be there when I arrive.

I sink into the mattress and try not to think about how much I have riding on the pageant this afternoon.

It's not enough to be in the pageant. I need to be crowned Apple Queen.

It's the only way I can leave the Flock.

CHAPTER

11

Claire

Now

IT'S A BREEZY, blue-sky day, the kind that makes September in northern Michigan enviable. Sometimes I resent that the month in which the worst things of my life happened is beautiful. I want it to be full of driving rain or moody clouds to match my memories of this time.

Henry squeezes my hand as we weave through the people clumping in front of booths. It's the third day of the fall festival, and I reluctantly agreed to attend after Henry begrudgingly asked me as he scrambled eggs for breakfast. It was a test, I knew, so I pretended like the festival didn't remind me of Lollie.

I didn't attend the festival ten years ago, when Lollie was crowned Apple Queen. After trudging to the event with my parents yearly, it felt cruel to have missed her big moment, to have to see her silky red dress in newspaper ink only. But her participation was a secret, up until she won. Her charming, expressive face was splashed across the local news, on television and in print. Her name hit the radio airwaves after her win, then again a week later when she went missing.

Now Henry leads me down Main Street. Crafters hawk knitted potholders and baby hair bows. Farmers sell cheese, apples, and blueberries from downstate. There's nothing I want, but Henry buys a half pound of fudge after cooing over a sample.

Main Street isn't usually so busy; Iola is too far from the interstate, and its winters are too harsh, for the town to attract many new people. Arbor State keeps Iola alive. We can see the tree-studded campus with its redbrick buildings and tall spires in the distance.

In the stretch between Zink's Hardware and the shuttered Arcadia Cinema, in the heart of downtown, we stroll past the scarecrow walk. A line of six-foot-tall scarecrows decorated by businesses and families adorns the street.

Henry points out a *Wizard of Oz*–themed set of scarecrows. "Just think: in a few years, the Kettler family might have a submission too. Can you picture our little tot decorating one of these?" he asks, smiling.

I bite my lip.

Is he being unreasonable, or am I? I don't exactly have the best track record when it comes to making decisions. When you've failed so monumentally, it's easier to let someone else dictate your choices. Safer.

I can almost see the late Dr. Diehl tottering through the crowd and tapping me on the shoulder. *You're now a recovering people pleaser*, she'd say. *Get comfortable with the guilt, and it'll become less powerful. You'll feel resentful if you don't take a stance on what you want.*

But I'm not sure what I want, and I've carried guilt for years. It's never become more comfortable, only heavier as I've gotten older. The image I conjured of Dr. Diehl disappears, and I'm left with the expectant but frustratingly patient smile of Henry as he daydreams about having kids.

A troop of Apple Blossoms scurries past us. Dolled up with stiffly sprayed hair and generous makeup, the Blossoms are the littlest beauty queens. Even the toddlers sparkle in that showy, confident way I never will.

I was plain growing up, with white-blond hair that blended with pale skin. A washed-out ghost of a girl. Even now, with my salon highlights and toned limbs from days spent laboring in the garden, I'm unremarkable at best. I'm bland, even for a librarian. I don't sport vintage frames or short bangs or funky-colored tights. I'm still a ghost.

The Blossoms collect in a swarming group up ahead, near the side of the stage. Their mothers fuss and primp. Everyone, from the girls to their mothers, is shrill and antsy. I recognize Jeannie Orr and Sara Singh, both girls I grew up with, preening over their own little beauty queens.

The Apple Queen contestants are there too. They don't take the stage until the evening, so their hair and makeup aren't outsized like they'll be once the pageant begins. Still, their posture is enviable, and I feel a stirring of jealousy even at my age.

"I'd like to watch this for a few minutes, if you don't mind," I tell Henry when he tugs me forward.

He glances at the drama of the crying, stomping girls waiting to take the stage.

"I'll go ahead to the farmers' market down at City Park. Meet me there?"

I nod and give him a quick kiss, grateful to be alone to watch the pageant. I linger behind a row of metal folding chairs as the first little girl takes the stage. She struts with a practiced sway of her hips while her mother stands just off the stage, shouting directions at her as if the gathering crowd isn't there.

I can't help but let my eyes linger on the row of Apple Queens. I conjure an image of Lollie sitting here herself all those years ago. I wonder if it was sunny as it is today, if she could feel the warm metal of her sunbaked chair through the silk of her dress.

I wonder, for the millionth time, if she was worried about what Dom would say when he found out she had participated in the pageant. Lollie, as the Flock's chief recruiter, was the only member Dom allowed to use one of the vans and leave the Bird Haven regularly.

There was nothing physically keeping us at the Bird Haven—something outsiders never seem to understand—but by September, after a summer with Dom and the others, I was afraid to leave, even if I had the means. To leave would have been to abandon our created family, and I considered the outside world evil by then. The others did too. But Lollie was free to come and go as she went to scout out new girls for Dom.

Was that why she entered the pageant initially? To recruit pretty girls to lure more men into the Flock?

The Apple Blossoms parade onstage, showing off choreographed steps and doll-faced makeup—both learned from YouTube tutorials, no doubt—and when the last dance number fades from the loudspeaker and the crowd disperses, I step forward.

At the judging table sits April Davies. She's practiced at maintaining her poise, but I catch her surprise in the way she lifts her eyebrows just slightly when she recognizes me. Elaine Hollis's daughter. She was friends with my mother. She has the same silvery blond hair I'd have expected my mom to sport, and she's plumped with age in a way that my mother's cancer never allowed her to do.

"Claire!" she says, her eyes darting around me. Whether she's searching for a toddler I might have entered into a Blossoms pageant or she's just mindful of being seen with the town pariah, I don't know.

"Mrs. Davies, hi. Do you have a moment?"

April glances around once more before gathering her tablet and purse from the judging table. She ushers me to the side of the stage, where we're obscured by cheap, weather-resistant curtains.

"Can I ask you a few questions about the Apple Queen pageant?"

She runs her eyes up and down me conspicuously now that we're alone. "Oh, hon. The pageant is really more for younger ladies."

I laugh. "I'm not trying to participate, no. I just wanted to see if you remember one of the contestants. Laurel Tai? She won ten years ago."

April's face hardens. "Of course I remember Miss Tai. I remember all the girls," she corrects. "What is it you want to know, Claire?"

"Just . . . what do you remember about her?" I pause, searching for words. April looks impatiently at her phone. "Lol—Laurel—she was a friend. But I didn't see her win the Apple Queen crown. It was obviously something that meant a lot to her, and it happened just before she went missing. I'm trying to make sense of her final days." I pause when I realize I'm rambling. "Anything you remember is appreciated."

April sighs. "The Apple Queen pageant is an audition for adulthood. As judges, we look for personality, substance, creativity, and yes, beauty. Miss Tai had those qualities in spades. She had that thing, that spark about her. When she walked onstage, it was *bam!* She was irresistible. She was going places. That's what we saw. That's what I remember."

So she saw it too. "Did she seem distracted or upset in any way?"

"No, no. She was the perfect queen."

"Do you remember anyone in the crowd paying special attention to her or fixating on her in any way?"

April's eyes narrow. "I watch the girls, not the crowd, Claire. I'm not sure what's prompted these questions, but please don't drag the Apple Queen pageant into this."

"Into what?"

"Into this search for answers, or whatever it is you're doing." She hoists her purse onto her shoulder and turns. "And Claire? Don't use the phrase 'went missing' when you talk about Laurel. It rubs people the wrong way. She didn't *go missing*. She didn't disappear into the ether. She was taken, and she was found dead in this town, next door to where she grew up. In a town that loved her. You of all people should know that."

As my mother's closest confidant scurries away after chastising me, I think that maybe I could have been in the Apple Queen pageant after all.

It takes a heavy dose of poise to keep from falling apart.

12

Laurel

Then

THE APPLE BLOSSOMS are a little too loud when I take the stage. I wink playfully at the crowd while the mothers herd the little girls away.

My posture's perfect, this I know. My shoulders align with my neck, my back isn't rounded, and my knees aren't locked. I keep my hands at my sides, careful not to let my sweaty palms brush against my silk dress.

At a gas station just outside of town, I sponged myself off as best I could, doused my roots in dry shampoo, and parted my hair on the opposite side it normally fell, just to give it extra volume. I applied foundation and eye shadow I'd swiped from a drugstore with a light hand, knowing the fluorescent lighting in the bathroom was deceiving. Besides, in a sea of beauty queens, I'd stand out more with less makeup. My dress demands a natural face anyway—the color's so bold, the cut so formfitting, anything more would be overpowering. When I finally slipped it over my head behind the curtain of the boutique's tiny dressing room, I knew it was a winning dress. And now, standing on the stage amid girls taped into sparkly dresses, painted with excessive cosmetics, I couldn't be more confident that I stand out, in the best way.

"Welcome," one of the judges calls in a loud, clear voice. It's Bethany Frasier, last year's winner. Back from Chicago, her strawberry-blond hair as bouncy as ever. "Please introduce yourself."

"Good afternoon, everyone. My name is Laurel Tai. While I live in Iola now, I'm originally from Estivant, so I recognize many faces in the crowd today," I say, offering a natural smile and lots of eye contact. "I'm an adventurer at heart. I'm always ready to explore and experience something new. I enjoy back-packing, caving, rappelling, and anything that gets my heart pumping."

One of the judges, a woman with blond hair spun with silver, glances at a clipboard on the table. "Thank you, Laurel. Our question for you today is, what's the biggest challenge young girls face today?"

I open my mouth to answer as a wind gust sends my long hair in a cyclone around my face. "Oh my," I laugh, and the crowd joins in. I flick my neck to toss my messy hair over my shoulder. My eyes lock with an older woman in the center of the audience, who—is it my imagination?—winks reassuringly.

"Once, decades ago, there were only a few defined tracks for a woman's life," I begin. "Go to school, marry a man, and have a family. Now we can live anywhere, look like anything, and love anyone. While young girls are undoubtedly grateful for these opportunities, the abundance of choice can feel para-lyzing. We're overwhelmed. Choosing a path that feels authen-tic, outside of the influence of what we see and hear, is our biggest challenge. We're privileged in that we're not handed a defined direction for our lives anymore, but instead we're tasked with being brave, genuine, curious, and adventurous. And, as social media continues to gain popularity, we're asked to broadcast our identity before we even have a chance to find out who we are."

When I hear the audience clapping their approval before I finish, I know the Apple Queen crown is mine.

* * *

A photographer for the *Iola Press* directs the beauty queens in how to stand onstage, growing frustrated as the girls jockey for position near the front. He places me squarely in the center, then separates me for a series of solo shots.

The afternoon sun has started to settle in the sky, and my bare arms prickle with the impending drop in temperature. I can't imagine covering my dress with a sweater, or ever taking it off, for that matter.

I spent too much on this dress. A summer's worth of money, collected from Claire's dad, nearly gone, in hopes of the bigger payout: the grand prize. I feel guilty that I used his money to compete in the pageant, but now I'll have the means to leave, which is what he intended the money for anyway.

I make my way over to one of the judges. Her name tag says APRIL DAVIES. She has the type of motherly body that gives good hugs and hints that bakery is always available in her warm kitchen.

"Congratulations, Laurel. You gave a lovely interview, and the crowd really picked up on your energy onstage. You were magnetic," she says, tucking her clipboard under an arm.

"Thank you. Regarding the prize . . ." I begin.

"Yes, I'm sure you're wondering!" She cuts me off with a hearty laugh. "We'll send a check to the address on your application first thing Monday morning."

One of the girls, usually Faith or Morgan, treks down the trail to the Bird Haven's mailbox every day. I can't risk them seeing anything addressed to me. Dom will take my check before I have a chance to cash it and escape.

"Oh, I see. Is there . . . is there a way I can pick it up here in town? I'd hate to risk it getting lost in the mail."

April cocks her head just a touch. "Sure, dear. I can give you a call when the check is ready and we can meet up at, say, town hall?"

"Why don't I call you?" I offer, thinking of my derelict phone that doesn't make or receive calls.

She's quiet for a beat, and again I imagine her as a mother as she studies me. "Just a moment. Let me get you a card."

She stoops and pulls a shoulder bag from below the judges' table. After a moment, she hands me a business card.

"Call me if you need anything at all, Laurel," she says.

Again she holds my gaze, and I blink to stave off the tears that threaten to form. When older women slide into protective mode, it fills my heart with a lonely longing for a family that cares.

Even before my dad left and my mom remarried a humorless man who disapproved of me from the start, she wasn't the type of parent to get on her knees and play with me. She had a short fuse and looked at me as more a burden than a joy. It feels like we traded hurtful words the moment I learned to speak, and it only got worse when she became a single parent. Truth be told, I've never missed her since I left home. I miss the girl I could have been had she been different.

The lively bustle of the crowd pulls me back to the moment. The troop of Apple Blossoms is back, and the little beauty queens unabashedly ogle the runners-up who mill around the stage. I say goodbye to April and make my way to the Blossoms.

"Can I take a picture with you?" a twig of a girl with stiff coils of curls asks.

I laugh, and forgetting everything I've studied about pageant posture and poses, I crouch beside her, teetering on my heels.

"I'd be honored to take a picture with you. What is your name?"

"I'm Viv," the curly-haired girl says.

I pull my neck back to take a closer look at her.

Viv. My little sister's name.

It's not her. This girl is younger. Viv was only eight years old when I left home, but who knows how much she's aged in the last two years? Would I recognize her in this crowd?

I press my cheek into her formal hairdo and smile for her mother's camera phone.

"I like your dress," Viv says, more shyly than I'd expect from a Blossom. The girls are trained to project confidence, so they're loud and assertive before they can form complex sentences.

"Thank you," I say, tucking a curl behind her tiny ear. "I like your smile."

"I want to be just like you when I grow up."

My smile falters.

Since I was a little girl, I've loved seeing women who are comfortable with who they are shine onstage. Beauty queens are charming, expressive, and eager, qualities I've always had in spades. They sparkle.

Lately, I've looked at the pageant as a stepping stone. The generous prize money that comes with the Apple Queen crown will help me start a new life in a new city, away from the Bird Haven and Dom.

What I didn't count on was being a role model to this little Blossom and girls like my sister just a few towns over.

Sometimes I feel as if I have more to apologize for than to be proud of. Am I worthy of being an aspiration?

*　*　*

Johnny and June's is too far from Arbor State's campus to attract college students, but it's a favorite of the locals. The Monday night crowd, though, is more bedraggled than those who frequent the hole-in-the-wall on the weekend.

Men sporting scruffy beards and women with years of wrinkles creasing their hard faces line the bar. The wardrobe is mostly flannel. I'm about twenty years younger than most of the regulars, but that doesn't stop the drink offers from coming.

I face the mirrored back of the bar so I can see men before they approach. Tonight's not about recruiting; it's about fundraising.

Once I find a mark, I'll guide us to a high-top away from the bar. I'll sit too close and touch his arm just enough to suggest I'm open to a nightcap. I'll insist we not open a tab. Instead, I'll ask for a drink, and then another, collecting his cash to pay each round at the bar. I'll pocket the change. I won't make much this way—maybe fifty dollars—but it's not bad for a night of flirty drinking.

Tonight, though, unapproachable men down cans of Pabst beer, never taking their eyes off the Monday night football game playing on the television above the bar. They're the type to count their change, so I sip a tumbler of Sprite and wait.

It's funny, being here, after the high of winning the pageant this weekend. I thought being the Apple Queen would feel like being love-bombed all the time. How Dom must feel in our adoration circles when we shower him with worshipful praise.

Instead, I've spent the last two days anxious and, if I'm honest, a little resentful. The Flock doesn't know I won the crown, of course, but I feel inexplicably offended that I'm not being fawned over. The same way I felt insulted when no one acknowledged my birthday, even though I knew I never told them the date.

After all the photos and attention at the pageant on Saturday, I drove to a gas station outside of town, the same one where I'd gotten ready hours earlier, and wiped the makeup off my face until it was bare. I wound my hair into a tight bun and pulled on my clothes that smelled of lake water and sweat. I tucked the foundation in my bag but tossed the eye shadow palette and lipstick in the bathroom trash can. My beautiful red dress was nothing more than a crumbled tissue at the bottom of my tote bag. I stared at myself in the mirror until the joy of winning the Apple Queen crown was replaced with the familiar haunted worry I carry now. Only then did I return to the Bird Haven. I spent that evening, and all day Sunday and Monday, preoccupied and snappy. I was relieved when Dom insisted I go to Johnny and June's to fundraise.

It's silly, really. I didn't enter the contest to be in the spotlight; I entered it as a means to escape, unseen, to a place where no one knows who I am.

On the TV, the Colts score a touchdown against the Bears, and the camera pans to show the Chicago skyline when the call is contested. I can't help but think of Bethany Frasier frolicking in the city again. I wonder if she'll hang out with me if I go to Chicago too, now that I'm an Apple Queen like her.

The door swings open, sending an unseasonably chilly rush of air into the bar. I raise my eyes to the mirror.

Two young men enter, both in oversized Carhartt jackets and faded baseball caps. With them comes the boozy smell of a night spent drinking on back roads. Alone, one of them could have been a mark, but together they're a grating night filled with phony machismo.

I finish my Sprite and gather my tote bag, my red silky slip of a pageant dress rumpled at the bottom. I might not have found a mark tonight, but I can still bring home a little cash to appease Dom.

In the hallway by the bathrooms, a forgotten step stool is shoved into the corner. It must have been used to replace the too-bright bulb overhead, which now casts the hallway in an unflattering white-blue light. I set my tote bag on it and use my phone as a prop to look distracted.

A woman is the first to approach.

"Ma'am? I hate to bother you, but I don't have enough gas to get home. Is there any chance you have a few dollars to spare?"

She coughs into her sleeve. "There's a station a few minutes from here. If you've got enough gas to make it there, I can pay at the pump."

"Thank you. That's so kind of you."

The woman uses her elbow to open the bathroom door just enough to slip through. "Holler at me when you're ready to follow me to the station," she calls as the door bangs shut.

I bite my lip. It's a generous offer, but I need cash.

A few minutes later, one of the young men dressed in a camel-brown work jacket lumbers down the hallway. I straighten and bat my doe eyes at him, hoping the bad lighting doesn't make me look too haggard.

"I'm so sorry to bother you, but I don't think I have enough gas to get home tonight," I say with a self-deprecating shake of my head. "Is there any chance you could spare just, oh, five dollars?"

He runs a hand over his reddish-brown beard and studies me. His arms are too big to hang flat at his sides, so he takes up most of the narrow hallway.

"Well, I'll be damned. Don't tell me you spent all your prize money already."

"I—excuse me?"

"You're the Apple Queen, right? You've been all over my Facebook feed this weekend," he says, pulling his phone from a pocket on the front of his button-up shirt. With a few swipes, he opens the app and turns his phone to me. "Here. This is you with my niece."

Cheek to cheek, I'm smiling next to the little curly-haired Blossom on his phone screen.

"Don't you get some money for winning?" he continues. He slides his phone back into his pocket and smirks. "Didn't think I'd run into a beauty queen begging for money in a bar just two days after her big win."

Tears threaten to fall. I grab my tote from the step stool and angle my body to slide past the man.

Outside, the night air smells like burning leaves. I jog across the gravel parking lot to the Flock's older-model white van. I start it up, and when I see that I still have half a tank of gas, I wonder how far away from here I could drive.

It's always embarrassing to beg for money from strangers, but I've never been recognized before.

If I had the prize money, I could leave now. I'm desperate to escape the Flock, but I know that tonight I need them. I can't explain to them why I'm so humiliated, but they'll envelop me with unquestioning warmth, like a family, when I return.

As I drive home to the Bird Haven, I remind myself that I'm not afraid to leave the Flock, that the outside world is not evil.

But as tears stream down my cheeks, I have a hard time believing myself.

CHAPTER

13

Claire

Now

A FERRIS WHEEL CHURNS slowly on Main Street. The week-long fall fest is still underway, and traffic is diverted from downtown Iola. As I pull out of our carport, I take a left down Elliot Street and leave the carnival and campus in my rearview mirror. I'm heading north today. To the Bird Haven.

My interview with Arlo is scheduled for three o'clock, but I leave the house at two knowing that I'll get jittery as I approach the sanctuary. I wonder if Arlo planned his arrival in town for the time of the year when I'm most nostalgic for Lollie, when the fall festival is in full swing and I'm reminded of the future she could have had after she was crowned Apple Queen.

I'm only a few minutes into the drive when my phone pings to announce the arrival of a new podcast episode. I've been waiting days, so I plug my phone into the dashboard and hit play.

Daisy Shea's throaty voice fills the car.

"Bizarre, scary stuff was happening long before Laurel's murder. Dominic bred fear and dependency among us. It was hard to leave, but it wasn't impossible."

I signal to turn although there's no traffic. Everyone's at the festival, blissfully watching a professional pumpkin carver or sipping cider brewed by the ale house on Main.

A tinkling of piano keys and Arlo's voice: "Welcome to *Birds of a Feather*. I'm your host, Arlo Stone, and I'm joined by former Flock member and defector Daisy Shea. Daisy, you're one of the few people who survived life at the Bird Haven with cult leader Dominic Bragg. What can you tell us about what was happening there, leading up to the Flock's demise?"

I grip the steering wheel. Daisy wasn't even there in the final days or even the final weeks. She's a fraud, I think angrily. She betrayed Lollie then, and now she's getting ready to do it again, this time for an audience.

"Well, Arlo," Daisy purrs, her voice sticky sweet, "another person might paint a picture of the Flock as a 'found family' who really just cared about a simple way of life at the Bird Haven. And that's what we were when I was there. Everyone was nurturing and supportive. We weren't dangerous. But that's not the story I can tell you anymore, because I saw what the Flock was becoming, and that's why I had to leave."

"What did you see the Flock becoming?" Arlo prompts. I wonder if he sees through her self-serving monologue like I do.

"The Flock reflected Dominic's growing paranoia."

Arlo interjects. "Now, some people think that Dominic Bragg's paranoia was in response to the media circus surrounding news of Laurel Tai's abduction and murder. But you're saying he, and the other Flock members, were paranoid before that happened."

"Oh yes," Daisy agrees. I can also see her enveloping Arlo in her scented cloud of vanilla and lilies as she nods vigorously over the microphone. "Have you heard about the intruder drills?"

*   *   *

I listen to all forty-two minutes of Daisy's interview, alternating between anger, frustration, and nostalgia. She gives Arlo a good sound bite when she announces that Dom was "drunk on his own grandiosity." She speculates that Dom staged intruder drills so we'd be afraid and obedient, too scared to flee. Arlo notes that tests of devotion are a common practice among cult leaders. The episode ends with Daisy's damning accusation that I'm involved in the Flock's deaths and a snippet from my father's interview, recorded a few days ago.

"Claire could have been diagnosed with depression. She had no meaningful relationships and no educational program. It's not surprising that she took the identity Bragg offered her."

I seethe at his words and debate canceling the interview, but I see Arlo's sporty hybrid parked outside the metal gates blocking entry to the Bird Haven. He waves his hand out the window when he sees me approach. I smooth my hair in the mirror and gather my purse and phone reluctantly. I wonder if Arlo timed the release of Daisy's episode until right before our interview to fire me up. He doesn't know, though, that my father makes a habit of diminishing me, just usually not for a global audience.

The gravel crunches under my feet.

"I trust you know where to go from here?" Arlo calls, his voice a little too chipper.

Being here, secluded, under the big sky with no noise but birdcalls, I already remember more. I could tell Arlo which bird sketches hang on the walls of the ornithologist's cottage where the Flock lived. I could point out the best spots for viewing hawks, eagles, falcons. Instead, I step around the gate, letting the overgrown tree branches claw at my arms, and follow a well-worn path to the main grounds.

I head down the path, Arlo nipping at my heels when the trees crowd the walkway. He clutches a device in his hand; I assume it's a professional recorder, better than an app on a cell phone.

"So, normally, I find a quiet spot to sit and let the person I'm interviewing just talk. I find that people give way more information than I expect," he laughs. "But I can tell you're not like that. So, I want to do something a little different."

"What's that?" I ask as I hold a branch back to keep it from snapping in Arlo's face. We're getting close now.

"Are you familiar with the game twenty questions? I'd like to shoot off some questions to you while walking around the grounds. You can just tell me what comes to your mind first, a word or a sentence. No need to elaborate. I know you said you have trouble remembering, but maybe being here will help."

"One-word answers?" This might not be so bad, I decide. Fewer words means less chance to say something I don't want broadcast to his audience.

"One word, ten words. It doesn't matter. Just whatever pops into your head."

We arrive in the clearing. I haven't been here since that summer. It looks eerily similar. The cottage still stands, looking a little worse for the wear. Dom's archaic wheelchair waits on the porch. A ghostly observer.

The grass is overgrown, and it's hard to spot the path down to the lake, but the mature trees are the same. Wires where the birds lined up in neat rows still hang suspended between the large oaks.

I spot a faded red birdhouse that Morgan and Faith built and nailed to a tree. The doors of the large cages where Raina nursed broken-winged birds back to health hang open at funny angles. One wall of the rickety fence that Jock erected around the vegetable garden has collapsed, but chicken wire still surrounds the rest. I look up. The sky is still larger than life here.

I can't believe how much I remember just being here. What would my therapist say if she were alive to see me? Would she ever admit she might have been wrong, that I may be able to access memories that have been hovering just below the surface of consciousness for years? Or would she plead with me to stop triggering myself before I unleash something dangerous in my mind?

"Isn't it a little unconventional, how you're recording this podcast?"

"How so?" Arlo asks, distracted. There's awe in his eyes, and I suspect it's to do with the Bird Haven's history as a crime scene instead of reverence for the beauty of the old bird sanctuary and the naturalist's cottage.

"Well, typically," I say, kicking the grass and looking down to hold the memories at bay, "wouldn't you record all the content, then return to a studio to piece together a story? You're conducting interviews, then airing them a few days later. How can you know the narrative of the story? It's like writing and publishing one chapter of a book at a time. What if there's a major plot development?"

"I mean, yeah, that's how scripted podcasts work," Arlo says. "This is a story about what happened to the Flock, but it's also about my investigation. Reviewing old leads, uncovering new ones. Seeing what emerges. Speaking of, you ready?" He holds up his recorder.

I look up and see Lido and Eden on the porch, picking at scabby knees, for a moment before they vanish. I nod.

"I'll record an intro later. Let's just dive in." He punches a button and holds the recorder near his chest. "Claire, we're in front of the main cottage on the grounds of the Bird Haven. Who lived here?"

The wooden siding has grayed with time and one window is boarded up, but otherwise it looks as it did ten years ago. "Um, Eden, Sunny, Helena, the twins. Most of the girls, really. And Dominic, of course."

"Where did the others live?"

I turn and point. "There were two sheds, one near the cottage and one closer to the lake. We emptied them and stayed there. At one point, there was a trailer and an old RV. And on warm nights, some of the guys, Vinny and Lido especially, would pitch a tent."

"Where did you live?"

"I slept in the shed closest to the house with Lollie. Laurel."

Arlo and I tromp through the grass and peer in the window. He tries the handle, and it creaks open. There's a soiled mattress on the ground. A hairbrush, some magazines. A maroon hat that brought out the brown in Lollie's eyes.

"Did you share a bed?" Arlo asks. His voice is deeper, more articulate, when he's recording.

"Yes."

"Did you and Lollie talk before falling asleep at night?"

"Yeah, of course."

"What did you talk about?"

Life after death. "Um," I hesitate. "Just, whatever girls talk about."

"Were you ever romantic with each other?"

Those lips, her smell, her warmth. "No." My cheeks color, even after all these years.

"What did you see the night she was taken?"

"Nothing. I slept through it." I see a tack nail above the mattress. It used to pin a photo of Lollie's little sister to the wall, but it's empty now. I look away.

"Why didn't you report Lollie missing?"

"I was looking for her. I thought she wandered off in the night. I thought it'd be better if I found her."

"Okay, let's switch gears," Arlo says, letting the shed door swing closed with a bang. He leads me back down the path. Is that Goldie kissing Hunter in the brush?

"We're standing in front of what looks like a garden," Arlo says, bringing me back to the present. "What was grown here?"

"Vegetables, mostly. Um, tomatoes, cucumbers, zucchini," I say, picturing them on the vines clear as day, Helena industriously tending to them. "We tried planting sweet corn, but that didn't go so well," I laugh.

Arlo smiles. "What else did you eat?"

"Um, our diet was mostly vegetarian, but we ate a lot of fresh shellfish, and we were, you know, well fed."

I don't mention how I got sick at the scent of a cooked meal after I left the Bird Haven.

"Who did the cooking?"

"Oh, the girls, mostly. We worked together. But Thomas did a lot too."

Gray-haired and stooped, Thomas was the older member of the Flock when I lived at the Bird Haven. He, like most of us, was separated from his past. He could be tactless and quick-tempered, especially when Faith and Eden ruined a dinner dish. But near the end, most of us were overemotional and aggressive too.

"Who was the funniest person?"

Arlo's found the path now. He leads us past the garden, around the cottage.

"Oh, probably Vinny."

"Was Dominic funny?"

Dom, funny? No. He did know how to humiliate you to gain a few laughs, though. "I wouldn't call him funny. He was playful, though. He had a special connection to animals. He was wise. Philosophical."

I wince. I gave too much away about Dom. But Arlo continues. His eyes are sharp as he takes in our surroundings. I look up in the trees for the first time, suddenly wondering if Arlo planted cameras around the Bird Haven before I arrived. Filming footage for a possible documentary. But all I see are leafy limbs and bird nests.

"Did the girls get along?"

"Yes, we were a family," I say automatically.

"Did anyone have a problem with Lollie?"

"No, everyone loved her. She was pretty, outgoing . . . a wonderful person." I keep my answer short when I feel a lump form in my throat. My words are insufficient and achingly bland for someone as electric as Lollie.

"Let's talk about the day the Flock died. What was the weather like?"

Arlo is leading us down the path to the garage where I found the Flock, I realize. I close my eyes and remember that day.

"Warm, sunny," I say, eyes still closed. I can almost feel the mosquitoes swarming my legs. "It had rained a lot the night before."

"What did you do that afternoon?"

"I napped. And walked down by the lake."

"Who did you talk to?" Arlo asks.

"No one, really. I was kind of off in my own world after Lollie went missing."

We're approaching the garage. The afternoon sun glints off the door of the steel building.

"Did you see Dom?"

I hesitate. "No, not that I remember."

"What time of day was it when you found the vans in the garage?"

I squint, imagining. A bird lands on the roof and titters at us. I remember the sound of the birds. They seemed to echo, roar, that day.

"The sun was just starting to set."

"How tall would you say the grass was?"

I frown. Who cares? "Um, about this tall, I guess." It prickles my ankles.

"Which door did you use to get into the garage?"

"The side door."

"Did you try the roll-up door?" Arlo's questions are coming faster now.

"Yes, I tried that first."

"Was the light on?" he asks, pointing to a motion light near the side door.

The building shimmers. I close my eyes, remembering. "No, it was dark when I left the garage."

"Did you have anything with you?"

"Just the key."

"Did you know the door was locked?"

"Yes, I'd tried it earlier."

We're at the entrance now. It's a gaping wound; the door's been removed from its hinges and leans against the wall just inside the garage. I expect the vans to be there, the hose to snake from their closed windows and exhaust pipes. But it's empty.

"So the Flock was locked in. They didn't commit suicide. They were murdered. One more question, Claire," Arlo says. "Why didn't you die with everyone else?"

CHAPTER

14

Laurel

Then

ON THE DRIVE back to the Bird Haven, I let my tears flow freely. I scream into the windshield until my throat is raw. I hate myself for my weakness.

My cheeks are itchy, my eyes red and puffy, when I park the van in the shed and pick my way through the overgrown grass to the cottage. Piano music wafts from the open windows. The porch creaks underfoot, announcing my arrival, and the tune ceases as the Flock's ears prick in my direction.

"Everyone, it's me," I call before turning the knob.

Dom's paranoia is growing, the intruder drills becoming more frequent, and I don't want to be mistaken as an outsider before I have the chance to escape in a few days.

Lido looks to Dom, who nods. Lido returns to the keys, tapping out a bright, brassy sound. It's more jarring than harmonious, but no one seems to mind.

It's late, but the girls are still awake, braiding each other's hair or drawing in sketchbooks.

Raina and Morgan pore over an old issue of a health magazine, which, like the piano music, is unsettling; with our poor sleep, unvaried diet, and nonexistent exercise routines, we're hardly the picture of well-being. Most of the girls have stopped menstruating, which has mostly been regarded as a relief. The outdated plumbing system couldn't handle the flow of more than a dozen young women synced on similar schedules anyway. Dom says it's a good thing: we're becoming pure.

The stack of decade-old magazines is one of the only references to outside society most of the girls have. Unlike me, they rarely leave. And tonight, when I return looking as rattled as I do, they don't have any desire to venture into the evil outside.

Dom sits in his wheelchair, stroking the mangy fur of his pet rabbit.

"Lollie, you're back. I've been waiting for you. I've prepared a private dinner for us," Dom says in his soft-spoken, feathery way.

As the wheelchair creaks under his shifting weight, my heart seizes. A private dinner. While usually it's an honor to spend time with Dom one-on-one, tonight I worry that it's a threat.

Reluctantly, I follow Dom from the cottage to the old RV, a Coachman Cadet from the seventies. The rig hasn't been serviced in years. Its tires are flat, and I'm sure its engine doesn't turn over anymore. Through the curtains on the back windows, there's a light glow that tells me Thomas is inside.

Orange and yellow stripes run down the camper's exterior. Dom swings the door open, and we enter. Thomas sits at the breakfast nook, drinking from a mug as he pores over one of the naturalist's books. A curator of birds, the original owner wrote an authoritative eight-volume study of migratory species. Of all the members of the Flock, Thomas is most interested in viewing and listening to the birds that still stop on this tract of land.

Thomas closes his book and tucks it under his arm, bowing his head to his chin as he edges past Dom and I. Quietly, with his folded way of walking, Thomas leaves the RV. He's the oldest Flock member, and he doesn't interact with the others much. I'm not sure why he's here, except that he likes a quiet place in nature to reflect and pass his retirement. Like all of us, Thomas must be here because whatever Dom tells him—whether it's spiritual, political, or something else—resonates with him.

A thick fish soup simmers on one of the burners of the camper's small stovetop. Dom lifts the lid, releasing a billow of steam and the scent of shellfish and onions. He ladles it into small white bowls rimmed with a navy-blue stripe.

We settle at the Formica table. The seat padding in the nook has flattened over time; the fabric's dated brushstroke pattern is dotted with years of spilled food.

I swirl my spoon around the bowl. It's a heavy cream soup, filled with shellfish and pureed vegetables. A thick bisque like this is not an everyday meal; it's richer than anything the girls mix up in the kitchen.

"What did you think of my sermon this morning? Did it speak to you?" Dom asks as he ladles a spoonful of soup into his mouth.

Across from me in the small booth, Dom is slight, his shoulders narrow. His amber eyes focus on me.

I lick my lips. "Yes, of course. Every word."

For hours, Dom waxed poetic about transcending into high vibrations, forming a bridge to a simpler existence within the illusion, awakening our consciousness. Littered with the Flock's own terminology, it'd be impossible to understand as an outsider.

"I was speaking to you today. I worry that you're a comfort seeker in search of the power of now. I want nothing more than to harness your energy of pure being as we embark on our transcendent journey together."

I lower my eyes and stare at my lumpy bowl of soup. The scent of seafood is nauseating in these cramped quarters. Already I have indigestion from hours spent sipping free soda at Johnny and June's, waiting for a mark. I feel sick under Dom's scrutinous gaze.

"Lollie, your family never understood your spirit and sensitivity. That's why you're here with me," Dom reminds me.

I bite my cuticle.

"I know things that no one else knows," he continues. "If you were truly enlightened and committed, you wouldn't seek out false opportunities."

From a pocket inside his denim jacket, Dom removes a piece of paper. He sets it beside his spoon and steeples his fingers together.

The photo's grainy but unmistakable: me in the silky red dress now crumpled at the bottom of my tote bag, accepting the Apple Queen crown just two days ago. Clipped from the Sunday morning edition of the *Iola Press*.

I sit very still, afraid to move or breathe.

"No one's ever recognized how wonderful you are, Lollie. You don't need false validation from the evil outside. Here, you're swimming in love and light and freedom. Someday you'll understand," he says.

Gingerly, with just the tips of his long, thin fingers, Dom picks up the photo and begins to tear it into tiny scraps, letting each one flutter into my bisque soup. He leans across the table and kisses my forehead.

"When you lose your ego, you gain reality. Eat this and you will understand. And remember: I'm with you always."

As he moves through the narrow galley of the camper to the door, I stare at my bowl as the soup absorbs the newspaper. My forehead, where Dom kissed me, remains hot to the touch.

* * *

I spend the next day in an anxious haze. Dom didn't see a need for me to leave the Bird Haven, so I didn't get a chance to call April Davies to ask about my check for the prize money.

My insomnia lingered all night. I haven't slept in days. Near daybreak, my aching muscles succumbed to painful spasms, waking Claire in the bed we share. She tried to calm me by brushing my hair, but when the boar bristles pulled clumps of dry hair from my scalp, she offered to fetch a book from the cottage and read to me, like she does for Dom.

I do my best to join the Flock in collecting vegetables and hiking to an old copper mine, but I feel disoriented all day. With a heavy chest and a tight throat, I wheeze as we slowly traipse through the woods in thin-soled tennis shoes.

By nightfall, I want nothing more than to slip into a deep, dreamless sleep, but Dom summons us to the fire pit. Everyone, even Thomas, gathers around the pit.

Dom, in a collarless linen shirt, floats around the Flock, placing his hand on our shoulders and foreheads. Whispers. Bowed heads. The evening breeze sends his shirt billowing like a kaftan. He directs Lido to return to the cottage. Moments later, a fast, metallic tone warbles from the open windows as Lido pounds on the piano keys with a dramatic rise and fall in volume.

Dom holds one hand to his heart and one in the air as he sways to the music.

"I sense the doubt in your heart," he says, his voice tender. "I feel a deep disharmony from your soul."

I scan the group. Is he talking about me? Please, no.

Dom closes his eyes, lowers his head, and begins to hum.

"My Flock, there's a traitor among us."

A few of the girls gasp. I bite my lip.

"You know who you are. Please stand," Dom instructs. His voice is louder now, more serious.

A hush falls over us. Even the birds are silent. The only sound is Lido playing the piano in the cottage.

Raina bumps my shoulder as she struggles to her feet. She picks her way unsteadily through our legs as she makes her way to Dom.

"Raina, I gave you my home and my love. I sensed your soul's discontent when we met, but it didn't deter me. All I asked from you was loyalty," he says.

Even with the fire's distorting glow, I can see that Raina's cheeks are flushed. A sheen of sweat covers her forehead and upper lip.

Dom turns to address us. "It came to my attention that Raina recently corresponded with her former family. It's my understanding that she divulged information about our sacred mission here. It's traitorous, yes, but that's not what concerns me. Raina's revealed dark, dark secrets about how her family treated her in the past, and in a moment of weakness, she was lured in by their evil manipulations."

I sat by her when she penned her autobiography. Lies, all of it, in an attempt to one-up the others girls' tales.

Raina's eyes are glassy and unblinking as Dom turns back to her. He presses his forehead against hers. Her dark hair and his greasy curls intertwine. He begins to chant, quietly at first, then louder. Lido bangs away on the piano keys, and we hold our collective breath. As the music climbs to a crescendo, Dom begins to lift his arms from his sides into the air above their heads.

As Lido crashes into a finale, Dom's voice rises above the chords, loud and strident. "Drop dead!" he commands.

He brings his hands down on Raina's head and pushes her to the ground, where she lands heavily in the grass.

"Let this be a warning to you all. Do not defy me."

*　*　*

Dom spends a few hours consoling us. He holds our hands, stroking them gently. His voice is tender, disappointed yet reassuring. Eyes darting between Raina's motionless body and Dom's billowing kaftan, the girls are both enchanted and terrified.

The evening's served its purpose: Dom's secured loyal, obedient followers.

Thomas and I, we're the only Flock members who have seen this before. Years ago, the summer I arrived at the Bird Haven, Dom drugged a troublemaking older man to make a point about loyalty. Then, as the drug's effects wore off, he resurrected him. I didn't know he'd drugged him to prove his paranormal abilities to us. But now I've seen his drawer full of tranquilizers and sleeping pills, hypnotics and sedatives. He's not above toying with our health to secure our loyalty. While Dom's chastised others for experimenting with drugs before they ever arrived at the Bird Haven, he rampantly self-medicates and secretly sedates anyone he considers to be challenging him.

Raina had the same stumbling, glassy-eyed demeanor of that older Flock member, so I know that he'll resurrect her too.

What worries me, though, isn't Raina, still unmoving by the dying fire. It's Dom's growing paranoia, and the sinking realization I might not be able stave off his obsessive suspicion long enough to escape.

CHAPTER

15

Claire

Now

"WHAT DO YOU mean, the door was locked?"
"The roll-up door and the side door were both locked. I used a key to get into the garage."

"Okay. So why is that such a big deal?"

I sigh and rub my forehead. Henry—he's trying to understand. I pounced on him the moment he walked in the door, tears running from my swollen eyes, and he sits next to me on the couch now, still in the bland button-down he wore to work today. I wear my equivalent of a baby's security blanket: a kelly-green eyesore of a T-shirt that Henry bought me when we went to a roller derby when we first started dating.

"No one knew the door was locked. And Arlo says that if it was locked, that means it wasn't suicide, that it wasn't voluntary. Now it's murder."

"Claire," Henry groans, "first, Arlo doesn't know anything. He's trying to sensationalize his podcast to get more listeners and ad revenue. A locked door doesn't necessarily point to murder." He pauses, ruffling his hair. "I'm having trouble understanding why you think this a big revelation. Do you mean to tell me that the police never asked if the door was locked when they interviewed you back then? You found everyone. The police must have had you walk through the details at the time."

My mind flashes to the hours of questioning from both local and federal agents. The rooms more spacious and light filled than crime-based TV shows led me to believe, the officers gentler. Between my clinical diagnosis confirming memory loss, my hard-nosed lawyer, and my father doing his part to shield me from only the most critical meetings, there was little I could offer at the time.

"Yeah, I talked to the police. Of course I did. But I couldn't really tell them anything. I was already in shock. The only thing I could remember—" I halt, thinking of Eden's eyes and vomit-soaked hair. I shake my head. "Look, this is bad. Trust me."

I stop short of telling him I've ruined my life. Again. When I look at Henry, his eyes are sad and I can't tell what he's thinking. He holds me while I cry and offers to make dinner.

I shouldn't have agreed to the interview. I know that now. I berate myself for being so stupid. I thought that by speaking to Arlo, I could help him find answers to the questions that have haunted me for ten years.

Who killed Laurel? Why did the Flock die? Why did I live? And where's Dom?

Before Arlo's arrival, I assumed I might never know the truth. I might never recover my memories, and I might never have a day where I didn't look over my shoulder, expecting to see Dom or Lollie's killer or a townsperson ready to hurl an insult at me. But now it seems he's cracked the door to the past. If I step through, I might finally know the truth. If I don't—well, it may not matter, because Arlo is here to tell a story, and I'm at the center of it. I still need to protect myself.

If Arlo can't find the truth, there may be someone else who can—at least someone who might know about Dom.

I open a private browser on my phone and load a Reddit thread about the Flock. There's one user who posts frequently and responds to others with self-assured ferocity. DetroitDoll.

Henry's back is to me while he stands over the stovetop, boiling pasta for a late dinner. I click on DetroitDoll's profile and click "Send Private Message." My phone pings with a response minutes later, while Henry is straining the noodles. I punch down the volume on my phone and peek at the reply before entering the kitchen.

DetroitDoll wants to meet tomorrow.

* * *

In the morning, I call in sick to work at the library and avoid the garden at my father's house. I allow myself hours of uninterrupted worrying after Henry heads to campus for the day. I float, willingly losing touch with reality as my mind drifts to the past. I text Cecily Lofton, asking her if she's ready to meet yet. I remember more after visiting the Bird Haven with Arlo, but I still want to talk to Cecily to find out what she remembers about the days after Lollie went missing.

Reluctantly, I dress and get in the car. DetroitDoll asked to meet at an antique store in Torch Lake, a drive that takes more than two hours.

Twin wagon wheels mark the entry to the parking lot of the Rocking Horse, a boxy antique mall off Lincoln Road. Gravel crunches under the tires as I pull in. There are only two other vehicles in the lot: a rust-stained maroon minivan and a white pickup, its bed stacked high with wicker chairs.

A bell chimes, announcing my arrival. Near the door, a heavyset man sits on a barstool near an old-fashioned cash register. When I approach, he flicks off a cheap task lamp and sets down a buffalo nickel.

"You must be Claire," he says.

I startle. "Are you . . . DetroitDoll?"

He chuckles and nods. "That I am, that I am. Thanks for coming out."

"Um . . . thanks for meeting with me." I look around. He's not at all what I expected. I conjured an image of a frizzy-haired woman, wild-eyed with remorse for not joining the Flock when it existed. A woman enamored with Dom. This man, he's tall, with a bulging belly that strains against his quarter-zip sweater. "What's your name?" I ask.

"I'd rather not say. I don't want to share personal details."

I bite my lip. He's probably the owner of this shop; it'd be easy enough to find his information online. Is he a threat, or am I?

I look around. The shop's quiet and empty save for a metallic clatter. A dealer stocking his antiques booth with vintage auto parts. Who buys old mufflers?

A sparkling display of vintage carnival glass catches my eye. My mom collected the beautiful iridescent pieces, and my gaze lingers while I search for a rare purple piece out of habit. A lump forms in my throat before I turn back to DetroitDoll.

"I saw your posts on the discussion forum. In more than one thread, you've said that you know where Dom is now. Can you tell me what you think?" I ask.

The man puckers his lips. "It's not what I think. It's what I know. Come on," he says, gesturing toward a small office behind the register.

Once inside, he shuts the door. He seems bigger in here, amid the old dolls and glassware awaiting price tags. The room smells like burned popcorn, and a tuna sandwich languishes on a plate near a ledger book.

"So you never lived at the Bird Haven. Right?"

"No, never. But I know more than most people. Including you, probably," DetroitDoll says.

"Probably," I agree with a small smile. It goes unreturned.

"I immersed myself in Dominic's teachings after the Flock died. I've been tracking him down ever since."

"His . . . teachings?"

DetroitDoll stares at me. "Dominic understands that we, as humans, crave clarity. He offers a path through the turbulence of these uncertain times. We needed him ten years ago, yes.

But we need him so much more now. Social injustice, violence, cruelty—it's so much worse now than it used to be. Dominic . . . he's clarity. He sees through all of the seductive, overwhelming choices we're faced with today. Do you remember his wisdom? He has an awakened consciousness."

Yes, I remember. His amber eyes seemed to penetrate me; he knew my thoughts and feelings before I did.

"I mean, yes, he was charming. Infectious even. But he was still just a man," I say, quoting my old therapist.

"No, Claire, he's more. I'm surprised to hear you say that, given how much time you spent with him, but I understand that external forces have influenced you in the years since," Detroit-Doll says. "Do you recall much about Dominic's childhood?"

I shake my head and perch on a cluttered countertop.

"Dominic had two near-death experiences as a child. He was born dangerously premature and barely survived. Then he survived a house fire that killed his family. These events opened up his psyche at a young age. He's not your average man. He's elevated."

To me, the Flock offered solace during a time when I longed for comfort and stability. But the girls worshiped Dom.

"Most people think Dom ran off and changed his identity when the Flock died," I say. "If he's alive, he'd have to keep a low profile. How did you find him?"

The man pulls out a metal folding chair and settles into it, pleased to see I'm not contradicting him. He wears thin glasses that dig into his pudgy cheeks, and he breathes with a slow, wheezy cadence.

"Like I said, I've been researching. Tracking. I'm confident I've found him."

"Well, where is he?"

DetroitDoll laughs, a loud bark in the small room. "I'm not going to jeopardize his safety by telling you where he is."

"Why did you agree to meet me, then?" I huff. "I told you I want to find out what you know about Dom. That's why I'm here."

"I could talk about Dominic for days. Tell you all the things people want to know from you. But I agreed to meet out of curiosity. You're Claire Hollis. You're infamous."

"It's Kettler now," I say weakly.

"Well, whatever your name, you're a survivor. You and Dominic are the only ones who truly know what happened that day at the Bird Haven."

On the counter, a row of clocks, all set to various times, manically tick away the seconds out of sync. My head is buzzing.

I leave DetroitDoll in his chaotic office and hurry back to my car, breathless with annoyance and disappointment.

He wouldn't tell me where to find Dom because he thinks I'm a threat. He sits in his shop full of forgotten junk, romanticizing life at the Bird Haven. If I'd stayed, he'd have reminded me how attentive and playful Dom could be. But he'd leave off how manipulative Dom was too. DetroitDoll wouldn't mention how Dom preyed on weakness. Exploited us. Tested our devotion.

Not for the first time, I wonder how I overlooked so many red flags. Was I really so desperate to believe in something, anything, that I ignored the warning signs?

I spot a notification on my phone. A new episode of *Birds of a Feather* is out. I fast-forward through the haunting music that builds to a jarring crescendo. I realized yesterday why the opening chords unsettle me; they're reminiscent of Lido playing on that old monster of a piano in the cottage. Lido banging away on the cracked, out-of-tune keys: it's a memory I didn't know I had until the podcast stirred it free.

Arlo's familiar voice fills the car.

"Welcome back to *Birds of a Feather*. I'm your host, Arlo Stone, and today I'm joined by someone very close to this case, Dr. Grant Hollis. Dr. Hollis is the medical examiner for Blair County, and he teaches mortuary science classes at Arbor State University in Iola."

Another voice, this one more familiar than Arlo's: "Thank you, Mr. Stone. I appreciate the opportunity to speak with you today."

I can imagine my father's ramrod-straight posture, tweed sport jacket, and short clipped beard as clearly as if he's in the car with me. I switch gears and pull the car off the road, listening to my father try to shut down Arlo's prodding questions with curt responses.

"Dr. Hollis, there's one thing I can't get over. Why, *why* did you perform Laurel Tai's autopsy when you knew how closely connected she was to your daughter?"

"What you and your listeners may not understand is that, as a physician, I determine the cause of death from a medical standpoint. It's black and white. I'm not involved in investigating the death scene or talking to witnesses. I make no assumptions. I deal in facts."

Arlo's voice rises in pitch, and I can tell he's frustrated by my father's response.

"I think 'black and white' becomes gray when your daughter's involved in the case. Wouldn't you agree?"

"I wasn't aware that Claire had a friendship with Laurel at the time."

Arlo scoffs, the sound jarring through the tinny speakers. I lower the volume and hunch closer to the steering wheel as I begin to drive toward the highway.

"At the very least, you knew that Laurel was a member of the Flock and that Claire lived there too. Is that correct?"

"I didn't know where Claire was at the time. I knew only that she left home. I didn't know Laurel either."

Instinctively, I hit the brakes, then glance in the mirror. No one behind me. Thank goodness. He's lying, of course. I accelerate again, listening as Arlo tries, unsuccessfully, to grill my father. He's no better at arguing with him than I am.

I drive fast, bumping over rutted country roads, anxious to return to the safety of home. It was a mistake to meet DetroitDoll.

I could have gotten hurt, or worse. Except everyone seems to think I'm the danger. When Arlo's interview with me airs, my reputation will only sink lower. My heart aches as I think of the pain it'll cause Henry. Maybe it'll shut down talk about having a baby, at least for now. Why would he want a monster to be the mother of his child? All I could offer a baby is a legacy of tragedy.

The episode continues, but Arlo doesn't get more out of my father. I don't know if his interview helps our family, as Dad claimed, or not.

"Don't miss our stunning next episode. Sole survivor of the Flock, Claire Kettler, shares a bombshell revelation that unravels everything you think you know about this case. Subscribe today so you don't miss a moment of *Birds of a Feather*."

Now my recorded voice wavers. "I just can't shake the guilt I feel," I say, and music swells and fades.

CHAPTER

16

Laurel

Then

I HAVE A GUT feeling that this time it isn't a drill.

Claire and I huddle together on our mattress, chins tucked over our knees. Another shot rings out, and a moan escapes Claire's lips.

It's full dark in the shed. We don't know how long we've been under siege or how many nighttime hours are left to endure. In the quiet moments, we can hear that even the wildlife has fallen silent, listening. We hardly dare breathe.

When the first shot roused us from sleep, Claire clamored to the door.

"No," I whispered, pulling on the hem of her shirt as she scrambled off the mattress. "It's not safe."

The window is too high to see out of, so I drag the bucket of rock salt below it to peek out. From this vantage point, I can see only the dark shadows of the tree line. Another shot echoes outside and I drop down, tumbling off the bucket and banging my shin on a metal shelf. I feel it in my chest and ears. That one was close.

"What should we do?" Claire asks. Her cheeks are streaked with trails of dried tears.

"There's nothing to do but wait," I reply.

From the direction of the cottage, the sound of breaking glass erupts. Even from this distance, we hear the girls scream in unison. I picture them huddled together in the living room, just like Claire and me.

Tree branches crack as footsteps run by the shed. We squeeze hands so hard it hurts.

Bang! Something heavy smacks against the shed's wooden door. I jump. Claire cries out. My hand darts to cover her mouth before I know what I'm doing. Eyes wide, we stare at each other, waiting. The footsteps retreat.

The deep-bass boom of a rifle explodes into the night.

Claire whimpers. My heart's beating so hard my chest aches. We've had intruder drills before. The last one was recent, the night Jock joined the Flock. But we've always weathered them together, as a group.

Tonight I'm separate from the others, and it sends a paralyzing swell of fear washing over me. If this is what happens when I'm at the Bird Haven, with so many people around to protect me, what will happen when I try to go off on my own to a big city?

* * *

By dawn, the gunfire has ceased and Claire has fallen asleep on my lap. It's hours until there's a knock at the door. I roll Claire's sleeping body off me and lurch to the door. My legs tingle with numbness. I hold on to the walls for support.

"Lollie? Claire?" a voice calls through the door. It's Vinny.

"We're here," I respond. My lips are dry and cracked. My throat burns. I'm desperate for a drink of water. I push on the door, but it won't swing open.

"Are you okay?" Vinny asks.

"Yeah, we're safe. Is everyone else okay?"

"Yeah. We've got some broken windows to board up, but no one was hit. You've got, uh, a dead animal blocking your door. A pretty gnarly raccoon. It's, uh . . . its guts are spilling out. I'll go get something to move it so you guys can get out," he says, his voice muffled through the door. "Fuck the outsiders, right?"

"Right." My voice is small.

I lean against the wall. Who are these outsiders who are threatening us?

In the past, the intruder drills have done little more than instill fear and dependency in us. But this, an all-night siege with broken windows and dead animals, this feels different. Did Dom stage this attack?

If his paranoia is growing, it won't be safe here much longer. And the real threat isn't a shadowy evil outsider; it's our prophet of false promises.

* * *

Later, the girls form a weary troop as we haul the laundry to the lake. The sound of wind chimes dangling from the porch fades and the birdcalls become louder as we go deeper into the woods.

Morgan leads the way, Faith, Claire, and I trailing behind. Raina usually joins us, but she hasn't been herself since her "resurrection." She lies on the nubby couch stroking Dom's pet rabbit, not stirring for meals or adoration circles.

I carry Dom's sheets and the thin towels we all share that never seem to dry. The cottage has a washing machine and dryer in a little wood-paneled nook by the kitchen, but they're waiting for new parts that'll never come. Thomas inspected them long ago, but Dom said we won't be reliant on outsiders for our basic needs. So we tromp through the trees to the lakeside every few days to do the wash.

On the rocky shore, Morgan shakes off a golden-yellow T-shirt and drops it in the water alongside the armful of laundry she's hauled here. It lands in a mucky bloom of algae.

Faith huffs. "We're trying to clean our clothes, not get them even grosser," she says as she stomps through the water, stopping a few feet from the shore. She wears an oversize gray shirt and underwear but no pants. She drops a pair of shorts into the water. Patches of red stand out on khaki; I realize she's scrubbing blood from the mutilated raccoon off Vinny's shorts.

"What does it matter? It's not like we even have soap," Morgan says slowly. Her thin hair splays over her bare shoulders, and her bangs hide her eyes.

"Hey, I can trim your bangs for you when we get back, if you want," I offer. I wring water out of a communal washcloth.

Morgan flicks her neck to send her hair from her eyes. "Nah, that's okay."

I've noticed this in the girls more and more lately. They seem almost indifferent about their appearance. Not everyone's secretly competing in beauty pageants, I remind myself.

Their apathy might have struck me as little more than a frustration if not for Dom's growing need for control. They shrink, and he grows stronger. His words more worrisome, his actions more dangerous. He's breaking them down, indoctrinating them into his weird otherworldly beliefs about transcendence and all that nonsense, and now he's leaving them so weak they can't resist or leave. It's horrifying, really, to see how Dom's hypocrisy and lies go unchecked. Am I the only one who's clearheaded enough to recognize that the man we believe in is growing increasingly paranoid? That he's becoming more erratic, demanding absolute control and unapologetic about how to get it?

Out here, isolated from reason and judgment, the girls have become everything I was trying to escape when I left home two years ago: sheltered shells of women without a voice or a choice. I need to think of a reason Dom will let me leave the Bird Haven tomorrow. I need to call April Davies about the check for the prize money. The urgency to leave feels like a black mass in my gut.

"Earlier, in our adoration circle, I wanted to thank Dom for protecting us from the outsider attack last night, but I couldn't find the words," Faith says, breaking the silence we've lapsed into. The late-afternoon sun sets the water in a shimmery glow behind her. "Not, like, the right words. Any words. I couldn't remember *words*."

Claire and I exchange a glance.

"I've been having memory problems too. But I've also not been sleeping, so it might be related to that," I say.

"Yeah, I've been achy lately. To the point of spasms. It hurts too much to sleep." Faith dips a sock, gray with age, into the water and watches water drip slowly from the toe. "I haven't slept for days. I'm all . . . disoriented."

"That should all be pretty easy to fix, though, right?" Claire says.

"If you know how, please tell me," I say. I've confided in Claire about my mounting health problems for weeks.

Claire looks at me, then Faith and Morgan. Morgan's face is impassive. She holds her body rigidly as she dips a pair of under-wear in the water. She may be here in body, but not in mind.

"Well, Dom explained it the other day, by the bonfire. He said that feeling bad is just a symptom of disloyalty. If you believe in him, he can heal you. I mean . . . you saw him bring Raina back to life, after all."

I sigh and try to catch Faith's eye. She's been here longer than Claire. She must see the absurdity of her belief in his sup-posedly supernatural powers.

"Yeah, I saw his phony resurrection. Look, Dom's healings aren't biological. If you feel better after talking to him, it's all in your head. He doesn't have some big, logic-defying power, guys. It's all a show. Come on," I say, my voice coming out harsher than I intended.

Their faces are slack, and instantly I know I've gone too far. Claire looks as if I've slapped her.

These passionless girls: they're not my allies. One of them will tell Dom about my lack of belief. If he was angry enough at Raina for contacting her family to make her *drop dead*, what will he do to me?

17

Claire

Now

THE NEXT MORNING, Sharon fusses over me when I return to work. She observes that I look peaked and recommends a strong cup of herbal tea. Lourdes keeps her distance, calling over from the reference desk to ask if I'm contagious.

Routine, boring tasks take up my morning. I search for books patrons claim to have returned, realphabetize the kids' section, discard the oldest issues of the magazine collection. Normally, I'm bothered by the endless, unfulfilling tasks of the library. I could have offered more, been more. But an unremarkable, weak-minded college dropout doesn't deserve a flashy career, I argue to myself these days.

Today, though, I welcome the mindless distractions that my job affords. I can't get DetroitDoll's words out of my head. I've tried to break free of these very thoughts for years. He ignited a dangerous longing in me.

I love Henry. I do. But sometimes I crave the breathless intimacy I felt in the Flock. Henry offers comfort and security, but I still feel a squeeze of panic when he gives me space. How can I tell him I want that smothering love that makes me forget who I am? He'd worry I'm slipping, and maybe I am.

The way the Flock seduced me, showered me with attention, in those early days—it felt good. My therapist used to prattle on about how love-bombing was just conditioning, the pleasure just free-flowing dopamine and endorphins. All of it manufactured feelings of unity and loyalty. Psychology and chemicals. But she'd never felt the warm glow of Dom's attention. Never had the chance to finally feel seen.

DetroitDoll's dreamy yearnings are echoing in my mind when a middle-aged woman approaches the circulation desk with a single book in her hand. I give the book's spines a final pat as I finish straightening them on the shelves and hurry over. When I reach for the book to scan it, I startle.

1984. How many times did I hold this book in my hands at the Bird Haven? I must have read it to Dom at least a dozen times. That was my job in the Flock: I read to Dom. Others did the wash, grew vegetables, chopped firewood. But I recited the words in this dystopian classic to him almost every night.

He told me I was sharp-witted. Darkly funny. I remember it now: the way his gaze lingered when he told me, the warmth of his fingertips on my bare arm. I haven't shelved or checked out this book in years, I'm sure of it, or I would have remembered it sooner.

The woman looks oblivious to my discomfort. She hands me her library card, and I see she has a few dollars in fines on her account. With a few keystrokes, I override the fines. It's something I do more often than Sharon knows. It's silly, but I always imagine it's my small way of atoning for the hurt I've caused the town of Iola.

When the woman leaves, I spend the rest of my shift wondering if I should reread *1984* when she returns it, if it'll jolt any old memories to the surface. The words will lure me back into Dom's orbit, I know. But is that what I want?

* * *

After my shift, I'm trimming spent leaves from a cluster of hosta plants when my father arrives home. His shiny dress shoes click up the walkway. While the dress code in Iola is camouflage and Carhartt, he must be the only man in town who wears a suit every day. Men don't even dress up for church here anymore.

His shoulders sag when he spots me crouching in the garden. Has the sight of me always drained him? Maybe it'd be different if my mother were still alive. She'd buffer him from my disappointments and stress, and his pinched face would offer a welcoming smile when I visited.

But his expression is stern, and he tosses a terse "Let's talk in the kitchen" over his shoulder as he marches up the stairs to the porch.

The kitchen is still painted a cheerful green and my father hasn't replaced the old floral dish towels my mother embroidered by hand, but it doesn't have the warmth it had when she was alive. The box of powdered doughnut holes, a fixture when I was a kid, is missing, and the windowsill is empty of a row of fresh potted herbs.

I lower myself into the chair nearest the pantry and wait while my father fills a water glass.

"Okay. Out with it, Claire. Say what you want to say," he says over his shoulder, facing the window over the sink.

"Why did you lie?"

He takes an agonizingly slow sip of water before he speaks.

"Would you prefer I implicate you even more in this mess? I'd say you're doing a pretty good job of that yourself."

"I'm involved in this whether I like it or not," I say. "And I just think lying is going to make it worse. If it comes out that you lied on the podcast, people will be even more suspicious of my involvement."

"It's time you distance yourself from all this, Claire."

With a sigh, I throw my head back and look at the ceiling. There's a tiny bug crawling along the top of the wall, darting in and out of shadows cast by the waning afternoon light.

"You shouldn't have said you didn't know I was living at the Bird Haven or that I was friends with Lollie. Laurel," I correct. "I mean, Laurel's mom is probably listening and can dispute what you said. And people will believe her more than us."

My father sets his water glass in the sink and crosses his arms. His face looks tired, lined. Hard. "What I know, Claire, is that you were troubled then. You lived only in the present. You joined this . . . this group—God only knows why—and you adopted their hedonistic disregard for consequences. I've spent ten years trying to get you to understand that you have a future. And that it's worth living."

"I know that. I'm not suicidal," I respond listlessly, still watching the bug on the ceiling.

"I can help you find a new therapist, if that's what you need," he says.

I think of Henry, his ruffled hair standing on end as he questioned whether my dad manipulated the outcome of my therapy sessions so I wouldn't remember. To protect me, he and Dr. Diehl said at the time. But what if it wasn't me they were protecting? I see them whispering in the hallway, but I can't be sure if it's a hazy memory returning or simply my imagination amid Henry's conspiracy talk.

"I'm capable of finding a new therapist if I want to start that again," I say carefully.

"Quacks are a dime a dozen, Claire Bear. You have to find someone you can trust. When Bunny died, you were still early in your sessions. Perhaps it stunted your recovery. I'll put in a call to Dr. Collins for you."

"I'm fine," I drawl.

It's always been like this: he lectures, I respond, and he refuses to listen. I feel like I'm a teenager again. The only differences are a decade's worth of lines on my face and a group of dead friends.

"What does Henry say about all this? I thought you two were thinking of starting a family."

"He wants to, but I'm not ready," I admit, finally looking at my father.

He levels his gaze. "That's the first sensible thing I've heard you say. You're not ready to be a mother."

His words send stinging needles into my heart. I look away, wounded and confused. He's echoing my thoughts, so why does it hurt so much to hear them spoken aloud?

I look out the window and see sunny clumps of ranunculus brightening the garden. My mother planted bulbs each fall and marveled when they sprouted after the cold spring rolled around. I still remember the way she pointed out where to dig, her long fingers covered with cheerfully patterned gloves. By the end of the season, holes had been ripped in the fingertips, so I bought her a new set every Mother's Day.

My mom died while in hospice care during those murky days between when Lollie went missing and when the Flock died. She never had to know what happened, and for that I'm grateful. A reporter caught me off guard shortly after my return and printed my words, screaming them in a headline: "Flock Survivor Says 'There's No Future.'"

It was misinterpreted, like so much I said at that time. While most people thought it meant I'd known about the Flock's suicide plan, I meant only that we'd lived in the present. Because, as a teenager, is there any other way to view life?

I couldn't see an adult version of me. Married, vacuuming, pretreating stains, flipping pancakes for a gaggle of kids. I still can't see it. Every day, I worry that someone will reveal the truth: Claire's an impostor. A fraud.

A selfish liar.

* * *

At dinner, I decide to tell Henry about DetroitDoll's theory that Dom is still alive. I don't mention that I met a man off the internet a few hours away.

"So, there's this group that posts on Reddit, and one of the more active members claims to have found Dominic," I say, careful to use his full name. Showing my impartiality.

Henry pokes at a slice of meat loaf on his plate. "The center's a little red on this. I think it's undercooked."

We both look at it in silence. It's true; the glaze has burned to an unsettling brown, while the center is a raw red. Wordlessly, I take his plate to the microwave.

"So what do you think about that idea? That he's alive?" I ask, leaning against the counter as the microwave timer ticks.

"I don't know, Claire. I don't think anything about it. I don't think about him. I don't think about the Flock. I don't think about you in the Flock." He ruffles his wavy hair. "I don't know what you want me to say."

"I'm just making conversation." An insistent ding tells me the meat loaf is ready. It's no longer red, but it'll be a long time before Henry can eat his green beans without burning his mouth. Steam billows from the plate when I set it in front of him.

"People are talking about all this again because of the podcast," I say. "One of the big questions is, where's Dominic? And I'm just telling you that I found someone who thinks they know the answer to that."

"Are you going to try to track him down, then?" Henry asks.

"No," I say automatically.

He studies me for a disarmingly long time. I hear kids ride bikes down the sidewalk out front, and a lawn mower start up. My eyes are trained on my plate and my own uncooked slice of meat loaf. I can't bring myself to look up.

"Have you ever really loved me, Claire?" he says finally.

My head snaps up. "Yes, of course!"

And it's true. He helps me be a better version of myself while still loving me, despite my flaws. He's smart, honest, and kind. He's the first man I felt comfortable enough with to wear my glasses and forgo makeup. When I thought I was above the silliness of dating and too broken for anyone to want to get to know, he was there, quieting my mind and helping me find myself.

My eyes widen, searching his face, willing him to believe me.

"I think a part of you can't let go of Dominic. And that's why you don't fully love me, not like I love you. And I think that's why you're stalling on starting a family of our own. You can tell me I'm wrong, but it's what I feel," Henry says, his voice both hard and vulnerable. "Now some stranger gave you a glimmer of hope that Dominic is out there, able to be found, and you want to know what I think about it. What do you want me to say? Give you my blessing to go find him?"

Henry pushes back from the table with a loud scrape. He empties his uneaten plate in the garbage can beside the refrigerator and leaves the kitchen. I listen to his footsteps trudge up the rear staircase and fade when he reaches the second floor.

I leave the baking dish to soak in the sink and tiptoe, scared to make a sound, upstairs to take a long, hot bath. I pinch myself when I feel myself begin to float, desperate to stay here, now, despite the pain. I cry cathartic tears and finally emerge, puffy eyed and red skinned.

The lumpy window seat in the reading nook serves as my bed tonight. My breath fogs the window. It's nearly fall, and nighttime temperatures are dropping.

It takes hours to fall asleep, and even then, it's fitful. Jarring fragments of dreams shake me from slumber. I dream of Henry rubbing my back, telling me he wants to start a family. Then his face thins out and his features melt into Dom's. He murmurs that I'm different from the others, that he could see me having his children. When I wake, I'm not sure if it was a dream or a long-forgotten memory. My neck and back ache as I stretch my curled body.

The house is quiet. Henry's left for work without saying goodbye. Our bed is made, his pajamas folded neatly on our dresser to wear again tonight. I wander downstairs and find my phone charging in the kitchen. It's a tiny show of thoughtfulness from Henry that gives me an unreasonable amount of hope.

Notifications on the home screen alert me to an overlooked alarm—I'm late for work—a missed call from Sharon, and a new episode of *Birds of a Feather*.

I curse as I tap Sharon's name. The library's recorded message picks up, and I punch zero to reach my boss.

"Sharon," I say breathlessly. "I'm so sorry. I missed my alarm this morning. I can be at the library in twenty minutes. Fifteen."

"Oh, Claire," she says. Motherly and disappointed at once. "I hate to have to do this, but I must ask you to go on unpaid leave for a while. I think there's a lot going on in your life, and I'd prefer you to address your personal issues. I'm sure you understand."

"I . . . no, I don't understand. Sharon, please. It's just this one time. I'm never late, you know that. I'll stay longer today. It's no problem."

"It's not just this . . . misunderstanding, dear," she says in a measured voice. "It's the publicity around you right now. And the unpleasant encounter with a patron recently."

I search my mind. Mrs. Tai. Sharon must have heard about her visit to the library to make copies for Lollie's vigil.

I plead with Sharon for a few more minutes, but she's firm. She promises to call when she feels I can return.

My job at the library is unfulfilling, yes, but I'm a socially clueless bookworm. It's perfect for me. I like helping the people of Iola, if even in a small way, and Lourdes keeps things interesting. What will she say when she finds out I've been put on involuntary leave?

What will Henry say?

Nerves make my hand tremble. The motion lights up my phone screen again, reminding me of the notification of the new podcast episode. My episode. I groan.

I fast-forward through the ads and introduction. Arlo's twangy voice warbles through the speakers.

"Listeners, the information I'm going to share with you today is going to challenge everything you think you know about this case. We know that, in 2012, fourteen members of the Flock died of asphyxiation from carbon monoxide poisoning. For ten years, we thought they died of suicide. Today, Flock survivor Claire Kettler will tell you a different story. This is never-before-heard, breaking insight into one of the worst cult deaths in the twenty-first century. This is *Birds of a Feather*."

Could this day get any worse?

CHAPTER

18

Laurel

Then

DOM AGREES TO let me recruit at Silver Dollar Lanes. He's hesitant, but I convince him that weekday-afternoon bowlers need to be saved too.

I pat on my secreted concealer to hide the dark circles from another restless night. I drive out of my way to Hovey's, a greasy spoon with the only working pay phone I know of. The breakfast crowd has cleared, and only a few old men pace the black-and-white linoleum for free refills of Coke.

April Davies's business card in hand, I dial her phone number from a pay phone near the bathrooms. "Pick up, pick up, pick up," I chant.

"Hello, this is April," a singsong voice chirps.

Relief floods my chest. "Ms. Davies, hi. This is Laurel Tai, from the Apple Queen pageant."

"Laurel, thanks for calling. I thought I'd have heard from you earlier in the week. I have your check ready to go. Are you available to meet up this afternoon?"

We make plans to meet at town hall in two hours. After we disconnect, I leave Hovey's and drive a mile northwest to a rocky pullout along old 26. I emerge from the van and walk to the low guardrail buffering me from the thousands of acres of trees and water below. The view is breathtaking.

The leaves will begin changing colors soon, but I won't be here to see it. When do the leaves change in Chicago? It doesn't matter, I realize, giddy. I'll be in the city, miles from a dense forest.

I'll leave tonight, I decide, as I head back to the van. I carry my pouch stuffed with what little cash I've stashed away—a few hundred dollars—and once I have the check from April, I'll just keep driving. I'll have the clothes on my back and this old van. I doubt Dom will report it missing, at least not right away. If I find the right chop shop outside Chicago, I can sell it for parts to make a little extra money.

It's my last afternoon in Iola, I realize. I debate driving to campus for one final look around, but I can't shake my guilt for all the times I've manipulatively trolled the tree-lined paths looking for a recruit or a mark.

Reluctantly, I steer into the pockmarked parking lot of Silver Dollar Lanes. Not to recruit, like Dom instructed, but to reminisce.

It smells like stale beer and the mineral oil coating the lanes. The entryway carpet is threadbare; it probably hasn't changed since I stood here with my dad so many years ago.

A league member, he came here every Tuesday night. When my little sister Viv was born, my bone-tired mother shipped me off with him for a few hours of alone time. It became our ritual.

It's still meat locker cold in here. I rub my arms as I look around. I don't want to waste even a few dollars on renting shoes and a lane. I find a seat at a high-top table near a concession stand and settle in, one eye on the clock and the other on the bowlers.

Once Dad got used to me tagging along for league night, he allowed little indulgences: a quarter for a gumball, two dollars for a plate of nachos. It smells like that gooey, yellow-orange cheese now. Superstitious, I scan the lanes in search of him.

Dark hair, a few days' worth of stubble, an untucked flannel shirt.

He's not here, of course. After he left us, I biked here from Estivant every Tuesday night for months. He could leave my mom, me, and Viv—somehow, I could understand this—but his bowling league? Never.

I asked his teammates if they knew where he was. At first, they ruffled my hair and set small bills on the plastic chairs so I could buy a snack. When they began to avoid eye contact or hurry to the men's room when I came by, and I knew it was time to give up hope of finding my dad.

Silver Dollar Lanes still holds the ghost of him. The lunchtime bowlers shuffle down the lanes like he did, swig beers like he did. Coming here on my last afternoon in Iola feels poetic. It's time I let go of him and the hurt he caused and move forward.

I'm edgy. Nervous. I haven't slept in days, and my memory's getting spotty. Even Dom commented on my lack of focus this morning. I'm terrified I'll trip up and reveal my plan, or that Dom will intuit my deception.

"Hey!" a voice rings out. "Hey, you. You can't be here!"

I turn. Her hair is stick straight and her lips glossed, but I recognize her instantly: Daisy Shea.

I raise a hand in defeat. "Daisy, look, I'm not here to cause any trouble."

"Get out of here, Lollie," she calls. She's wearing a polo shirt a few sizes too big for her, and I realize she works here, assigning lanes and doling out shoes. "No one here wants to join your freaky cult. You need to leave."

"That's not why I'm here," I exhale, already defeated. I rise to my feet. Daisy won't step away from the counter, so we face off, a duel of former best friends turned enemies.

"Listen. I'm sorry I gave your confessional to your parents. I shouldn't have done that. I'm sorry."

"Yeah, that was a shit thing to do. What about the cemetery plot calls?"

"What?"

Daisy scoffs. "Please. Don't act like you weren't behind it. Those really scared us."

"I don't know—"

"I don't believe for a *second* that you don't know about them or that you weren't the one making them. Come on. All those calls, day and night, asking if we wanted to buy a cemetery plot for me? That was freaky as hell, Lollie."

"Jesus," I breathe. Dom's paranoia has only grown since Daisy left. What will he do to me when he realizes I'm gone?

Daisy lowers her voice. "I don't want anything to do with you or the Flock."

Words bubble in my chest. I'm desperately lonely for someone to confide in. I could confess that I'm running away—tonight—and ask for her help. A few extra dollars, a forgotten hoodie from her car, even a granola bar would be a relief. But I'm feeling as superstitious as I am cautious, so I don't tell her that I get it, that I'm defecting too.

I could have avoided so much pain if I'd left with Daisy months ago. Now I'm only a few hours away from shedding this skin and becoming someone new.

It's funny, I think, as I edge around Daisy to leave: becoming someone new was the allure of the Flock in the first place.

*　*　*

Town hall is a small building with dark wooden siding and garden beds overflowing with canary-yellow daylilies. I spot April Davies sitting under a covered picnic shelter nearby.

She stands to wave me over. It's windy, but her shellacked helmet of white-blond hair is picture-perfect. She has enviable posture, and I wonder if she's a former beauty queen herself.

"Laurel, hello," she calls.

"Thanks for meeting me," I say, breathless. The traffic lights were out on Main Street thanks to last night's storm, and I'm running a few minutes late from the backup.

"I have the check for your prize money here," she says, offering a sealed business envelope to me. "With your phone connection issues, what's the best way to keep in contact with you?"

I'll take Dom's burner phone with me when I leave, but I don't know how long it'll stay active.

"I'll give you my number, but if anything changes, I'll let you know," I say as I stuff the envelope in my tote bag. The red pageant dress is still crumpled at the bottom.

"Okay. We have a few events coming up that we'd like the Apple Queen to attend. The library's announcing a book drive, and the Apple Blossoms are hosting a daddy-daughter dance. Then there'll be a float in next month's Halloween parade. It's customary for the queen to participate in events around town, as I'm sure you know."

"Of course." I nod. I'll be gone by then, but as long as the check doesn't bounce, it doesn't matter if I can't fulfill my duties.

April talks a little longer, sharing meaningless town updates and weather commentary, all while fixing me with an appraising eye. I can tell she's reluctant to part ways.

She offers to treat me to coffee at a shop on Main, but I decline. We say goodbye a few minutes later, and as I'm brushing my hair from my eye, I catch sight of a familiar figure leaving town hall.

I turn toward the parking lot but it's too late.

"Laurel!"

"Dr. Hollis, hi," I say. I keep my shoulders squared toward the lot and turn only my head, so he understands I'm in a hurry.

"I'm glad I caught you," he says, tucking a sheaf of papers under his suited arm. "There's something I'd like Claire to know. Could you tell her for me?"

No, I want to shout. The check practically throbs in my tote bag. I'm not going back to the Bird Haven.

"What is it?" I inject a coolness into my voice, striving for indifference.

"It's her mother. She has cancer, as I'm sure Claire told you. The outlook isn't good. She has a few days left, a week at best. A hospice worker's staying at the house with her now." He glances at his wristwatch. "In fact, I don't have much time to talk. Elaine's in and out of lucidity, but it'd mean a lot to her if Claire would come back to say goodbye."

A sigh deflates me. "I'll make sure she knows. And Dr. Hollis? I'm sorry."

He opens his wallet and hands me two hundred-dollar bills before striding to his silver sedan. I tuck the bills beside the envelope with my prize check.

Sitting in the Flock's old white van, I strum my fingers on the steering wheel for what feels like ages. A glance at the dash, though, tells me time's barely creeping forward.

Shift into drive, head south for eight hours, and arrive in Chicago after nightfall.

Or head back north to the Bird Haven one final time to let Claire know her mother's dying.

I wipe the sweat off my neck and shift gears.

19

Claire

Now

A TEXT FROM LOURDES the next morning sparks a fresh wave of tears. Let me know if you need anything. Here for you. xo

I spent the night crying. Henry held me, our fight forgiven when I told him I'd been put on temporary leave at the library. He cursed Sharon and vowed to look into the legality of her decision, but soon he realized I didn't need someone to match my anger. I just needed to feel his weight around me, secure and comforting.

He offered to stay home from his trail ride planned for the afternoon, but I waved him off when I saw the way worry widened his eyes. I can't face pity, not from my husband.

When Lourdes's text arrives, I spend fifteen minutes with my fingers hovering over the phone's keyboard, unsure how to respond. If I had the courage to talk to her now, she'd wag her ring-bedazzled fingers and insist I pull myself together.

One look in the mirror tells me she'd be right. My hair sports the outgrown highlights of a woman who once tried. My face is longer, narrower, than I remember. I look gaunt. Haunted. A few swipes of concealer hide the redness, but the puffiness around my eyes remains. My nails are ragged, with torn cuticles and dirt staining the tips.

I could go to the hair salon today, I decide. Stop wallowing. *Try* for once. I'll bring a book so I can avoid small talk with the stylist. I call Lucia's Salon, down on Dutch Lane by the Rodeway Inn. It's out of my way, but it might be quieter than the shop downtown.

A woman answers, her voice eager and bright. But after I'm put on hold, she returns with a steely tone to inform me that they have no availability—not today, not for me.

Stunned, I hang up. It's naïve of me to think I can continue to live in Iola. I've been a pariah for years, and now it'll only get worse.

I feel dazed as I hunt for my keys and a scarf. Despite the bright sun, it's deceptively cool today. I need fresh air. As I turn the key in my car's ignition, I glance up at our house. I expect to see a spray-painted slur marring the siding of my Queen Anne Victorian. But the beige siding is intact. It won't be long, though, I realize, until someone defaces our dark-red door. *A devil lives here*, they could write.

Sometimes it helps to think of all the ways I could be hurt before others speak them. Preparation for the inevitable.

I spend a few hours sitting on the rocky terrain of the harbor. The lighthouse looms on the shore nearby, and the ferry chugs on the choppy water of the lake. There's an old Native American footpath not far from here.

My eyes are heavy. I haven't slept well in weeks, not since I first saw Arlo at the library. Every night, I'm drained. Mentally exhausted. I'm ready to drift into blissful unconsciousness, but my brain won't turn off. With heavy-headed fogginess, I try to reconstruct memories. Something, anything, that will give me an answer to my friends' deaths.

When I lie beside Henry, my mind latches on to memories of Lollie's eyes, the way they crinkled at the corners when she smiled, and I start to drift to sleep, but Eden's wide, unseeing eyes invade. I spiral until our bedroom begins to lighten with the first inklings of dawn and Henry awakens, oblivious to my sleepless, troubled night.

The cool breeze blowing off the harbor lessens my fatigue. I let the water's rhythmic lapping at the shore hypnotize me. I dig my nails into the pebble-filled sand and toss rocks into the lake, wondering how anyone ever gets them to skip across the water with more than a graceless plop.

At two o'clock, after I've been at the harbor for three hours, I tromp back up the trail and return to my car.

Fayette Avenue becomes Main Street as I wind around campus and near the heart of downtown Iola. I pass the historic county courthouse and a veterans' memorial. The road narrows. Ahead, a few vehicles are parked in the street, motionless as the traffic lights flick from green to yellow to red.

I squint through the windshield—the afternoon sun's glare highlights how dirty it is—and try to see around the cars. Was there an accident?

Drivers emerge from their cars and form little clumps in the road. I watch a woman point a flabby arm into the air. I lift my gaze, following it.

Above Main Street, a cable is suspended across two lanes of traffic. It stretches from the second story of the Arcadia Cinema to a run-down pub the college kids frequent.

Hanging from it are birds. Big, black birds—crows, maybe, or ravens. A half-dozen birds strung up by their curved talons. Wings dangling. I count six carcasses, but the birds' wide wingspans, hung tip to tip, leave no gaps on the wire.

There are words on the Arcadia's marquee. It's been shuttered for years, reading FOR SALE for as long as I can remember. But today the cinema's marquee proudly advertises, *Now Playing: The Birds.*

The limp wings sway in the breeze. Their blackness blooms wider as my vision darkens. I grip the steering wheel and blink rapidly, trying to keep from fainting.

More vehicles, more people gather. A police car winds through the maze of onlookers, its lights whirring but siren silent. I stay in my car.

I can't tear my eyes from the birds, the marquee.

I know it's a warning about the Flock. And I know it's meant for me.

* * *

"Now we take you to footage of this afternoon's macabre scene in downtown Iola," a newscaster reports.

My footsteps thud on the wood floor as I race through the foyer into the sitting room. Henry is on the couch. He sets down a bicycling magazine when I enter.

"This, this," I say breathlessly, reaching for the remote. "Here it is. Listen." I punch up the volume.

". . . several dead birds hanging over Main Street today, and vandalism to the sign of the old Arcadia Cinema, which has been closed since 1997. Police say this is nothing more than an ill-advised prank by a group of students at Arbor State University. No word yet on if any charges will be filed against the students . . ."

"A prank?" My shoulders drop, and my arms hang loosely at my sides. I wilt onto the couch beside Henry, crumpling his magazine. I rub my eyes with the sleeves of my oversized sweater.

"Claire, look," Henry says. He leans forward.

On the screen, it's me. I'm ten years younger. Paler, skinnier. My hair long and unwashed. I'm unsteady and I look dazed. My father, grim faced with hair that's not yet turned white, clutches my elbow as we leave the police station. This isn't footage from my first visit to the station; that wasn't worthy of news coverage yet. For weeks my father escorted me to interviews, and I never lost that numb, stunned expression.

". . . believe this misguided prank is in response to recent publicity around the 2012 deaths of cult members known as the Flock. Shown here, surviving member Claire Hollis exits the police department alongside her father, Blair County medical examiner Grant Hollis . . ."

"Oh," I moan. "So much for staying under the radar."

"This is good, though, isn't it?" Henry asks as he lowers the volume on the television when the news turns to blaring commercials. "It's not meant for you, after all."

"No. Now everyone's paying attention."

Henry rubs the crease between his eyes. "Maybe someone knows something. And the attention from this cruel prank and the podcast too—maybe it'll stir up some answers finally. Put the whole thing to rest."

I stand and pace the room, past the built-in shelves and over-stuffed arm chairs that are never sat in because we never have company.

"Everyone wants to know the same things. Who killed Lollie? Why'd the Flock die, and why'd I live? And where'd Dominic go?" I pause to peek behind the heavy curtains. No lights brighten our backyard, so I can't see the scrubby grass or generous woodpile at this time of night. Still, a part of me expects I'll see someone back there, watching. Waiting.

A specter's haunted me for years. Eyes on me while I garden in the yard, load groceries into my trunk, shelve books at the library. It's an unsettled prickled-neck hair feeling, being watched. I don't tell Henry. I deserve the scrutiny, the glowing target on my back, the fear.

Henry shifts on the couch. The newscaster returns, reciting details of a charity bake sale. Her voice is a low murmur now.

"I know the answer to one of those questions, but I've never told anyone," I say, letting the curtain fall back into place. "I killed Lollie."

20

Laurel

Then

A s I STEER the van through the tree-lined road back to the Bird Haven, I debate penning a letter to Claire and leaving it in the mailbox for her to find.

But we've been too close this summer for me to tell her that her mother's dying by way of a note on the back of an old receipt.

I park on the roadside, before the trees open to the clearing with the cottage. I'll tell Claire and hop back in the van as quickly as I can. I worry not parking in the garage will rouse Dom's suspicion, but maybe I can catch Claire before he knows I'm back.

I check our shed first. Claire's not here. Biting my lip, I scan for anything I can stuff in my tote to bring with me. I settle on my photo of Viv tacked above our mattress. I slip it off the nail and smooth the little rupture in the top of the picture before sliding it into my back pocket.

I hear voices from the open windows of the cottage. If I enter, Dom might see me, and then it'll be harder to leave again. I tiptoe to the window and peek in, hoping to catch sight of Claire and wave her outside.

She's at the kitchen counter, shoulder to shoulder with Sunny, blocked partially by Eden's wide frame. They're chopping vegetables. Even out here, I can smell the familiar scent of seafood stew wafting from a large pot on the stovetop.

Her back is to me, but I can see Eden's face, and the twins at the rickety kitchen table too. They're all crying.

Leave, a voice in my head screams. Leave now, while they're distracted. Put a note on Claire's pillow and hurry back to the van.

I step onto the wraparound porch so quietly the wood doesn't creak under my weight. I feel paralyzed.

As my head continues to scream, I turn the doorknob and enter the cottage. Jock and Helena shuffle a deck of playing cards between them by the coffee table. Lido sits at the piano, fingers poised above the keys in silent song. Even Thomas is here, whittling a small piece of wood in his hands. I see Dom's mangy rabbit on the couch but not Dom himself.

At the entryway to the kitchen, I try to beckon to Claire, but she doesn't see me. I can tell now that she's crying too.

What's going on? Does everyone know about Claire's mother already?

I touch her shoulder and she startles, nicking her knuckle on the knife blade.

"Oh no. I'm sorry," I say as I reach for a rag of a dish towel on the counter.

Claire dabs at her eyes first, then holds it to her bleeding finger.

"What happened?"

"You didn't hear?" Claire sniffs.

The other girls stop chopping. The twins look up.

"It's Raina. She tried to kill herself."

*   *   *

Vinny found her in the lake, the girls tell me.

He was fishing on the shore when he saw her emerge from the forest and hunt up and down the shoreline, collecting rocks.

She stuffed them in her pockets and even the hood of her sweat-shirt before wading into the water.

"I thought that was only something that happened in, like, books," Goldie whispers. She recently let Sunny chop her curly hair into a short pixie, and it doesn't suit her. She's too gaunt now, and it adds a haunted severity to her features.

"Is she okay?" I ask, my voice hitching in my throat.

"Vinny pulled her from the lake, but not before she lost con-sciousness. He gave her mouth-to-mouth. He said she choked up a bunch of water and then threw up. He carried her back here. She was super weak and pretty dazed," Sunny says.

"Where is she now?"

"Up in Dom's room, with him," Eden supplies. "He's heal-ing her."

I exhale noisily and look around at their faces. Tear-streaked and somber, yet serious. They still believe Dom can help her.

"This is crazy," I say. "Raina needs medical attention. Dom can't do anything for her."

Eden snorts and furrows her brow. "I mean . . . are you seri-ous, Lollie? We just watched him bring her back from the dead a couple days ago. If anyone can heal her, it's him."

"No," I say, a little too loudly. From the living room, Helena and Jock look over. "Don't you see? That phony resurrection is the reason she tried to kill herself. Dom spends a whole night berating her for being weak, tells her to *drop dead*, for God's sake, then brings her back, all the while telling us how amaz-ing it is to return to the dust? It's like he's romanticizing death. Encouraging it, even."

The girls are quiet. Claire casts a warning glance to the stairs, as if she expects Dom to materialize after my blasphe-mous words.

"She *is* weak, Lollie. That's not Dom's fault." Eden raises her chin defiantly.

I shake my head and catch Claire's eye. I tilt my chin toward the hallway and mouth *please*.

I leave the girls tittering in my wake. Now I have no choice but to leave. Questioning Dom, vocalizing my disloyal thoughts: I'll be ostracized immediately.

Claire meets me in the hallway. The weak glow from a wall-mounted light casts dark shadows on her pale face.

I take her hand. "Come with me," I whisper, leading her out of the cottage.

Inside our shed, Claire's hesitant to sit. She hovers by the door.

She's not like me. She'd rather be right than popular, and she's dismissive of emotions. Distant and hard to get to know, Claire hasn't bonded much with the other Flock members since she got here a few months ago. She finds small talk pointless, and the girls' conversations have only gotten more trivial, since they never leave the Bird Haven.

But here, in the shed, we talk about big things, just she and I. Purpose, ethics, God, and death: we cover it all, lying beside each other night after night. Is happiness just a chemical? Is one lifetime enough?

So it seems fitting that on my last night here, I'm the one to tell her this harsh truth about her mother.

"I saw your dad today," I say, sitting on the low mattress. I rub the sheets between my fingers and look up at her. "He said your mom only has a few days left, Claire."

She blinks rapidly. Her white cheeks turn a mottled red. She gulps, trying to find words.

"The cancer's spread, and she's in hospice now," I continue. "Your dad thinks she has a few days, or maybe a week at most. He says she's not very lucid right now—she spends a lot of time sleeping—but he still wants you to come say your goodbyes. We can take the van tonight, and I can drop you off at your house."

To my surprise, Claire shakes her head. Her blond hair, lank with grease, hangs limply to her shoulders.

"I don't want to see her actively die."

"But . . . she's your mom," I say. Even I'd visit my mother, a judgmental woman who disowned me. Claire chose to leave, and her parents want her back. "I get that you don't want to see her in pain. Seeing her now won't change all your memories of her, though. Later, you might feel sad or even, I don't know, *guilty*, if you don't say goodbye."

"It'd be selfish of me to go. It'd be too disruptive," she says, still lingering by the door.

"They *want* you there, Claire," I argue.

"I-I-I . . ." She stutters and grimaces. "I-I'm not going," she says loudly.

I realize returning to the Bird Haven tonight was a mistake. Claire doesn't want to hear about her mother, and news of Raina's suicide attempt makes me hesitant to leave this surrogate family I've built. It would have been better if Claire didn't know about her mom and I didn't know about Raina.

I reach into my tote bag and finger the bony rabbit's foot key chain. I think of Dom stroking his bunny, sitting in his creaky old wheelchair. He'll haunt me forever. I need to leave now.

Hoisting my bag on my shoulder, I stand. I'm face-to-face with Claire when our eyes meet. I'm ready to reach for the doorknob and shoulder past her when she lets out a heaving cry and collapses into my arms.

Her weight makes my knees buckle. I guide her to the mattress and stroke her hair while she sobs.

What was I thinking? That I'd tell her this terrible news about her mother and escape the next minute? It'd be cruel to leave her now.

Besides, I know Claire: her mind's never at rest. She'll tumble this news around in her head, becoming preoccupied. Without me to talk to, she'll isolate herself from the other girls in the Flock. They already think she's arrogant, rude.

She's said before that her parents wanted her to be adventurous and independent—more like me, really—but she feels as if she's always making the wrong decision in their eyes. This time, I agree. It's a mistake not to say her goodbyes.

Claire cries herself to sleep, and I lie beside her for what feels like hours. Listening to every sound and staring into the darkness. My head pounds from exhaustion and anxiety. My stomach aches, but not with hunger. Is it worry, fear?

An owl hoots, and somewhere in the woods, a branch snaps. I create a storyline in my mind, imagining walking down the streets of Chicago by tomorrow evening. When twilight sets in, the buildings will sparkle. I'll start over, away from this communal trauma of the Flock and its narcissistic leader. I'll discover a new world, build a new family.

I sink into my imagination and let the film in my mind carry into a dream.

* * *

I'm in a state between sleep and wake.

Is it morning or night? A shadow stands over me. Beside me, I can feel Claire's body is rigid with tension. She's awake. I blink, but my mind is foggy, and I can't place who's in our shed with us.

It is another intruder drill so soon? Outside, it's quiet of gunfire and shattering windows.

The shadow breathes fast and shallow. He reaches and yanks me to standing. I stumble, disoriented. My mind's not thinking fast enough. Even my limbs aren't working right.

He stuffs something in my mouth and jerks me toward the door. I stagger, hitting my head on a metal shelf. He throws a shoulder into the door while wrangling me.

I remember the gutted raccoon at our door just a few days ago. An omen.

My arms prickle with the sudden cold. He tightens his grip and leads me away from the cottage, into the woods.

Twigs and pebbles jam into my bare feet. I scream into the rag in my mouth, but it's muffled. It gets darker.

I try to clear my head. Two thoughts circle their way through my mind, getting louder with each loop.

The first: Dom said disloyalty would attract evil.

The other: I wouldn't be here tonight if not for Claire.

Louder now, screaming in my mind.

Then: silence.

Part 2

21

Claire

Now

HENRY'S FACE DOESN'T register surprise, so I repeat myself: "I killed Lollie."

Now his eyes narrow slightly, but he doesn't break my gaze. Has he suspected I killed her all along? Why is he still in the room with me? Why has he ever been with me?

"What happened?" he says finally, quietly.

I perch on the arm of the overstuffed chair, then pop up again, pacing.

"I always said I never saw the intruder, but that's not true. I woke first, and I saw him standing over our bed. I sat up. He said my name, Henry. *Claire.* One word. He had this flat, low voice. I'll never forget it." I pause, remembering the way his disembodied voice carried through the shadowy darkness of the shed where we slept. "He wanted me, and I shook my head. And he took Lollie instead."

The TV volume rises when the commercials return. Henry looks away as he reaches for the remote and turns it off. The silence is enveloping.

"So . . . what? You misled the intruder, and he took Laurel, then later killed her?"

I feel a crease form between my brows. "I was the intended target. I know it in my soul. But I was scared, and I shook my head when he said my name. He took Lollie, and when he realized his mistake, he killed her. But really, I killed her. I let him take her."

"Who would have wanted to take you?" Henry leans back into the couch, crossing a leg over his knee. Getting comfortable, not running scared.

I stop pacing and trace a finger along one of the built-in bookshelves. It's adorned with picture frames I haven't bothered to update in years. Dust balls up on my fingertip.

"If I knew, Lollie's murder wouldn't still be unsolved. I didn't tell the truth then, and the police have looked in the wrong places for years. They looked at people in the pageant circuit, people who knew Lollie. But that's wrong. Everyone loved her. It's me he wanted that night, not her."

"You're loved too, Claire."

I look up. Henry's brows are knit together, and his eyes look darker, more mournful, than usual. Visions of this moment have danced in my head for years. Since we started dating, I worried how I'd tell him about my role in my best friend's death. Of all the scenarios I imagined, I never expected he'd stay calm, supportive, inquisitive. I don't deserve him.

"Lollie's death triggered the Flock's suicide. I have the blood of so many people on my hands. They were supposed to be my family, and I killed them all."

"Don't talk like that, Claire," Henry says, leaning forward.

He's off the couch and at my side in an instant. I melt into his warm sweatshirt. His fingertips are stained black, and he smells like printer ink. He's achingly normal, solid and reassuring.

"I wish you would have told me this sooner. I hate to think of this misguided guilt digging deeper into you every day," he says.

I pull away. "It's not misguided. I'm at fault."

I shuffle in slipper-clad feet to the kitchen, where I begin opening cabinets and drawers. I don't know what I'm looking for, but it feels good to move. I pull a stack of coupons out of a drawer and toss them on the counter. I begin to toss the expired ones onto a pile.

Henry follows me. "Can this wait, Claire? We don't need a twenty-percent-off coupon for Tres Caminos right now," he says as he bends to pick up a flyer that's drifted to the varnished maple wood floor.

I unleash an unbridled squeal of frustration, slamming the rest of the stack onto the countertop. "Fuck," I breathe. "I feel like you never grasp the weight of what I tell you. My actions killed my best friend and, in turn, everyone in the Flock. That's a big deal. Someone wanted to take me that night instead, Henry. I've had a target on my back for ten years. I live in a constant swirl of fear and guilt. Every day I remember what I did, and I alternate between relief I'm alive and just wishing he'd come back and take me. Finish it all, finally."

I've crumpled the coupons in my clenched fists. I catch a glimpse of myself in the reflective microwave door. I look feverish.

Henry sighs as he rubs his forehead. "Then let's figure out who would have wanted to take you and why. Did you know something about the Flock or Dominic? Were you involved in something dangerous?"

My blood feels like it's pounding in my head and a sheen of sweat has broken out above my lip, but Henry? There's no tension in his body, and somehow it makes me even angrier that he's so practical, not intimidated or flustered by my revelation about my role in Lollie's death.

"No. For years I've turned over everything I can remember, but you know my memories are all jumbled and spotty. I don't know why the intruder wanted me, but I know he did." I walk to the trash can and toss handfuls of wrinkled coupons inside. I lean against the massive, heavy-topped worktable in the center of the room. Original to our Victorian, it now serves as our kitchen island.

"It seems like your memories are starting to return, though. Maybe you only thought they were lost. If we talk through this together or even get you a new therapist, if you'd feel more comfortable with that . . ." He trails off, a thoughtful squint lining his face. "How'd you get involved with that old therapist, anyway?"

"Dr. Diehl? She was an acquaintance of my dad's. She was good at what she did, and he said she could be trusted."

"Well, any therapist you see would be bound by confidentiality rules, Claire. You were an adult by the time you saw her. Something about her and what she told you doesn't sit right with me," he says, drumming his fingers on the table. "From the start, she told you that you couldn't—and shouldn't—access your memories of what happened. I get that you had this diagnosis, and memory gaps aren't unusual for PTSD. That makes sense to me. But it seems like remembering would help you heal, if you did it in a safe way. But she told you the opposite. That it'd be dangerous to remember. She made you scared of your own mind. Don't you think that's unusual?" Henry asks, ruffling his hair into spikes.

"What would she have to gain by telling me that if it wasn't true?"

"Maybe it's not what she had to gain. Maybe it's what you or someone else had to lose."

"Like what? And who?"

"Your dad?"

I open my mouth, and Henry holds his hand up. "Hear me out." He looks up at the ceiling, collecting his thoughts. "When you returned home that first day, you were reeling from the shock of finding your friends. You also found out your mom died of cancer while you were gone. Do you think that in that state, you said anything to your dad that he would have worried would incriminate you? Or affect him in some way? What if he set you up with that therapist and influenced her because he didn't want you to remember? Maybe you said something about the intruder taking Lollie or targeting you, and he didn't want that to get out."

My mind spins. When I first returned home, I told my dad everything I remembered leading up to finding the Flock in the idling vans. I've been intimidated by him and angry with him for the ways he infantilizes me even as an adult, but I've never doubted his intentions before.

"Look," Henry continues. "I don't want to make things weird between you and your dad. Or me and your dad, for that matter. But you need to stop relying on him and taking everything he says as the truth." He points a finger at me and back at his chest. "We're partners. Let me help you figure this out so you can finally move forward. I mean, I'm ready to start the next chapter in our lives. But you, and all this—sometimes it seems like you're content to muddle around in murky memories and punish yourself for choices you made as a teenager. You can't define yourself by something that happened ten years ago."

I want to reassure him. He wants me to move forward, but there's no way to make closure of something so complicated, so traumatic. The ashes of my grief will always be there.

"So what do I do?" I ask, my voice barely above a whisper.

He shrugs. "Look at the facts? Figure out what was really going on there. Not just when you were there, but before. Because maybe you're not thinking far enough back. Didn't you once tell me that people in the Flock were dying before Laurel was abducted and before the suicides? You've said there were weird health problems, right?"

"Yeah, we were sick that summer, but I don't know what that has to do with anything. I don't think it's related."

"Maybe it is, Claire," Henry argues. "People were dying before Laurel and the Flock, even though those were the ones that got all the attention. We know that for sure. If we can figure out what was happening with those health problems and early deaths, maybe we'll find a clue to Laurel's killer."

22

Dominic

Then

WHEN I WAKE, my leg is twitching uncontrollably. I don't know if it's because I took my medication or because I forgot. I rummage through the detritus on my desk to find the bottle and shake two pills into my mouth, dry-swallowing the lump.

It's still dark in the room, but it's not late. Sheets of rain beat at the windows, casting the room in shades of gray. A body lies in a tangled heap on the hulking four-poster bed. I step forward, eyeing her.

The sheets reek of unwashed bodies and sex, though not from last night. No, I've spent the night pacing and watching. Deciding.

If only she hadn't done this.

She was unwell, but aren't we all? After her secretive attempts at reaching the outside were publicly reprimanded with a demonstrative of what happens when the Flock question me, I thought she'd fall in line. This overly dramatic suicide staging in the lake, though: it's as if she's learned nothing.

Still, I'm lucky Vinny was there to pull her from the water. The last thing I need is more questions about people dying here right now.

Raina stirs, grunting and rolling over in an unattractive mess of bent limbs and greasy hair. I turn to the window, rubbing my chin as I survey the grounds.

The rain started only an hour or two ago, but the low areas are already flooded. The old RV sits in a veritable pond. If it had any chance of running before, it doesn't now. The tree line is thick, but a glimpse of white along the roadside catches my eye. I strain to see through the downpour, not bothering to conceal my nakedness in the window.

There's something there, but I'll need to get closer to see. I shrug on my jacket and pants and cast another glance at Raina. She may have made it through the night, but I still have a challenge ahead. Her attempt will make the others question our mission here. Best case, they'll use it to strengthen their belief in me while turning on her for her disloyalty and weakness. Today we'll have an honesty circle to gauge their reaction to it all.

Out of chaos, there's always opportunity to capitalize on. Turbulent times are ripe for finding troubled souls, naïvely idealistic, searching for a chance to be a part of something bigger. Tonight and every night, I'll tell them I know their fears, I sense their pain, I see their minds. I promise eternity. Soon, I become immortal.

Downstairs, the girls lope around the living room in various states of undress. Goldie touches her nipple as I pass, and I make a note to bring her to my room when I return.

Outside, there's a heady, earthy smell in the air as the rain beats down. My pants blacken with mud as I head toward the roadside.

Parked partially in the brush is one of the Flock's two vans. Alarms ring in my head as I stagger forward. This shouldn't be here.

I fling open the door. It's empty. What's it doing out here, out of the garage?

Lollie.

I don't bother to knock on the shed door. Inside, it's dark. The day's little light filters through a window near the ceiling. Rain batters against the thin walls. Claire sits on the mattress as if she's been expecting me.

"Where's Lollie?" I bark.

"I don't know," Claire says, her voice barely more than a whisper. She doesn't meet my eyes.

Something's wrong.

I step farther into the shed, letting the door slam behind me. Water drips from my hair onto the concrete slab of a floor. I survey the space, taking in the garden tools, fishing poles, faded life preservers, and dozens of birdhouses suspended from hooks in the ceiling.

Beside the mattress is Lollie's bag. I snatch it up, dropping things on the wet floor as I rummage through it: the van's keys on a lucky rabbit's paw key chain, a zippered pouch wadded with cash and a check, a red dress I recognize from the pageant debacle.

"Tell me again. Where's Lollie?"

"She's gone."

"What happened?" I try to keep a steel edge from invading my voice. Claire's in a precarious state, and I need information.

"Someone came in last night and took her."

My eyes narrow as I study Claire. Is she lying? Covering for Lollie?

When I saw the newspaper article touting Lollie's pageant win, I knew it was just the beginning of her secrets. I'd sensed she was pining for the outside, and when I saw her smiling for an audience of hundreds at the Podunk town festival, I assumed it was only a matter of time before she left us. Me.

Did she run off in the night, or get outside help to leave? Maybe. But why leave the van parked on the side of the road?

"Who was it?"

Claire shakes her head. "I don't know. I was asleep," she says in a pitiful, childlike voice.

"You were asleep? How do you know someone took her, then? How do you know she didn't leave on her own?"

"I . . . I . . . ," she stammers.

"You're lying." So much for the pandering niceties. "Whatever you're not telling me, I will find out. I already know it, in my unconscious. I'm going back to the house to tap into my inner knowledge. I hope that, for the sake of your transcendence to the next plane, you divulge your truth before I unearth it."

I start for the door and have only begun to turn the knob before she's on her knees. Crawling across the concrete to my feet.

"I'm so sorry," she whimpers. "It was a man, but I don't know who he was. He just came in and took her while we were sleeping."

"Did she know him?" I finger the trail of hair leading down my stomach to remind Claire that I'm the man here. The master.

"I don't think so, no. She struggled."

An outsider. My stomach curdles with an unsettling mix of satisfaction and fear as I realize my visions are coming true. The end is nearing.

As Claire grovels at my feet, I understand I own her now.

"Lollie has been taken, and it's your fault. The burden of this guilt will be a heavy weight to carry. I'll save you from the coming persecution as long as I can. You're not to tell anyone that the outsiders have captured Lollie. Not even the Flock can know, not yet."

I leave her crying on the floor of the shed, only to return to more damaged girls in the house.

I need to find Lollie before anyone realizes she's missing. Once people find out the Apple Queen has been kidnapped in her sleep, the townspeople and media will descend.

Demanding. Prying. Destroying.

* * *

With Raina deposited downstairs in the care of the girls, I have time to think. I close the blinds, remove my clothes, and recline on the bed with a pencil and paper. I relax my muscles and let energy run through me like a river. In a deep meditative state, I feel my unconscious mind open.

When my channel is clear, I try to tune in to Lollie's frequency to locate her physical being, but . . . silence. Instinctively, I know this means she's transcended from our plane. My mind starts to wander, to *interpret*, but I guide it back and let the process consume my being.

The gaps between my thoughts are wide. I feel separate from myself as I dissolve. The writing flows, a stream cascading through my hand. I'm channeling my soul's wisdom.

The pencil stops moving. I feel limp. I open my eyes and see the paper is covered in overlapping symbols and words.

There's little need to decipher it. I've been automatic writing for years; the patterns are sharp and clear. The message is both authoritative and malevolent.

We're marching toward the end, but I see now that Lollie's disappearance is the trigger. She's set into motion the Flock's ruin.

It should have all been so simple. I've always known I was different, even as a child. It's not so much that I knew I was special, as so many talentless, mediocre children are told by their equally unimpressive parents, but I knew I was *better*. I ached to make others see this. It wasn't until I discovered social psychology that I realized there's a veritable playbook for making others understand I'm elevated above them. Leaders have been doing it for years. There's a formula for gaining power, money, and people. Look to the greats, and you'll see there's a step-by-step guide to securing devotion.

All you have to do is offer a chance to belong. Recruit vulnerable people. Tell them what they want to hear. Give them a dream. Build a community of bruised people. Then seclude them until they become dependent on you. Require sacrifice:

money, real estate, independence. Test their loyalty to ensure commitment.

I've done all that here. But then our growth slowed and the money stopped flowing. I imagined there'd be ballooning followers by now, an upgraded compound, maybe even an influential political role not unlike Jim Jones when he was the darling of California liberals.

It's laughably common to want money, power, and people. It's why men fight wars. But if I fail here with my Flock, what can I do so that, inevitably, everyone still sees my power?

I ruminate on this, and what to do, until hours later when the sound of the banjo pulls me from my room.

Downstairs, Lido's banging on the piano keys, a deep funereal dirge filling the room, while Vinny plucks a chirpy twang on a banjo. The discordant sound is unsettling, but the others don't seem to mind. Sunny hums, in her own musical world, while Helena sways to a rhythm that's not there.

It's the banjo that catches my eye. Old, dented, and missing a string, the sight of it transports me.

My grandfather played it in the evenings, after his shift at the delicatessen. He'd leave loaves of hard, crusty bread beside his key ring on the console in the entryway, and we'd scatter, letting him settle into his favorite chair. His fingertips forever smelled of briny pickle juice, and his black button-down shirt inevitably had a few sickly red-meat stains. He'd wipe his nose, and ours too, with a soggy handkerchief, more out of habit than necessity. My sister was the only one to pipe up and put an end to the disgusting habit. By then, his hands had taken on a tremor and his eyes were rheumy. I didn't think it was worth asking him to change when he had so little time left. Better to be himself, bad habits and all, then succumb to what others wanted.

As Vinny strums the instrument, another string snaps. He laughs, a braying sound that sets my nerves on fire. Before the others realize I've joined them downstairs, I snatch the banjo from his hand and cradle it to my chest.

"That's enough."

Their laughter stops, and even Lido stops playing. Goldie, in her vulgar way, shouts something unintelligible from the kitchen.

"Oh, Dom, thank God you're here," she says when she pokes her head around the corner. "We're worried about Lollie. We haven't seen her all day. Do you know where she is?"

I set my grandfather's banjo beside a cabinet in the hallway, slowly and deliberately. Buying time as I look for Claire to read her expression. What's she told them?

But she's not in the room that I can see, and that in itself is likely what's tipped them off that something's wrong.

"Yeah, Lollie was supposed to help with the wash today, but she wasn't here," Faith offers. "And Claire was all edgy and quiet. Something's up."

"Did Claire say there's any reason to be worried about Lollie?" I ask.

Goldie and Faith exchange a look.

"She didn't have to," Goldie retorts, as brash as ever. "Even when she leaves to recruit or run errands, she's only gone a few hours. No one's seen her since last night."

I pick my way through the girls lounging on the floor to sit in my chair. It creaks under my weight. I debate what angle to take here: tell them Lollie was taken, that she left, or that she's expected to return shortly? It's too soon to give anything away, I decide.

"It sounds as if you've manufactured a crisis that doesn't exist," I say, cocking my head and letting my eyes bore into Goldie, then Faith.

As if punctuating my words, an eerie scream pierces the night. Even Thomas, who's been whittling in a chair in the corner, looks up, alarmed. The girls huddle together as the men race to the window. Vinny picks up a shotgun resting near the door. A few voices call my name, and Eden's at my side in a moment, whimpering.

"Is that Lollie?" one of the twins asks.

Again, the alarming cry rings out. It sounds like a woman screaming.

Tears stream down Morgan's normally impassive face. I sigh.

"That's not Lollie," I say. I keep my voice quiet and measured, so quiet that I repeat myself.

"How do you know?" Sunny demands.

The scream cuts through the darkness again. Vinny throws open the door and thuds out onto the porch, shoeless and shirtless.

"He's right," Thomas says from the corner. He raises his voice to be heard over the growing cacophony, something I refuse to do. "That's no human. That's a red fox."

"A fox? No. No way," Goldie says, striding to the window.

"It's probably just hunting or mating," Thomas adds.

I see the tension start to slip out of the others' muscles. They begin to back away from the windows, which at night carry only their worried reflections anyway. They ease back to their spots, eyes more alert than usual. Thomas's words, spoken so infrequently, carry weight.

"The Bird Haven isn't the set of a horror movie." I aim for reassurance with an undercurrent of threat: the formula for bringing the Flock under my wing every time. "Lollie's not screaming in the woods."

My mind flicks to my attempt to channel Lollie's energy this afternoon; I know she's not in the woods, at least not *alive*, screaming. But Claire? Could she have screamed just now if she found something disturbing related to Lollie's disappearance?

As if on cue, Vinny racks the shotgun and shouts something into the darkness.

"Stop, stop! Wait! It's Claire," Helena, nose pressed to the window, screams.

Claire stumbles past Vinny as his chest heaves, the gun dangling from his limp arm. He murmurs back at her with blank eyes, and I realize how close he must have come to shooting her. But she seems not to notice.

"Did you hear that?" she pants.

"We heard the red fox, if that's what you mean," I say, turning up the corner of my lip into a smirk.

Eden chuckles, and Jock shakes his head. Loyal.

"A fox? No, but it sounded like . . ." She trails off when she catches my eye.

"Lollie's not with you in the shed, is she?" Goldie asks from where she stands under Hunter's arm near the couch.

Claires shakes her head. I can smell her greasy, lank hair from here.

Eden must smell it too. "Claire, you smell bad," she says, wrinkling her nose theatrically.

Claire blinks slowly. A film slides over her eyes. A haunted veil of guilt. What's she not told me yet?

"I smell like Claire."

23

Claire

Now

S UNNY WAS THE first to hallucinate. I remember that now. We'd been irritable for weeks, with aching muscles and growing insomnia. But the hallucinations were terrifying and harder to ignore. Sunny had tremors by then, and a gash on her forehead from one of the many times she'd lost her balance. We'd all been growing clumsier as the summer waned, and it was getting harder to know if we were in pain because of our frequent falls or if the sickness caused that too.

The first time Sunny hallucinated, she screamed that she was drowning and clawed at Jock's face when he tried to help her. We were all huddled in the sitting room of the old cottage on a particularly rainy afternoon when it happened. Even Dom was there, sitting in the rickety antique wheelchair that had once belonged to the ornithologist. It was Dom's throne.

The sickness was frustrating. We could never find the right words. We stuttered. We were disoriented. Words echoed in our heads, and we became clumsy, uncoordinated.

But it was scary too. Our chests felt heavy, our limbs numb and tingly. Hot and cold felt reversed. We saw things that weren't there.

Yes, it was getting worse in the weeks leading up to Lollie's kidnapping and the Flock's deaths. But I don't know how our mysterious health problems could be connected. Henry thinks there's a link, but I'm not so sure.

It took a few months, but eventually my symptoms went away too. Living back at my childhood home with my father ushering me to see Dr. Diehl and preparing my meals, I began to feel better physically. Emotionally, mentally, I was tortured, but I regained my balance, hot became hot once again, and words stopped echoing in my head.

Arlo's mentioned our health problems in his podcast, but I wonder how much outsiders know about it.

From my nest in a wicker chair on our sun porch, I dig my phone from the pocket of my cardigan. I open a private browser and pull up the Reddit thread about the Flock.

I scroll until I find a post—by DetroitDoll, of course—about the sickness.

Health problems were abundant among Flock members. Some have called them "mysterious," but I can put the puzzle pieces together. Many members were anxious and depressed about their former lives before living at the Bird Haven. These mental health issues affected their sleep, which exacerbated body pains and affected their memory. Dominic was helping them overcome their anxiety and depression, which would have solved the rest.

His theory accounts for some of the symptoms we had, but not everything. I don't think sleep loss would have made Lollie feel like ants were biting her all over. I think there was more to it than that, but I'm still unsure that it was connected to the deaths.

I click on DetroitDoll's profile. A list of all of his posts and comments appears. My eyes flick over the words, trying to find any indication of his source of information.

After reading the posts, I'd wondered if DetroitDoll *was* Dom, until I saw his hefty frame and sagging cheeks in person. When I visited the antiques shop, DetroitDoll said he'd found Dom. He wanted me to believe that's where he's getting his insider knowledge. But now that I've met DetroitDoll, I can't imagine Dom confiding in him. He always favored younger, more malleable people. Even though DetroitDoll clearly worships Dom, I have a hard time believing Dom would come out of hiding for him. If he's still alive, that is.

So where's DetroitDoll getting his information? I scour his posts, looking for a clue pointing to the person he thinks is Dom.

I rule out any users spreading misinformation, but several pages in, there's a post that catches my attention.

Laurel's kidnapping and murder was a catalyst for what happened to the Flock, but it's unsolved. Who killed her and why? I know police wouldn't point a finger at a rich white guy, but did they even look into the connection between Laurel and the county medical examiner Grant Hollis? They were seen meeting up at Arbor State regularly in the weeks before her kidnapping. He's a mortician. He'd know how to cover up evidence.

I read it several times, and each time it sends a fresh wave of prickly doubt up my spine. I knew Lollie had seen my dad once. On her last night, she returned to our shed with news that my mom was in hospice. She urged me to see her, to say goodbye, and I refused. I guess I never thought about it too deeply, but I assumed that was a one-time meeting. I never would have thought that Lollie had been seen with my dad on campus multiple times before she was taken.

The accusation that my dad was involved in Lollie's death is ridiculous, of course—the intruder said my name, after all. I would have recognized my own father's voice and build, even in the dark. He didn't take Lollie. But why did he meet up with her? Who saw them together?

I click on the user's profile. DontLookDown. There are only a handful of comments and no identifying information. No other mentions of Lollie or my father. But this is clearly someone who knows something.

Henry's words echo in my head. Is he right—did my dad influence my recovery because he didn't want me to reveal something to the wrong person?

Midday sun pours into the room. I'm too hot in my sweater, but I don't mind. I gaze out the window into the yard. I'm no closer to finding the person who DetroitDoll believes is Dom, but now I have even more questions.

How well did my father know Lollie before he performed her autopsy?

*   *   *

By four o'clock, my neck aches from scrolling the discussion board for hours. I'd planned to go to the grocery store in Lapeer to get chicken and fresh vegetables for dinner, but now Henry will be home before I have time to make it there. I jam a hat over my unwashed hair and hurry to the local store down the street.

Lollie's face greets me at the door. The automatic doors open and close and Lollie toys with me, sliding back and forth in a game of hide-and-seek. Her vigil is coming up in a few days. Finally, I step into the store and pluck a spare flyer off the bulletin board, folding it in half and tucking it under my arm as I turn and hurry back to my car.

When I'm safely locked inside, I unfold the flyer and study it. Her picture catches me by surprise, and my chest tightens and my pulse quickens. But when I expect to see her, I feel nothing but gaping emptiness, like my heart's been removed because it can't hurt for her anymore.

I open a voice app on my phone—something Henry installed to ward off telemarketers—and am grateful my name and number are concealed when I dial the number on the flyer. I wait only two rings for Diane Tai to answer. She's slightly breathless, but I don't remember if that's the way she always sounds.

"Mrs. Tai," I say, "I'm calling because I think you should cancel Laurel's memorial vigil."

A sharp intake of breath. "Who is this?"

"I'm . . . I'm just a concerned citizen. It's too dangerous to have this vigil now. After that so-called prank downtown yesterday . . ." I trail off. "It's not safe, Mrs. Tai."

"Why? Are you planning to do something?"

"No, of course not. It's just, with the podcast and all the publicity and now those birds downtown . . . It's not safe," I repeat.

"I'm not going to live in fear. If my daughter's killer wants to make himself known at her vigil, then I welcome it."

I glance at the screen of my phone. She's ended the call.

The parking lot is filling up. The slow but steady stream of dinnertime stragglers convinces me to give up on chicken and vegetables. I'll pick up fast food on my way home.

When I glance in the rearview mirror, I catch sight of deep frown lines etched into my forehead. They're not from yet another unpleasant chat with Lollie's mother, not exactly.

It's that barking, definitive way she talked to me. Just as Lollie used to describe it. As I talked to her mother, I traveled back in time. Became teenage Lollie, back when she was still known as Laurel. Before Dom and the Bird Haven.

With just a few words from Diane Tai in her authoritative tone, I felt hopelessness and frustration bubble in my chest.

I spent years distancing myself from the narrative about my upbringing that I built while with the Flock. Dismantling the false story I told myself about my past to justify the way we lived there. Now I worry that Lollie's wasn't a false story after all, and it sends me into a spiral of doubt.

Because while I was in the Flock, Dom worked hard to help me repaint my personal history. I was a disappointment, my parents uncaring, cruel, and capitalistic.

My therapist stripped down his lies until I was no longer a failure, my parents no longer villains. But what if Dr. Diehl didn't have my best interests in mind but my father's? What if he had something to hide and me regaining my memories would put him at risk?

What if my father is hiding a dark secret after all?

24

Dominic

Then

I SPEND A SLEEPLESS night pacing my room. The damn fox screamed for hours, setting my nerves on edge. With every howl, the need to find Lollie became more urgent.

There are two possibilities: she chose to leave, or she was forced to leave.

If she chose to leave the Flock, where would she go? Certainly not back to her family. Daisy made sure of that when she defected; her bitter spite served only to sever Lollie's ties with her family with a satisfying finality.

And what about Daisy? Would Lollie have turned to her to help her leave? Sure, they were best friends here once, but all that changed when Daisy decided to betray me while Lollie stayed loyal. Girls don't rebuild burnt bridges so easily.

Who's the man Claire saw in the shed that night? Plenty of people have stayed a few days or months at the Bird Haven before deciding enlightenment wasn't for them. They trudged back to their small, predictable lives and myopic dreams. I took them under my wing, so to speak, but they resisted the opportunity to fly to new levels of awakening, to be timelessly free. Could one of those disillusioned men have returned for Lollie?

If Claire's right, though, she was taken. The thought sends me into a light-headed feeling of unreality. With a clenched heart and jittery hands, I breathe, trying to elevate myself to a place of knowing instead of feeling. I try to bypass the noise in my head, the roiling in my gut, that tells me that Lollie was taken by an evil outsider intent on provoking the demise of the Flock.

All that attention from winning the Apple Queen pageant: it'll be my downfall. Without it, no one would look for her if she's truly missing. But now she's in the public eye. She'll be expected to be places, shake hands, kiss babies—whatever it is pageant girls do.

I shake out a handful of pills that help me focus. There's a rattle in the bottle; I'll need someone to go into town for a refill soon. Lollie's job.

I spill the contents of her tote bag on my bed and rifle through them. The dress smells like the essence of Lollie. Intoxicating, citrusy. The same heady scent she left on my sheets night after night after she arrived here.

Her flip phone is wiped clean, with no indication of where she may be. In her purse, there's makeup, a hairbrush, and breath mints I never saw her use. There are tampons and little packets of towelettes. A nail file, some loose ibuprofen, and my rabbit's foot key chain with keys to the vans.

A business card bears the name and phone number of a woman named April Davies. I study it. I'll track her down to see if she can lead me to Lollie, but chances are she's related to the pageant in some way. This woman may come looking for Lollie before I can find her.

There's an uncashed check made out to her. I set it aside, wondering if I can have Goldie use Lollie's ID and deposit it into my account.

A zippered pouch is stuffed with cash. A few hundred dollars. It's a decent amount of money for a girl without a job. I toss the bills on my desk.

The cash is needed. While the land is owned by my family and the bills go through my parents—they believe they're funding a wayward sensitive son as he lives "off the grid" but not a dozen plus of his followers—I still need money to feed everyone. At first, money flowed from the older recruits and financed the Flock. They sold their cars, stocks, even homes to be here. It's been more than a year since they died, and now funds are running dry. Now it'll get even worse without Lollie around to fundraise from drunk, potbellied men at the bars in town.

There's no way Lollie would choose to leave without this money, but its presence tells me she was readying to go somewhere.

Yes, the money proves she was taken. Our reckoning is coming.

* * *

It's Goldie's raised voice that finally rouses me from my room. She's standing within the fenced perimeter of the vegetable garden with dirty knees and hands on hips, shrieking at Eden.

Eden's on the porch. Her jowly cheeks flap as she trades insults with Goldie across the yard. With so little food, I thought she'd have lost some weight by now.

"Dom, thank God." She's breathless. "Goldie's just, like, investing her energy in doubt and fear right now. I'm choosing courage and faith, like you'd want, Dom."

I put my hand on her neck and caress her curls reassuringly. She's got a sticky yearning to please, and though it's what I want from the Flock, it's more grating than satisfying coming from Eden.

"What's this about?" I ask.

Goldie flings a zucchini at one of the twins and stomps from the garden. She's tiny but fierce. After Lollie, I thought Raina was my biggest problem, but maybe I was wrong and it's Goldie.

"Something's happened to Lollie. She's still missing. And fucking Eden here can't get her damn head out of your ass for two seconds to see something's wrong," she snaps.

Missing. If they think she's been taken, the situation will spiral quickly.

"Dom said there's nothing to worry about," Eden retorts.

Did I say that? I remember reassuring them that the screaming fox wasn't Lollie being tortured in the woods, but even I don't know it wasn't.

I scan the grounds. Claire isn't among the others; she must be holed up in the shed again. Jock and Hunter have stopped stacking firewood to stare. A hammer dangles from Helena's hand as she waits to affix a birdhouse to a post, watching. Lido and Sunny eye us wearily from a clearing where they practice yoga. The twins shield their eyes from the sun as they watch from the hammocks. Even Morgan, expressionless and aloof, tracks Goldie as she approaches me with fire in her eyes.

I expect Goldie to pound on my chest with her little fists, but she stops just short of me, panting. Her breath is rank, her skin a sickly jaundice yellow.

"Gather, everyone, please," I say magnanimously, widening my arms.

They settle on the wooden porch, some opting for the chairs or steps, others leaning against posts or perched on window frames. The day is sunny, and the birdcalls are loud. A perfect September morning.

"There's something you should know," I begin. I affect a silvery, gentle tone. I pour sorrow into my eyes and meet each person's gaze. I feel Goldie's fire extinguish.

"Out here, where we live quiet and free, I'm teaching you to renounce the chase. I'm helping you rid yourself of pride so you can become pure and humble. With my guidance, you're freeing yourself of want and desire. It's in this unclouded state of surrender that we'll blissfully move beyond to a timeless and eternal world without limits," I say.

The black mood that settled over some of their faces has morphed into something dreamy. I thought it'd be harder to romanticize death, to make them *yearn* for it, but it's all in the language you use. *Transcend, immortal, infinite*: these are the words that glamorize something that shouldn't appeal to twenty-somethings. I chisel away at the secrecy of death, remove the taboo. Make it ever present so they underestimate the gravity of what I'm leading them toward.

"I sense you're worried about Lollie, and rightfully so. In a misguided moment of pride and superiority, Lollie submitted herself to judgment of the vainest kind: she entered a beauty queen pageant. And Lollie, as you all know, is a beautiful soul despite these misgivings, and others saw that too. She won the pageant."

The Flock exchanges surprised chuckles and smiles. Pride in their own, even as I'm lecturing against egotism. I harden my voice as I continue.

"Lollie was taken from the safety of the Bird Haven by an evil outsider. I'm trying to channel her astral being, but we're not vibrating on the same plane. I fear the worst," I say, looking around at the Flock's ashen faces. Smiles wiped clean. "Unfortunately, Lollie didn't recognize the power of her desires. She manifested this and, in doing so, has put us all in danger. Just as she was targeted, we're now being hunted."

"How could Lollie do this to us? She's betrayed us all," Eden says. Always first, always loudest.

I raise a hand to my chest and take a few stumbling steps, as if overtaken by a radiating pain. The Flock quiets again.

I sit, lowering my head into my hands. "I take responsibility. I saw the signs of her betrayal, but I didn't stop her," I say. "At our honesty circle, Lollie told us all she felt sick. Her symptoms were a sign of disloyalty. Had she put her faith and loyalty in me and the Flock and not her own prideful vanity, she wouldn't have been taken. We'd be safe. Let this be a warning to you: now, more than ever, is the time to commit to me."

* * *

When the Flock breaks hours later, I'm ravenous. The pantry houses little more than bags of rice and crackers. I rarely leave the grounds, but there's nothing here that will satiate me.

A side effect of the medication, I'm sure of it. It tamps down the ghostly pain I used to feel in my limbs and keeps hallucinations at bay, but it leaves me starving and nauseated. It hardly matters; the rattle in the bottle tells me it's almost empty, but the pharmacy won't refill it for another three weeks. I've never been good at pacing myself.

Rabbit-foot key chain in hand, I slid into a pair of old men's work boots sitting in the hallway. The banjo still rests where I set it, its broken strings a mocking reminder of the Flock's lack of respect.

Outside, I start down the path to the mailbox, knowing that Lollie left one of the vans on the roadside for her escape but never got to set her plan into motion. It's less than two days since Claire said she was taken, but I'm no closer to finding out what happened to her.

I think of the business card in her purse. April Davies. When I go into town for food, perhaps I'll stop at the library to use one of their computers to look up where she lives. It won't be hard to find; Iola's too small to care about privacy.

Amid a plague of attention seekers and social and political unrest, isolating myself out here was the best decision I've made. Relocating from the chaotic world into the wilderness was freeing. Yet sometimes I miss the amenities of life outside. Internet, for one.

I can't help but think of how many more people I could reach with my message if I succumbed to social media. It's counter to what I teach, yes, but it's teeming with vulnerable people greedy for reassurance that they can change their lives while remaining lazy.

But the physical solitude of the Bird Haven is so important; it breeds dependence. Out here, I give my followers a dream and I measure their trust, commitment, and reliance. I adjust for what resonates. Could I do that on the internet? I could gradually build intensity, but how would I gauge their loyalty? I could reach more people and perfectly control my image. But without all-night orations, drugged resurrections, psychic healings, mind readings, and gradual, disabling sickness, could I secure their obedience? The best leaders know you need to isolate and make your voice ever present if you want total power.

The van starts right up, and the dash tells me there's a full tank of gas. It's even been backed up so it's facing the exit on the narrow gravel road. Yes, Lollie was planning to escape that night. I'm sure of it.

I hit the gas pedal, feeling vindicated in knowing that I'll use the money she squirreled away for myself today. After all I gave her for two years, I'm stunned she'd go behind my back like this. What's worse, her departure—intentional or not—has fractured the Flock.

I grip the steering wheel harder as anger overtakes me. The van bumps over a rut, and I hit my head on the ceiling. I release a primal scream, not unlike that ungodly fox's shrieks that bounced around my head all night.

My mind drills through the Flock's words after I told them about Lollie this afternoon.

Why didn't you see this in one of your visions?

Why aren't you doing anything to find her?

If you know everything, why don't you know where she is?

Questioning me. Second-guessing me at every turn.

I take a sharp left onto the pavement. The tires squeal as I peal away from the Bird Haven.

Looking wild-haired and shell-shocked, Claire ambled out of the shed as the others flung accusations and doubt. In a daze, she claimed she slept through it, and in the next breath she said it was too dark to see the man's identity. The Flock tore into her until her stories got more convoluted.

This morning I saw Claire as a liability, but now I see her as an opportunity. As the Flock villainizes her, batters her self-image even further, I'll step in. She arrived bruised but not broken, a ghost of a girl with little personality. I largely ignored her for the summer, not seeing her full potential. But now, as Lollie's disappearance threatens to undo her, I'll pour myself into the fractures of her mind so she's fully under my influence.

That's all there is to it: pluck someone from a turbulent situation, give them intense validation that they're separate, special, and watch them adore you. Their logic turns off and your power increases.

I'll mold her into what I need to survive the end of the Flock.

25

Claire

Now

IT'S ONE OF those fall days you dream about when summer drags on too long. Sunny, with a light breeze and just a hint of freshly mown grass hovering in the air.

Students stream down the walkways, and I match their pace, hurrying down the tree-studded path.

Designated as an arboretum, the campus is classically beautiful, with restored redbrick buildings, a performance hall too large for the university's two thousand students, and a scenic mountain biking trail skirting the perimeter.

Wilkins Hall, however, doesn't have the charm of the other buildings on campus. It's squat, gray, and windowless. It's hidden behind a dining hall, at the farthest point from where Henry and Cecily Lofton have their offices.

There's no smoke or ash, and few know it, but there's a crematorium built into the building.

In addition to his job as the Blair County medical examiner, my father teaches mortuary science courses here. He agreed to meet me during his break between advanced embalming theory and principles and practices of cremation.

He doesn't meet me in the lab, which is as sterile as the one in his examiner's office. Jam-packed with stainless-steel equipment and tables intended to hold bodies, the lab is designed for hands-on experience with mortuary tasks.

Instead, today, he ushers me to a room designed to look like a funeral parlor. I sit in an overstuffed blue chair at a laminate wood table beside a wall showcasing basic and premium casket options. To my right, there's a display of urns: glass and metal, bronze and marble.

"What's this about, Claire?" he asks as he takes a seat. "I don't have much time today."

It's always been this way. Dead bodies, work, his students: they all come first.

"How well did you know my friend Laurel before she died?"

My father sighs, but his posture stays erect. He's used to having difficult conversations in this room, even if it's just role-playing with students learning funeral service counseling.

"Someone saw you with her on campus before she died. More than once," I say. "Tell me the truth."

"I met with Laurel several times, yes. She approached me here in the lab. She told me where you were and that you needed money. I gave her some cash on more than one occasion."

I drum my fingers on the tabletop. There's a large binder of memorial programs and prayer cards beside my elbow. The thought of students, barely adults, learning to gracefully guide families through their worst moments isn't comforting; it sets me on edge. I lean back in my chair.

"You gave money to the Flock?" I ask.

"No, I wasn't financing a cult, Claire. I gave money to Laurel thinking it would be used to help you girls leave. I realized my mistake when I saw her dress."

"Her dress?"

He smiles ruefully. "Her pageant gown, the one she wore when she was named the Apple Queen at the fall festival. I knew

I'd been had when I saw her on the front page of the newspaper in that new red dress."

The newspaper ran a grainy photo, but it didn't diminish her radiance in that silky red gown with her hair loose around her shoulders.

"On his podcast, Arlo asked you if you knew Laurel before she died. You said no. He asked if it was a conflict of interest that you performed her autopsy. You said no," I emphasize, tapping the table. "If this gets out . . . Dad, this could look really bad for you. You were meeting regularly with a girl who was murdered. You were giving her money. People won't think it was used for a pageant dress. They'll suspect the worst—that you were paying her to keep quiet about something."

I pause and look up. Waiting. Leaving an opening, just in case.

"I answered your question, Claire," my father says, meeting my gaze. "Now, if there's nothing else, I have a busy day." He sets his hands on the table, ready to push away.

"Yeah, there is something else. What do you remember about the early deaths, the people you performed the autopsies on?"

"I thought we already talked about this."

"Well, you said you'd have Pamela pull their records in case Arlo asked about it on his podcast," I say.

He nods. "Yes, and I reviewed the files. Their manners of deaths were determined to be inconclusive."

"Inconclusive? All of them?"

There were five. A couple, two elderly women, and a widowed man.

"Yes, Claire," he says firmly, with the pedantic tone that was the soundtrack to my teenage years. "I don't have time to rehash this. I have a class at three and a body to autopsy. On top of that, I'm testifying in a trial in a few days, and I need to prepare."

He stands and smooths his suit. Behind him, an open casket reveals a plush pink lining. I follow him into the dim, low-ceilinged hallway and out into the bright afternoon sun. He retreats back into the darkness of Wilkins Hall, leaving me to wander campus.

This time I walk slowly, thinking. My father's words about a trial echo in my head.

He performs an autopsy anytime the cause of death is suspicious or unknown. It's not uncommon for him to testify to a victim's manner of death. He doesn't work for prosecutors; he works for the government. It's up to a jury to accept his opinion, but his testimony could sway a verdict.

I'm certain that Lollie's abductor meant to take me. What if the intruder targeted me because of something my father did or said?

26

Dominic

Then

WHEN I RETURN to the Bird Haven after bingeing at a drive-in diner, there's a small blue sedan with a dent in its bumper parked at the gate to the private drive.

My hackles rise as I get out of the van to inspect it. Oversize sunglasses sit in the center console, an adapter cord dangles from a port in the dash, and an air freshener advertising the local radio station hangs from the mirror.

I can't see through the trees, but I know a woman drives this vehicle, and she's on foot now. I slip a key into the lock on the gate and get back into the van. Branches whip at the windows as I drive fast down the narrow lane.

Though I expect to see someone milling around, nosing into windows and knocking on doors, the clearing is empty. I park outside the garage and jog to the cottage, feeling my lunch of beef Manhattan and mashed potatoes sloshing in my gut.

Inside, Raina naps, oblivious as my rabbit sniffs her fingertips. It crawls beside her arm, nose twitching, and she grunts in her sleep. Whoever's arrived at the Bird Haven, she's not in the cottage.

I catch the sound of laughter in the air, far away and unpredictable. I strain to listen, but I've had hearing problems for years. My mother thought I was just an irritable kid, and it took years before anyone diagnosed me with mild hearing loss. A slew of audiologists prescribed hearing aids, each one better quality than the last, but they sit in the cases at my parents' home in Forest Hills.

The Flock must be down by the lake. I kick off the old work boots, letting them land with a thud beside Raina, amused when even that doesn't make her stir. I take off through the weedy grass on foot. The path is well-worn, and before long the deep indigo of the lake appears through the trees.

I see the intruder immediately. She's young, with long, dark hair and olive skin. She's stunning. I think of the business card in Lollie's purse. Is this April Davies?

"Dom! Dom, you're here," Sunny calls, waving from the water. "Meet the newest member of the Flock!"

Rooted to my perch on the path, I let this girl come to me. On delicate toes, she maneuvers rocks on the shoreline. Her calves glisten with water, and her nose is shiny with sweat. With disappointment, I spot a beauty mark on her nose as she approaches.

"I've heard so much about you, Dom," she says. She laughs, and it's a gentle, upper-class tinkling sound, full of warmth. "I'm Cecily."

I hold her hands in mine and gaze into her eyes. That laugh again. This time, discomfort edges it. I stare longer, drinking her in. She's not April Davies, no. Why would a girl like this come here?

You don't have to be broken to want to be part of a group, but it's usually the disenchanted, overwhelmed, and gullible who make their way to me. It's a win-win: these lost souls are more likely to have pasts they want to hide, making it easy to blackmail them with their own secrets, and they rarely have anything to return to on the outside, making it less likely for them to leave or resist. It's hard to entice desirable people to join a group of broken misfits. Without Lollie to recruit girls with looks or money, what's Cecily doing here?

"You're interested in becoming a member of my Flock?"

She nods, offering an easy smile. Her teeth don't bear the briny film that so many of the girls here have grown accustomed to.

"Yeah. I've heard a lot about what you're doing here, and I think it's really wonderful."

"What are we doing here?"

She laughs again, but this time it's more of a surprised grunt. Her poise leaches out of her the longer I stare.

"You know, just this, this simple life of found family and spirituality, and um . . ." She glances behind her, looking for reassurance in the Flock. "And, um, transcendence and purity. Oh! And, um, awakening."

The beef Manhattan from Julian's turns over in my stomach. She's using my words. Instinctively, I know she's not to be trusted.

"How did you hear about us?"

Cecily's smile falters. With a curious tilt of my head, I wait. Did Lollie meet her before she was taken? Does she know someone in the Flock? Is the public talking about us?

"Here and there, I guess. I heard a group was living off the land at the old bird sanctuary, and I thought that was really cool. I came to check it out, and everyone told me about you and this, you know, family you've built."

I don't offer a nod or smile. Instead, I let my eyes, catlike in their golden color, bore into Cecily. She lets out an uncomfortable laugh and turns away, tottering down the rocky incline back to the water.

Instead of sensing my displeasure, the Flock surrounds her, the golden, happy stranger. I watch the scene only a moment before I turn away.

They slip further from my grip every day.

* * *

Picking my way through the trees, moving away from the lake and the splash-happy gaiety of the Flock with a new doe-eyed girl to invigorate them, I head to Claire and Lollie's shed.

I know before I pull on the door handle that Claire's inside. She wasn't with the others by the lake; I would have seen her blindingly pale skin beside the late-summer tans.

Inside, it smells more rank than it did just a day ago. For a manic moment, I wonder if Lollie is rotting in here. But the space is too small, and Claire too weak, to conceal a body.

I spent my lunch debating which member of the Flock I can trust the most. Certainly not Raina after her suicide attempt, or fiery Goldie or dead-eyed Morgan. They're all becoming too erratic, unsteady, to be trusted. Of course, Eden's hungry for my approval, but that doesn't instill confidence in me. Too-strong emotions are a liability.

But Claire, she's different.

She's been on my mind all afternoon. I thought I'd need to order the others to stay away from her so the social isolation could feed her growing distress, but she's separated herself from the Flock. I see now she really only stayed here for Lollie, and I need to fill that void if I'm to use her to my advantage. Only days ago I pegged her as weak, a liability. But now I see something else entirely: a quiet tenacity I know will serve me well.

"Claire," I purr. "You're not down by the lake with the others." I sit beside her prone body on the mattress and stroke her back through her dress. Her spine juts out under her translucent skin. "What I know, and what I think you sense as well, is that you're different from the others, and that's why you're not with them now."

At this, she rolls over, squinting in the dim light that filters through the lone window. She hugs a tattered teddy bear to her chest. A relic from her past—something I lecture the Flock about—but I ignore it this time.

"There's something about you, Claire. I see what Lollie saw in you."

There: a dreamy cast in her eyes at the mention of Lollie's name, before the realization she's missing sets in. Lollie is her weakness.

"She told me how special you are and how much she cares about you. She knew you were elevated. In you, she saw what others couldn't see." I rub circles on her back and continue in the same soothing voice my mother used when I was sick as a kid. Interweaving visions of Lollie with love-bombing is a sedative to Claire.

In one breath, I tell her Lollie confessed her love for Claire to me; in the next, I muse that I could see myself starting a family with her. She crawls to a sitting position, and I hold her shoulders and begin to sway her reed-thin body in time with mine. Rhythmic and reassuring, I drip longing and loyalty into her. She's spellbound.

When I'm done, I know she trusts me implicitly. And I know I can trust her for what needs to be done next.

*   *   *

As dusk falls, the girls trot out bowls of spaghetti topped with watery marinara. The portions are meager, but the Flock slurps it greedily.

It's far less than I ate for lunch, but seeing them gorge themselves sickens me.

Normally, I take pains to remind them to be thankful for their food, even when there's barely anything on their plates. It's a tactic one of my idols used: distort their perceptions to gain control. But today I remain quiet while I watch them.

Cecily nudges herself between Helena and Sunny at a picnic table in the clearing. She asks about the vegetable garden and how many fish the boys catch each day. She prods about sleeping arrangements, showers, internet access, communication with the outside, leaving the grounds, and past Flock members.

I can't take it. Appearances be damned. I take Eden's bowl from her hands and lift it above my head. Her jaw works like a fish gasping for air as she eyes her dinner.

"Starting immediately, we're going to begin fasting. It's time to cleanse ourselves spiritually. You need to be pure, emotionally, mentally, and physically. This meal is only polluting your body. From now on, we'll only eat food we grow or catch." I tip the bowl and let the noodles slide into a slimy pile on the grass.

"There's an evil entity that's trying to separate us and plant seeds of doubt," I say, avoiding Cecily's raised eyebrow. "Tonight, instead of an honesty circle, you'll come to me one by one. If you want to stay, you'll need to rid yourself of the poisonous, traitorous thoughts that have contaminated our family."

As I turn to retreat to the cabin, I pointedly step in Eden's spaghetti with my bare feet. Once inside, I peer through the window from a distance so the others can't see me. They've tipped their bowls into the grass too. Good. While pasta doesn't cost much, meals for more than a dozen people are draining what's left of my funds. What's better, a fast will leave them suggestible as I figure out how to navigate Lollie's disappearance and what it means for me.

I find my rabbit nosing around the kitchen for crumbs. With him in arm, I settle into the old wooden wheelchair, a relic from an invalid ancestor a century ago. I wait, but it doesn't take long.

Stockpiling secrets to use against others has always been a part of my process, ever since I was a kid biding my time, hiding in nooks around the house, waiting for my sister to reveal gossip to her best friend on the phone or my mother to do something I knew my dad wouldn't like. It's always been about gathering information, however innocuous. I send Vinny to the former houses of new recruits to search their families' garbage for information I can use in readings. I encourage the Flock to spy on each other. The truth is, it's not all that different from a salesman checking his database before he cold-calls you. It's easier to form an intimate connection with a little information. I hoard every detail until they think I'm blessed with otherworldly knowledge.

Hunter's the first to enter the cabin. He sits across from me, knees raised as his hulking body sinks into the faded red couch.

"Tell me every negative thing you've ever said or done," I instruct.

He confesses to swiping vodka from his dad's liquor cabinet, smoking pot in friends' basements, and forcing Goldie to have sex more than once. I tell him the alcohol and drugs at such a young age ruined his brain. He's impulsive and bad at making decisions. I tell him he needs to rely on me because he can't trust his damaged mind.

Jock comes next, and he confesses that he prefers anonymous sex with men. I tell him that while others find his actions shameful, I offer him a safe space full of understanding and love.

Vinny trots in and admits to theft, but it's nothing I've not heard before. A disappointment. Thomas is next, and he's always the confessional I dread the most. Maybe because he's older that the rest, his sins are darker than the others. He wants quiet absolution, so I give it to him.

Lido's disinterest in learning his ancestors' language morphed into shame and isolation. I remind him how much his family looks down on him for the pain he's caused them and that the Flock is his true family. He may be a failure, but I accept him.

The girls follow in a line, presenting themselves one by one for their confession and critique. Helena, Faith, Goldie, Raina. Eden and Sunny. Morgan and the twins. I draw out insecurities and call attention to their flaws. I pry and poke at their vulnerabilities. I play with their soft minds until I can see devotion dance in their eyes.

Claire's different now, of course. She enters the cabin a shivery, thin mess, her eyes puffy with tears. I don't need to break her down any further. I spend her session love-bombing her instead. I flood her with visions of the future and enough validation to patch her fragile self-esteem. I idealize her, and us together. Still, she leaves crying like all the others.

The new girl, Cecily, pokes a hesitant head through the door.

"Do you want me to come in too?" she calls. Her eyes scan the room, barely touching on me.

"Yes, of course. Come in, Cecily." I stroke the rabbit's coarse fur and wait for her to take a seat.

"I'm not really sure what I'm supposed to do. I'm kind of at a loss. Everyone else came out crying, so . . . what's going on in here?" She raises her eyebrows, looking more amused than concerned.

I can see now that this is a lark for her. Why she's here, I still don't know. But in the wake of Lollie's disappearance, her arrival is both suspicious and concerning.

"I just want to talk with you," I say, taking a different tack than with the others. "What do you think of the Bird Haven so far?"

"Oh, it's beautiful," she gushes, leaning forward, elbows on knees. An eager schoolgirl. "Everyone's really kind, and they have nothing but good things to say about you."

I eye her as I dig my fingers in the scruff of the rabbit's neck.

"Huh," I grunt. "You know, Cecily, I don't think you're going to be the right fit for the Flock. You can say your goodbyes, then I'd like you to leave."

She sits back, surprised. She scratches her head with a manicured finger.

"Why—"

"Nothing is real," I interrupt. "Our attachments in life, they're nothing more than projections on a wall. Our time here is fleeting, and we'd like to spend it alone, together."

Her chin tilts upward and her eyes narrow. Appraising. She stands and rubs her palms on her bare thighs, as if wiping away the memory of our couch touching her skin.

"That's a shame. I didn't even have a chance to ask you about Lollie yet."

CHAPTER

27

Claire

Now

THE FERRY DEPARTS from the northern tip of the peninsula shortly after seven in the morning, so I wake and dress before Henry leaves for work. Cecily Lofton texted last night to arrange to meet, and I jumped at the chance.

When I arrive, the ferry is docked in the marina. I park in a nearby grassy lot still blanketed with morning dew.

Across the harbor are small islands that constitute a national park. Home to abandoned copper mines and fisheries, the rocky islands jut from the deep-blue water like mirages.

A few passengers wait on wooden benches on the dock. Cecily is easy to spot in her bright-pink sweater and oversize sunglasses.

She pushes them over her head, into her glossy hair, as she approaches, her heels rapping on the dock. "Thanks for meeting me on such short notice."

"I wouldn't miss the chance to talk to you," I say, self-conscious of my outgrown highlights and ragged cuticles. I jam my hands deeper into my pockets.

Cecily laughs, a light tinkle like a delicate bell. "As a reporter and now a professor, people have said a lot about me through the years, but wanting to talk to me? That's not usually one of them."

Before long, the dock fills with park employees ready to be ferried to work and hikers eager to catch sight of a bald eagle or moose.

A deckhand ushers us onto the ferry. I'm grateful to see that the water's calm. Still, it's easy to feel sick with the constant gentle rocking, so I guide Cecily to a quiet bench on the deck in the cold, fresh air so I can avoid queasiness. I skipped breakfast, and now I'm not sure that was a good idea.

"You're probably wondering why we couldn't just talk on land, like normal people," Cecily says, a smile in her voice. She holds up her phone. "No service, no interruptions."

"No escape," I joke.

"These last few weeks have been crazy with the start of the semester, but I didn't want you to think I forgot about our meeting. I went over all my old notes and articles. You mostly want to talk about Dominic and Laurel, right?"

"Yeah, Dom and Lollie, of course—but all of it, really. There's just so much I don't remember. Some memories have started to come back since Arlo started stirring up the past."

"Right," Cecily says slowly. She looks out to the water as we pass tiny, rocky islets covered in orange lichen. "Judging from the latest episode of his podcast, it sounded like a lot of memories came back to you during your visit to the Bird Haven. Like remembering that the garage door was locked?"

When she returns her gaze to me, her eyes are searching.

"That day—all of it—it was traumatic," I explain.

Cecily watches me for another beat before responding. "I wasn't surprised to hear it. A part of me was waiting for it, I think. It's one thing for Dominic to have influenced the Flock's suicide, but it's another for him to murder them. I just . . . I just feel so guilty about all of it."

My neck snaps toward her. She's hunched against the wind, and her sunglasses have slipped back over her eyes. I want to ask her to take them off so I can better study her face.

"Why would you feel guilty?" I ask as a strange bubble begins in the pit of my stomach. Am I jealous, anxious, scared?

She sighs. "After I got that anonymous tip about Laurel's disappearance, I couldn't just show up at the Bird Haven. I deceived Dominic to get my foot in the door. But he was guarded. Totally suspicious about my motive for being there at that time. So when I broke the news of Laurel's abduction and reported what conditions were like for this cult at the old bird sanctuary, I mean . . . things blew up. Those early articles of mine fueled the media circus around the Flock." Cecily pauses, and when she swallows deliberately, slowly, I recognize that she's seasick. Her face is pallid, and her fists are clenched.

"I think he looked at all of us reporters like an invasion," she continues. "I outed him for his wild conspiracy theories and boasts of divine power. He'd taken pages from the books of famous cult leaders. He was doing it all: isolating, love-bombing, gaslighting, coercing, exploiting . . . the list goes on and on. We ruined everything he was building. We swarmed the Bird Haven, tried to interview the girls. The press angered him. He thought we'd tell lies, but the truth was more than enough. In his own logic, it was an excuse to initiate the extinction he longed for."

The hairs on my arms stand on end. "So you think he planned the deaths all along?"

Cecily considers. "I think there were a couple factors at play, but yeah, I think there was an undercurrent of premeditation all along. There was his draining bank account, and Lollie's kidnapping and murder, of course. But I don't think it was simply a desperate act. I think he always wanted to be famous in this way."

I picture Dom's face aglow in the light of the bonfire, his gaze boring into each of us as he stroked the fur of his wild rabbit. Was he planning our deaths even then?

"Did you . . ."

"What?" Cecily prompts.

"Did you try to interview me?" I ask, feeling pathetic for not remembering the reporters clearly.

"I don't think I did, personally. But yeah, I remember talking to Eden, Goldie, and Helena. Faith too. The guys were close-lipped, though."

Eden's corkscrew curls and Goldie's broken-winged birds. Helena's garden and Faith's demon. Their images flick through my mind like a frantic movie reel.

"Did they say anything about being sick?" I ask, thinking of Helena's newfound stutter, the way Goldie's hair was falling out near the end.

Cecily tilts her head and gazes up and to the left, as if she's watching the girls from the Flock up in the sky. Remembering.

"Yeah, they did, but they were all over the place. I used some of their info in one of my articles about the living conditions at the Bird Haven. I listed a litany of random health problems."

"What about the people who died earlier, before the rest of the Flock? Did the girls say anything about them? Anything about them being sick?"

Beside me, Cecily begins to rock back and forth. She closes her eyes and swallows again. "I don't remember the girls saying much about them, but I thought their deaths would make an interesting sidebar article. I wrote up some profiles, but the *Iola Press* never ran them because all the other deaths happened. It kind of overshadowed them, to be honest. I can dig them up and email you when I get back to my computer."

I thank Cecily and guide her to the railing of the ferry, where, along with another hiker, she retches over the side into the dark water. After, she pats her lipstick-stained mouth with a tissue from her purse.

"I just wish we could correct the narrative. I mean, he got what he wanted. People think Dominic's this charismatic cult leader who persuaded people to kill themselves. But I don't think they willingly died. I think they had no choice. This belief that they just marched blindly into a group suicide—it diminishes them, doesn't it? And it just makes me so mad that Dominic comes out of all this unscathed, really. Like, he got all the power and fame he wanted when he's nothing more than a cowardly killer." She huffs, her breath a white cloud. "There are a lot of unanswered questions, but more than anything, I'd love to know where Dom is now. Every time I see some spiritual guru on Instagram, I wonder if it's him, reinventing himself."

"You think he's alive?" I ask.

"Yeah, of course. I think he had too big an ego to kill himself and not call attention to it. I think he'll resurface one day, because he won't be able to stay quiet. All that cockiness?" She shakes her head, a gentle movement after getting sick. "I always thought that if there'd been a trial, he would have wanted to represent himself."

Yes, I can picture him strutting contemptuously in a courtroom. Peacocking for the jury.

Cecily studies the rugged islets as we pass.

"See over there? That's Cemetery Island," she says, pointing. "It's home to a bunch of mysterious grave sites."

Oh good, I think. More unsolved deaths.

*　*　*

After Cecily and I part ways after our four-hour ferry trip around the lake, I'm anxious to check my podcast subscription feed to see if Arlo has released a new episode of *Birds of a Feather*. It's been a few days since the episode with my interview aired, and I'm unsure how he'll follow it up.

A new episode hasn't posted yet, but my phone pings with an hours-old text from Henry once I'm back in service range. It's terse: Where are you? I need to talk.

With my foot on the gas pedal, I narrowly skirt around the curves of old 26 and screech to sudden stops at the red lights on Depot Street.

Henry is in the kitchen when I get home. He wears a pullover and sweatpants, and I wonder if he went in to work this morning.

Two plates of spaghetti with a side of garlic bread sit on the kitchen table. Tall water glasses leave rings on the table.

"You made lunch," I say.

Normally, I eat a few slices of turkey slapped between bread, with a smear of mustard if I'm feeling industrious. A hot lunch is as unusual as Henry's presence at home, in sweatpants, during the afternoon.

Henry shrugs, growing quiet as he does when he's upset. He pulls back his chair and begins to absently twirl pasta around his fork. I eye him, willing him to make eye contact, to tell me everything's okay. After a minute, I carry my plate to the microwave.

"My mom's in the hospital," he says to my turned back.

I whirl around as the microwave starts to ding. "What? What happened?"

"Her neighbor found her in the elevator this afternoon. They think she had a stroke. I don't know the extent of the damage. I'll drive down to Mission Falls this afternoon," he says, looking down at his cold plate.

"I'll come with," I offer, reaching for my glass. "I'm on leave at the library, so it's no problem."

"No."

I freeze. While I wait for him to speak, I nervously run my fingertip along the glass's rim. There's more, I know it.

"Right now, you, and your past, and this podcast—it's all added stress. I need to focus on my family," he says.

"I'm your family too," I say quietly.

He sets his fork down in a bed of spaghetti. "It's the lies and the sneaking around, Claire. I mean, where were you today? I needed you, and you didn't even text me back for hours. I thought we just talked about how we're partners, how I'm here to help you. That goes both ways. Sometimes I need help too." He sighs. "I'm going out of town for a few days. I'll stay at my mom's house while she's in the hospital. I've already packed."

With a listless tilt of his head, he gestures toward the door, where I see a nylon duffel bag sitting on the plush red rug in the foyer.

Before long, Henry empties his untouched plate into the trash, avoids eye contact while kissing me goodbye, and shuffles out the door.

From the kitchen window, I watch his sedan disappear down Elliot Street with a mix of hopelessness and relief. While I don't want my mother-in-law to have suffered a stroke, a part of me is happy I won't have to answer Henry's questions and return his disapproving gaze for a few days. The rockiness of our marriage these past few weeks is taking its toll on me, even though Henry swore he loves me, that he's my partner, just a few days ago. It doesn't feel that way when he leaves to tend to a family emergency without me.

When Henry's safely out of sight, I rifle through the drawers of his desk to find a notebook. I bring the paper to the heavy worktable in the kitchen as my plate of cold spaghetti lingers nearby. I begin to jot down notes.

Lollie's abductor meant to take me that night. I'm sure of it. I draw two arrows. Could I have been targeted because of my father's testimony at a criminal trial? Or could it be related to something I knew about the mysterious health problems and the early deaths of the Flock, as Henry suggested?

The accusation that my father met with Lollie on campus, giving her money, in the weeks before her abduction niggles in my mind. Could someone have seen them together and assumed *she* was his daughter? It might have been a mistaken identity, but I'd still be responsible for her death, since I didn't offer myself when the intruder said my name.

I need to know more about criminal cases in which my father's testified, I decide. I wish I could use a computer at the library, but I don't want to face Sharon and Lourdes.

My laptop is on the padded bench in the reading nook, its battery long dead. I snake the charger's cord from the outlet beside the toaster to my roost at the worktable in the kitchen. I open a private tab on my computer's internet browser, hoping it'll prevent my tech guru of a husband from knowing my browsing history.

I stand, hunched and anxious, at the worktable for more than two hours. My wrist aches from overuse. I find court transcripts bearing my father's name, but nothing stands out to me.

Looking back at my notebook, I hesitate. Slowly, I draw a line between my two theories. Could they both be right?

Maybe my father was targeted, not for his testimony but for his autopsy work. He was the one to perform the postmortems for the Flock members who died before the mass suicide, after all. What if someone disagreed with his conclusions about their mysterious health problems and cause of death?

Five people. Five inconclusive deaths.

I need to see those autopsy files.

CHAPTER

28

Dominic

Then

CECILY'S PARTING WORDS bury themselves in my gut. I knew she wasn't to be trusted. I spend the night pacing my room, dry-swallowing any sedatives I can find until I realize it's no use. Now's not the time to rest; I need to be sharp, alert. I switch to anything that might stimulate me, but my medication is running low, and the pharmacy won't refill the one I need most until later in the month.

By dawn, my mind feels like a murky swamp of swirling repetitive thoughts. My breathing is so shallow that sometimes I feel as if I'm drowning in the shadowy pit in my head. I gasp as if breaking through the water after a long swim. Reality is so hazy, my heartbeat so slow, I wonder if I'm being held underwater after all. If Lollie returned in the night to show me how it feels to die.

Because she's dead; I know it.

And now, in death, she's my undoing.

The worst part is, I did it all right. I drew from all the influential leaders. I grew my Flock. I gave them a dream. I gradually reformed their minds and offered them a chance to belong to something grand. I studied what Charles Manson, Jim Jones,

Marshall Applewhite, and David Koresh did wrong. I built a foundation to gain money, power, and people without needing to go down in a fiery shootout or board an imaginary spaceship. And yet—and yet. With Lollie gone, so goes any remaining chance I have at becoming one of the exalted leaders I've studied so extensively. As I see it, there's really only one way prove to everyone the power I had over the Flock.

An hour later, my room is bathed in harsh morning sunlight, and I feel only two things: dizzy and sad. Voices from downstairs curl under my door like smoke. Everything is ephemeral. A passing laugh, the fading notes from the piano. The Flock's signs of life vanish as they reach my room.

But one sound breaks through. Razor-sharp and insistent, a series of loud raps at the door rouse me. I struggle to sit. Voices, louder this time, tell me outsiders are here. The wooden stairs creak, and there's a hesitant knock at my door.

"What is it?" I croak. It's nearly inaudible. I try again. "What?"

The door opens and Goldie peers in. "Dom? The police are here. They want to talk to you."

I try to swing my legs over the bed, but my balance is compromised. I can't make it down the stairs.

"Send them up," I demand. Hazily, I wonder if there's anything I should hide before they enter, but the pills are prescription, and besides, they're already melting into my blood and exploding in my head.

Goldie's steps are so light I don't hear them on the stairs, but the police: I hear them coming up. Heels thudding, keys jingling, pants rustling. It all feels like an assault on my senses.

"Hi there. We're from the county sheriff's office. I'm Deputy Lassila, and this is Deputy Aho," the taller officer says as he thumbs a finger at his partner.

Their bodies block the brunt of the sun's severity, but still I shield my eyes and squint to see them better. Lassila has short-cropped gray hair, a moustache, and wire-frame glasses. He wears a dark-brown shirt with a tan tie, a mirror to the other officer, but Lassila's has creases ironed into the sleeves. My mind has trouble focusing. I stare at the creases and wonder if there's anything more pointless in life than ironing clothes.

"We're here because we got a tip about a young woman named Laurel Tai. We understand this is her last known residence. To your knowledge, is Miss Tai here now?" It's Aho who speaks. His eyebrows dwarf his features, and his nose looks like it took a hit in a bar fight. He stuffs his hands in his pockets as he watches me.

"Laurel? Who is Laurel? Who, really, are any of us, but for specks of dust shimmering in the sunlight?"

"Laurel Tai's lived here for two years, so cut the bullshit. We know you know who she is," Aho says. "Where is she?"

"In a universe where there's no end, only space, where is anyone? When is anyone?"

Lassila exhales noisily. "We got a tip that Laurel's missing. What do you know about that?"

"Knowledge is but a distortion of the mind in which minutiae trap us in a sheltered existence," I muse.

"This guy's a nutjob. Hey," Aho says, snapping his fingers in my face. "What are you on, guy?"

"We're not getting anywhere with him," Lassila says. "We'll have better luck talking to everyone downstairs."

"If you did something to that girl, or if you know something about her, it's better to tell us now." Aho's tone is unreadable; I can't tell if it's an opening or a threat.

They ask more questions, spend longer in my room than I'd like. When they leave, I fall into a dreamless, hazy sleep. Fragments of thoughts worm their way through my mind even as I rest. Subconsciously, I know I brought the end even closer to the Flock by talking to the police in my state.

When they talk to the others, they'll know Laurel's been missing for days.

*   *   *

When I wake hours later, the harsh morning sun's weakened, casting shadows in my room. A rank smell beside the bed alerts me to a puddle of puke that must have happened while I slept restlessly. My thoughts are still muddled, but now I feel something more than an empty sadness.

Fury, panic, and pressure built in my body while I slept. My muscles feel taut and painful. My breathing's unsteady, and my hand shakes when I lift a glass to my parched lips.

My memory of the officers' visit is patchy. But even though I didn't retain their words, their intention hangs in the air. It's only a matter of time before the persecution begins, and I'll be at the center.

The other deaths were overlooked, but I won't be so lucky with Lollie. She thrust herself into the public eye, and now they'll look for her. When they don't find her here, they'll turn their attention to me.

Many of the greats faced scrutiny, charges, or lawsuits, but it'll be hard to prove I've done anything illegal. The truth is, you can do some pretty egregious stuff and still avoid prosecution. No one here would accuse me of hurting Lollie, and they couldn't provide evidence anyway. But I can't have police poking around, asking about our living situation, beliefs, or even food supply.

Downstairs, the cabin is empty. I find Vinny napping in the sun while a few of the girls lounge on the porch. Out by the RV, I spot Thomas rooting through a tackle box.

"Gather everyone," I croak to Eden, whose legs are covered in coarse hair and bruises.

"Even Claire?" she asks.

I debate. No, I have to keep her separate from the others. She must know she's different for my plan to work. "Leave her be," I say with a shake of my head.

When the rest of the Flock's assembled on the porch, I spend no time with poetic abstractions. I feel as if I'm coming out of a trance; I need to hear, concretely, what has been said to the police.

"I need to know what each of you said to the police this morning." I place my palms on my thighs to quell the tremors that still overtake them.

A few of them exchange glances. Faith speaks. "We just told them the truth. That someone took her. An outsider."

"Yeah, and we explained that we didn't even know about the whole pageant thing either. We just found out about that," Sunny adds.

"If she was keeping that a secret, who knows what else she wasn't telling us? We don't even really know she was taken. She might have chosen to leave on her own. Maybe whoever 'took' her was someone she'd asked to help her leave," Eden argues.

I think of the pouch stuffed with cash, the uncashed check from the city of Iola, and the van's keys in Lollie's tote bag. Claire's admission that a man took her from the shed while they were sleeping. I know Lollie didn't choose to leave, not like this, but I'm grateful for Eden's devotion. It may be what keeps the police from declaring Lollie a missing person.

"Eden, come on. Dom told us she was taken by an outsider," Helena says.

"Yeah, but Dom, what did you say to the cops?" Goldie asks, cocking her head. "When they came down from your room, they seemed kind of pissed. One of the cops said you were drugged out and talking in circles."

"He called you the Riddler." Vinny smirks.

I dig my nails into my thighs. Fuck the officers. Undermining me in front of my Flock.

"We're on the path to enlightenment. I don't expect close-minded outsiders to understand the words of an upper-density spirit like me."

"They're just looking for some answers so they can find Lollie," Goldie replies.

"They won't find Lollie, but that doesn't bother them. They're comfortable living with doubt, with life's unanswerable questions outside their reach. But that's not you or me.

We're seekers here. We're ascending to an awakening, where all of answers to life's questions will be available to us. We'll soon know what happened to Lollie, because we're elevated."

Jock scrambles to me and begins kissing my feet. I stroke his hair. Perhaps I'll invite him to my room tonight.

"How do you know they won't find Lollie?" Raina asks. Her voice is as flat as her eyes have been since her suicide attempt. "Is she dead?"

"She wouldn't be the first person to die at the Bird Haven," Goldie says. She places a hand on Hunter's knee and turns away from me. "Remember the others?"

Those who have been here longest nod, slowly, almost dreamily. They're sifting through their memories now, trying to conjure the faces of those who died more than a year ago. There were five of them, and they offered little to the Flock but money, which is rapidly drying up.

"They were older people who were sick. This is different. Laurel was taken," Faith says. "It's good you reported her missing, Dom."

"He didn't." Goldie again, brash as always. "The cops said they got an anonymous tip about her."

They did say that, didn't they? I pluck their words from my foggy memory. It must have been Cecily who reported her missing. She's the only outsider who's been in contact with the Flock since Lollie was taken.

"Dominic, there's something you should see," Thomas says from the back of the porch, where he leans against a pillar.

Everyone turns to look at him. I can't remember the last time Thomas spoke up in a group session. He extracts a folded newspaper from the back pocket of his jeans. He unfurls it, glances down, and sighs. His bony shoulders lead the way as he walks toward me. The others part to let him through.

I take the paper but don't look at it.

"What's this?"

"With Lollie gone, I was fundraising in town this morning after the police left. I was, uh, getting some harsher words than I'm used to. I didn't know what was behind all that hate, but then I spotted this on a table at the diner. The *Iola Press* got a tip about Lollie too, and they published it. Third page, below the fold, but still, it's there. I think we're going to face some tough questions now that Lollie's missing," Thomas says. "And, uh, needless to say, I came back empty-handed today. Sorry, boss."

The paper's gripped so tightly in my hands the newsprint has transferred to my fingers already. First a visit from the police, now a newspaper article? Lollie's been missing only three days and already we're being dissected, ridiculed, and reviled.

If Lollie weren't missing, I could kill her.

I straighten, crumbling the grainy picture of Lollie in my hand. It's time to start making the thought of death ever present to trivialize it, to normalize it.

"What I need you all to know, when you think about Lollie or the others, is that their souls are now free to awaken because they're not afraid of death. You're not alive if you live in fear," I say, sweeping my arms grandly into the air. "I see the paths splitting before us. A life of fear, of being hunted. Or ascending into enlightenment with the Flock."

CHAPTER

29

Claire

Now

FRIDAY MORNING'S COPY of the *Iola Press* informed me that my father is scheduled to provide a second day of testimony in a criminal case involving a domestic dispute turned fatal. With him safely confined at the Blair County courthouse, I show up at the medical examiner's office shortly after the doors open to the public.

Pamela whispers on the office phone, tutting at her daughter—something about remedies for a baby's cold—and smiles sheepishly when she realizes I'm hovering nearby. She winks at me as she intones, "Remember: fluids, fluids, fluids!"

She hangs up. "Sorry about that, hon." From the back of her chair, she grabs a fleece vest and zips it over her scrubs. "We keep it so chilly in here, you'd think your father's trying to preserve me," she jokes.

Ah, morgue humor. I force the corners of my mouth upward and return a smile. "Well, it's working. I swear you're aging in reverse, Pamela."

She flaps her hand at me cheerfully. "What can I do for you, dear?"

"My dad wanted me to pick up a few files while he's out of the office. Those autopsies from ten years ago . . . do you have those on hand?"

"What, those cult people? Oh, um—I mean, those, uh, bird . . ."

"The former members of the Flock," I interject when Pamela's cheeks flame red. We're unworthy of respect, even in death, because everyone thinks we were weak and gullible. "He said you pulled the files?"

"Yes, I did, but that was a few weeks ago, before he was on that radio interview, or—what did he call it? I don't remember refiling them yet, so they should still be in his office." She pushes herself to her feet, and her chair rolls out behind her.

"The podcast," I say, already stepping back. "I'll grab them. It's no problem."

Pamela starts down the hallway to follow me, but her phone rings, tethering her to her desk. I follow a series of doors until I'm in the exam room where my father works.

I'm grateful to see the room is empty. His assistant labels samples, updates records, and performs unpleasant tasks like weighing organs to reduce the administrative burden of his work. She's not here now, but she could be nearby, receiving a body at the delivery dock in the back of the building.

My father's computer screen is dark. File folders are jammed into stacked organizer trays beside his mouse pad. I pull them out, careful not to let any loose papers escape. The first two stacks contain files for names I don't recognize, but the third pile catches my eye.

The five files on the top belong to the Flock members who died before the rest: a couple, Anna and David; two older women, Felice and Yvette; and one widowed man, Ian.

There are more files there too. I flip through the folders: Helena Fields, Raina Majel, Thomas van Nuys. Goldie and Eden's files bear their real names: Georgann Mills and Caitlin Aldridge, respectively. They're all here—all fourteen Flock members who died in the garage. My father didn't perform these autopsies, but he has copies from the FBI. Laurel Tai's file folder is mixed into the stack too.

Fingers twitching, I gather all the files and tuck them under my arm. I don't have much time; I have to read through all of the reports before my father realizes the files are missing.

*　　*　　*

With the files spread out on the kitchen table and a steaming mug of coffee warming my hand, I open the first folder. As I begin to orient myself to the format, my phone dings with a notification.

I grab it quickly. It's not Henry; he's still in Mission Falls with his mother. She's suffered a series of ministrokes since he arrived, and he's not sure when he'll come back home.

Instead, it's an alert that a new episode of *Birds of a Feather* has released. I open the episode and hit play.

I spend the length of the twenty-five-minute episode breathless as Arlo recaps the case and what he's uncovered, liberally replaying sound bites of my "revelation" about the locked garage door at the Bird Haven. It's clear that he doesn't have new information this week. He's biding his time, likely planning to record more at Lollie's memorial vigil tomorrow afternoon.

My attention to the podcast wavers, and I've started to sort the autopsy file folders on the table when a new voice interjects, drawing me away from the task. I tap the rewind button three times to capture the last thirty seconds of speech.

"This is a long-term and complex investigation. Our department is continuing a methodical and committed approach to ensure that any person or persons involved in the abduction and murder of Laurel Tai will be held accountable. I cannot speculate on new information, and I ask that the Iola community refrain from doing so as well." The man's voice is measured, patient. The police chief?

"I think that the people of Iola, and the world, deserve to know the truth," Arlo's nasal voice replies. "Claire Kettler confessed that the garage door was locked. That implies the Flock members died by murder, not suicide. Does your department have plans to reinterview her? Don't you think she knows more than she's admitted in the past?"

"I can't talk about what I think. Rather, at the right time, I'll talk about what I know."

Arlo continues to push the officer for an inflammatory remark about me, but he refuses to provide one. Still, I set my mug down when I realize my hands are shaking. The investigation is turning to me again. I need to figure out who killed Lollie before I take the blame for it.

I turn back to the files on the table. As I read through the autopsy files for the early deaths, I reference the series of unpublished profile pieces Cecily emailed to me after we met on the ferry. The articles remind me that these were people, not bodies.

Felice and Yvette were sisters. I didn't know that. Born in France, they were former seamstresses who never married and didn't have any children.

Ian Ward was widowed not once but twice. A ruined financial consultant forced to declare bankruptcy and sell his home, Ian let his money mismanagement drive his only daughter across the country, far away from his embarrassments.

Anna and David were the only married couple living at the Bird Haven. After their son died in a crash during a race at the county speedway, they quit their jobs, sold their home, and took up residence with Dom and the rest of the Flock. Cecily's article doesn't confirm that they gave the proceeds from the sale of their house to Dom, but I suspect that's how he funded the Flock.

While there's still so much about these people I don't know, I know one thing with certainty: they were all as enchanted by Dom as I was. Intuitively, I can sense it by reading between the words in their profile pieces.

They were vulnerable, overwhelmed, and content with separating from past trauma. Just like me.

The world scared them, and they became dependent and dedicated to Dom. Just like me.

The psychological similarities shout at me as I read Cecily's articles. The Flock members, we were all so alike.

There's another similarity too. This one weaves its way through all the autopsy reports: the early deaths, those who died in the garage, and even Lollie.

They all had trace amounts of a neurotoxin in their systems at their time of death.

*   *   *

The kitchen falls into darkness, the laptop emitting the only light by the time I come up for air. I don't understand any more about toxicology than I did a few hours ago, but after reading and rereading the autopsy files, I have a lead: Kat Kiley.

On each file, beside my father's narrow, pointed handwriting and illegible scrawl of a signature, Kat Kiley's name appears. As the medical examiner's assistant, she prepared bodies and transcribed autopsy reports. She worked with my father for a few years before leaving the ME's office.

I need to speak with Kat, I decide. She can explain what the presence of this neurotoxin means, if anything. I'm sure my father has her phone number, but he can't know I am speaking to her, just as he can't know I took his autopsy files home with me.

Without much digging, I find Kat on Facebook. She's divorced, lives in nearby Lapeer, and, judging from her profile picture, has lost her once-effervescent smile. She's a home care nurse now, I glean from her posts.

I hesitate only a moment before typing a message and hitting send. The phone's still in my hand when it buzzes with a response. She agrees to meet me after nine o'clock and sends an address that's closer than I expect—just a few blocks north of Main Street here in Iola.

By eight thirty, I'm so edgy and anxious that I debate walking to meet Kat. Henry's voice echoes through my head with a lecture on safety, so I decide to drive the few blocks. I leave the house first without my keys, then without my jacket. On my third attempt, I fasten my seat belt and let out a shaky breath before starting the engine. I'm not nervous to meet Kat. Rather, I'm jittery with anticipation of what she'll tell me.

I drive below the speed limit, but it still takes me only four minutes to arrive at 932 Forestview Drive. The road is dark, devoid of streetlights, but I spot the smoldering end of a lit cigarette as I leave my vehicle and head up the crumbly walkway to the house.

Kat Kiley waits on the porch, one hand buried deep in the pocket of her sweater while the other lifts the cigarette from her mouth. She turns her face to the moon to exhale smoke.

I recognize her, though she's older now and not as effortlessly pretty as she was when she worked at the medical examiner's office years ago. She wasn't antisocial or obsessed with death then; she simply needed a job, and her unflappable demeanor meant that dead bodies didn't bother her.

"You're probably wondering why I'm here."

"I'm curious why you wouldn't talk to your dad about a case, yeah," Kat says. She inhales from the cigarette once more before stamping it out with the toe of her boot. She gestures to a metal patio chair while she shuffles to an adjacent porch swing.

As I sit in the chair, a chill instantly shocks my legs and travels through my body. The day's warmth disappears so quickly once night arrives in the fall around here. I must cast a longing glance toward the house, because Kat catches my eye.

"I'd invite you in, but it's not my house. I'm a hospice nurse," Kat explains. "Mrs. Perry is nearing her final days, and I'm here to make her comfortable. She's sleeping now, but I'll have to go in to check on her soon."

A memory hurtles through my mind: Lollie sitting me down in our dark shed, birdhouses clanking overhead and mosquitoes feeding on my legs, to tell me my mom was in hospice. Her urging me to say goodbye. Me refusing to leave. Did my mother have a nurse like Kat with her at the end?

"I won't take up much of your time," I say, trying to shake off the memory and focus. "There were a few cases that were marked as an undetermined cause of death, but I think there might be a link between them. It's something I don't understand, and I think you might be able to explain it."

"If I couldn't explain it then, I doubt I can now," she says ruefully. "I hated when we had to put 'Cause of death: Undetermined' into the record. There were so many uncomfortable conversations with family that followed. Those cases are so frustrating. You can really drive yourself crazy."

"Did it happen often—an undetermined cause of death?" I catch myself gnawing on a fingernail and drop my hand to my lap.

"Most of the time, the examination leads to the truth. The office had a good success rate. It used to be that we had fewer than five percent of cases that wound up as unknown cause of death."

"Used to?"

"There was a time when our office had more inconclusive autopsies than usual," Kat says carefully. "I suspect you know that and that's why you're here, right? Otherwise, you'd be talking to your dad."

I purse my lips and study Kat in the shadowy darkness across the porch. Her skin is waxen, her face puffy. She was once so youthful, but now she exudes a solemn, cynical resignation.

"I want to know what you know," I say, hoping it's the right answer to unlock Kat.

She casts her eyes toward the darkened windows of the house and sighs as she digs into her pocket to retrieve her cigarettes. She lights one and puffs for a long moment.

"Dr. Hollis went through a rough patch when your mom was diagnosed, and then you left, and then, of course, your mom died.

He was making some mistakes, and there were rumors of an audit and administrative leave. But between me and some of the mortuary students, we were able to cover a lot of the cases that came in during that time." Kat lets out a hacking cough. "This is Blair County, so it's not like there were big, high-profile murder cases. Most were natural or accidental, or on the worst days, a child with an undiagnosed medical condition. Sometimes the cause of death was unknown, but those were uncommon, for the most part."

I lean back in my chair, reeling. "So my father was performing shoddy work and was going to be fired, so students started to perform autopsies?"

"No, I mean, I wasn't a student then. I was his assistant. Sometimes the students just, you know, helped out. It wasn't a big conspiracy or anything."

"What about some of the people who were in the Flock? Did students perform those inconclusive autopsies?"

"The Flock? What, that cult? No, the FBI did those."

"No, not when they—" I halt as images of their slack mouths, strewn limbs, and ashen skin invade my mind. "The early deaths, the ones who died before the rest." I fumble with my phone, my cold fingers clunky on the touch screen. I pull up a snapshot of an autopsy record and extend my arm to hand my phone to Kat.

"How did you get this?" she asks, squinting at the screen.

"That's Ian Ward's autopsy file. His cause of death was ruled as undetermined, and both you and my father signed the report. Is this someone you or a student autopsied?"

"Claire." She sighs. "This file is dated more than ten years ago. Do you have any idea how many people I've worked on?"

"Can you scroll down to the section that mentions trace amounts of a neurotoxin in his system when he died?"

Kat holds my gaze for a moment before looking down at the screen. She pauses and uses the fingers of her left hand to enlarge the image while the lit cigarette dangles from her right hand.

She clucks her tongue and frowns. She lifts the cigarette to her mouth and lets it hang between her lips as she opens an internet browser and begins to type. I sit on my hands to warm them and watch my breath rise in white puffs as she continues to read from my phone. More scrolling, then she looks up.

"This is a marine neurotoxin, which means that it's found in water. It's basically something that poisons the brain and the nervous system. This particular toxin is related to shellfish harvested during an outbreak of harmful algae blooms. So, when clams or mussels or oysters that contain this toxin are ingested, they can cause extensive illness," Kat explains. "Sometimes it's more gastrointestinal. Think nausea or vomiting. Other times, there are neurological symptoms, like partial paralysis or slurred speech. It's more common in coastal places like Florida or Texas, but it's not unheard of in freshwater, especially if the shellfish were harvested noncommercially." She looks up as she leans forward on the porch swing to return my phone.

"I skimmed a few research articles just now," she continues. "It sounds like cooking and cleaning doesn't kill the toxins, and they're undetectable by taste, so this guy, Ian Ward, he might not have known he was ingesting a poison. He would have felt the effects, but . . . he wouldn't have known what was causing it."

My mind swims. Those rainy afternoons at the Bird Haven, all us girls lying atop one another, moaning of pain and blurry vision and tremors. Our throats were tight, our chests heavy, our ears echoing, our hands tingling.

Could our mysterious health problems have been related to poisonous shellfish?

If my father didn't perform the autopsies himself, or if he failed to see the significance of the neurotoxin in the bodies, could that be the reason he and I, and mistakenly Lollie, were targeted?

Kat keeps talking, but my hearing becomes tunneled. My thoughts are racing.

Who could have wanted to expose my father's mistakes in these death investigations?

30

Dominic

Then

THE CLOUDS GATHER overhead, warning of another rainy afternoon. The wind's growing stronger, whipping Helena and Faith's long hair as they gather vegetables in the garden. The hammocks flap in the wind. Hunter wipes sweat from his forehead as he chops the firewood Vinny gathers. With one eye on the swelling clouds, Hunter hacks at the logs before the impending rain leaves them wet and unusable, leaving us without a warm fire for another night.

Eden wheels my antique chair to the porch, where I survey the work. There's an electricity in the air. Whether it's reflective of the visit from the police, the newspaper article about Lollie's disappearance, or my announcement that end-days are near, I don't know. But those members of the Flock who can work, are; the others lie in heaps inside, moaning about phantom aches and pains that could be cured if only they believed more deeply.

The wind chimes swallow the sound of Thomas's whistle, but I see him wave his arms by the RV to get my attention.

"Boss," he calls across the clearing. "A visitor."

My hearing impairment means I can't hear the crunch of tires on the gravel road leading into the Bird Haven. I nod as if I've been expecting someone, sip lukewarm water from a glass etched with lemons, and hoist myself from the chair slowly.

The wind picks up, taking leaves from the trees in a swirling cyclone. The leaves have started to change, but we won't be here to see the peak of the fall colors.

Trees gather at the edge of the clearing, forming a tunneled walkway to the gravel road. Sure enough, a black pickup truck bumps along the rutted road while branches scratch at its doors. I see the metal gate blocking entry to the Bird Haven is unlatched, the lock hanging uselessly from one side. Did I leave it unfastened when I went to town for lunch?

The truck stops, and a man exits. A patchy beard, smudged glasses, and a generic ball cap: I know this man. I release a breath I didn't know I was holding.

"Dominic," he calls as he strides toward me. "It's been a while, my friend. How've you been?"

"I'm doing fine, Mark. And you?"

His glasses sit too high on his nose. He pushes them up with one finger while straightening his crew-neck sweatshirt over his belly with the other hand. Even at a distance, he carries with him the unmistakable scent of fish.

"Doing okay myself. It's been a good season. Just caught some gems this morning. Splake and lake trout," he says. "Say, you still got your friends living out here with you?"

I offer no more than a nod.

"It's been a while since you've asked for a delivery. Are you using a different harvester for food? 'Cause, you know, I'm open to negotiating if it's about money," Mark says.

"No, I'm not interested. We're doing fine for ourselves."

He casts a glance northward, as if he could see the lake through the trees. "You're not . . . Are you catching your own fish to eat?"

"We have enough for everyone. We're fine," I repeat.

"I told you about the advisory, though, remember? There might be a toxin outbreak on the lake. Whatever you catch, it might be affected, might not. The university's got a team testing the game fish and shellfish. Whether you use me or someone else, I've really got to recommend you get your food from a harvester. Your friends could get pretty sick if they're eating contaminated catches."

Yes. They could get weak, confused, and dependent. They'd need someone to tell them what to do, what to think. They'd be compliant, too sick and too scared to leave—and it'd all be gradual. Subtle and slow, the damage done before anyone realizes. There'd be no stockpile of expensive drugs for law enforcement to trace one day.

The amazing thing, really, about the availability of information is that you can take a creative idea, pinpoint how it failed, and improve on it. Before Jim Jones's followers ever drank the Kool-Aid, he drugged them to make it appear he had divine powers. Aum Shinrikyo used a truth serum to indoctrinate, and psychedelics were a factor in the Manson family crimes. Mind-controlling drugs were indispensable to the greats, but what's even better is an undetectable, slow poison found in nature. Found right outside our door.

I curl my lips into a semblance of a smile. "The girls tend to a magnificent vegetable garden," I say. "Really, we're doing fine."

Mark cranes his neck, this time in the opposite direction, toward the cabin. The trees afford privacy, though, so after a few moments' hesitation, he tips his head in a parting gesture and climbs back into his truck. He begins a slow trek down the narrow road in reverse.

I stop to check on Helena and Faith's progress in the vegetable garden. It's true: this summer's yield has been better than in the past, but it's not enough for us to live on. The girls stack zucchini and tomatoes in a bucket. The cucumber plant looks as if it's rotting.

I haven't made it back to the porch when Thomas's voice calls out again.

"Must've forgotten something, boss."

I turn. Thomas points behind him, toward the road. Has Mark returned to lecture me more?

A caravan of vehicles inches down the road. Trucks and SUVs mostly, but a few sedans are mixed in. The first car drives past me. I bang on the passing window with my fist, and it lurches to a stop. The passenger window slides down.

"Are you the owner?" the arrogant driver calls, leaning across the front seat.

"Yes, and this is private property. You need to leave."

A woman with blond hair at odds with her skin tone opens the driver's door and climbs out. Her ample chest leads the way, and she follows as an afterthought.

"My name is Diane Tai. I'm Laurel's mother. I brought a search party with me to look for my daughter. I've got the Lions Club, the Rotary Club, and everyone else I could get."

"And law enforcement?" I prod, glancing at the parade. No police vehicles in sight.

"They're aware we plan to canvass the area today," Diane says vaguely.

I take this in. If the police aren't here to direct the search effort, they may not even believe she's missing. After they met me coming down from a mess of uppers and downers, they might speculate she left on her own accord: who'd want to stay in the wilderness with a "nutjob," as they called me?

I scratch my neck and cast a backward glance at the Flock. Those who were outside now gather at the edge of the tree line to watch the procession. This is not part of the plan, but can I spin it to the Flock? An invasion? A threat to our safe haven?

"You can search," I concede, "but leave us alone."

Diane sucks in a breath. No doubt she expected to put up a fight. She probably prepared a sound bite for reporters alleging that our refusal to let the search party look for Lollie points to our guilt; now she needs to rewrite her narrative as a victim.

She waddles back to her vehicle and turns off the ignition. One by one, the car doors behind her begin to open, and a flood of searchers gather in the clearing.

They eye the cabin, the RV, the shed, the birdcages. They drink in the details, as they've been instructed to do today. It's been years since the Bird Haven was open to the public. Perhaps a few of the older locals remember hiking to the birding platform or exploring the experimental area where my ancestors cultivated trees and plants not native to the area. It looks much the same as it did back then, but the vegetation is thicker and the birdcages are empty.

The Flock has migrated to the porch, where even the sickest of the girls huddle now, watching the group that's gathered with unabashed curiosity. Even Claire is out of the shed today, staring at Lollie's mother with a mixture of dread and loathing etched on her pale face.

"Okay, everyone," Diane shouts in a nasal voice. "Thanks for volunteering to search for my daughter today. I want everyone to write their name and contact details on this paper before the search begins." She waves a clipboard above her head. "Norman was kind enough to get a map of the area and print copies for everyone. We've separated it into grids."

She hands a sheaf of papers to a woman beside her, who scurries among the volunteers, handing out maps and whistles.

"Go slowly. Look at everything. Walk arm-length apart. Don't touch anything. Take pictures of anything you find. If you see anything suspicious, tag it and use your whistle," Diane instructs.

A man steps forward. "Look up and down. Don't forget about trees and ditches. Are the mine shafts on your property?" he asks, turning to me.

"No, but the only navigable access is through my property."

He turns back to the crowd of volunteers and talks at a quick clip. "We'll need to search there too. Remember, everyone: this is a wilderness area. Be alert and prepared at all times. Keep an eye out for animals and possibly poisonous plants."

"Let's go ahead and split into groups," Diane says. "Laurel's aunt Winnie will man the command post. She has flashlights, extra maps, whistles, phone chargers, a first-aid kit, a crowbar . . . what else?" She glances at a heavyset woman schlepping shopping bags to a folding table someone's erected. "If you need anything, let Winnie know. What I need . . . I need you to find my daughter today. Please."

The volunteers break into groups, armed with supplies, hiking boots, and mouths set in grim lines of determination. The wind picks up, carrying a cold undercurrent that makes the women pull their sporty jackets tighter around their bodies.

Slowly, methodically, the groups scatter from the clearing, leaving only the Flock and Aunt Winnie.

My skin feels like a wound current. I'm agitated, buzzing with fury and violation, as I cross the clearing.

"Do you think they'll find anything, Dom?" Goldie asks as I approach the porch.

"Nothing more than poison ivy and a head cold."

"We don't know where the intruder took her, though. There could be clues," Helena points out.

"Open your eyes, Helena. We're surrounded by intruders. This is not a drill anymore. The outsiders have invaded our camp. Just like I've warned."

"They won't be able to search in the rain," Eden says, pointing to the roiling clouds overhead. "Can you accelerate the storm? Then the evil outsiders will have no choice but to leave."

Right. Weather control, one of my many purported talents.

"Let them search. It doesn't make a difference now. It's almost time to transcend."

*　*　*

The days pass in a sludgy haze. The police come by more than once, officially naming Lollie a missing person. Diane Tai shrieks at us from beyond the locked metal gate daily. The media descend, using telephoto lenses to snap photos through the trees.

The Flock is plagued with sickness. They've lost their balance and the ability to find the right words. They complain of muscle pain, tight throats, and no sleep. They stutter, tremor, hallucinate.

It hardly matters; I've forbidden them to leave the cabin for fear of the eagle-eyed media. Though the disturbance was unexpected, I've woven it into my plan. Isolation, growing paranoia, outside threats—the truth is, the media are helping me strengthen the Flock's ever-increasing dependence on me. It's accelerating; we're hurtling toward the moment I'll become immortal.

The weak blue-gray light of dawn filters through the windows. From the kitchen, where she's simmering a pot of oatmeal, Faith turns up the radio. In the early-morning quiet, the host's voice fills the room:

"This is Holliday Jones on 780 WDBC Talk Radio. I have some sad news to share today. As many of you know, twenty-year-old Laurel Tai, a current resident of Iola and former resident of Estivant, has been missing for two weeks. Laurel was recently crowned the Apple Queen at Iola's fall festival.

"Early reports suggest that this morning, during the annual squirrel count, hikers found Laurel's body near Union River. Police have yet to confirm the news, but a press conference has been scheduled for this afternoon.

"The squirrel count is an annual event in which volunteers scour wooded areas and parks for sightings of the white albino squirrel with hopes of getting an accurate count of the population in Iola . . ."

31

Claire

Now

WHEN MY VISIT with Kat ends, I don't drive the four minutes it takes to get back to my house on Elliot Street. Instead, I find myself plucking a bottle of cheap white wine from the refrigerated case at a convenience store.

Henry's not home to judge me for drinking while I'm supposedly trying to get pregnant, but still I feel guilty when I hand the cashier a ten-dollar bill.

Bottle tucked under my arm, I fumble with my keys at the front door, then find I left it unlocked when I went to meet Kat in my flustered state. I leave my boots on the rug in the foyer, grab a wineglass and my laptop from the kitchen, then pad upstairs in the darkness.

It's nearly midnight when I pour my first glass. I consider texting Henry to ask how his mother is doing but decide against it, feeling superstitious that somehow he'll know I'm still up, drinking in our bed, while he tends to his ailing parent. I down the glass quickly, flush with shame from the disappointment I know Henry would feel if he could see me now.

My mind is whirling. Kat gave me much to think about, but that's not all: Lollie's anniversary vigil begins in sixteen hours. Tomorrow afternoon, the residents of Iola will converge under the covered picnic shelters at City Park to mourn the loss of someone they didn't love enough in life. Remembering her in that silky red dress when she was crowned Apple Queen, they'll all think they owned a part of her. Diane Tai will march between mourners, conveying her indignance that her daughter's murderer was never caught while concealing the reasons Lollie left her home years before she died. Arlo will thrust a microphone in the face of anyone who will talk, and believe me, they will—and they'll talk about me.

I have to go, even if Henry pleaded with me to skip the vigil before he left town. His coat on, his phone in hand, he looked fatalistic as he stood in the doorway and asked me to be safe while he's gone. He worried about another macabre scene, like the carcasses of dead crows strung up overhead on Main Street. I'm worried about that too, but this time it might not be a prank.

But still, it's more suspicious if I don't go. So I drink now, trying to calm my fluttering thoughts.

A refilled glass sits on my bedside table as I boot up my laptop and open a new document to take notes.

What do I know?

The Flock members had a toxin in their bodies when they died, but no one connected the dots because my father didn't perform the autopsies. Kat and other mortuary students from the college did cursory work so he wouldn't lose his job when his mistakes got noticed.

He was in a bad place after my mother was diagnosed with cancer, I know that. But despite what Kat said, I'd never thought my leaving to join Dom's Flock at the Bird Haven ever affected him. I'd thought he was relieved; I'd never thought it'd be a source of stress. But I was only nineteen then.

Maybe someone knew about the shoddy work happening in the medical examiner's office and wanted to spotlight the string of inconclusive autopsies. Could it be someone related to Felice, Yvette, Ian, Anna, or David—the early Flock members who died?

Perhaps someone wanted to draw attention to the Flock so that the media would descend and my father, the medical examiner, would snap out of his stupor and piece together why people were dying at the Bird Haven. What better way to draw my father's attention back to the deaths than to ensure I was dead too?

My mind reels. I down my glass.

If that's true and the intruder meant to take me instead of Lollie to draw my father's attention, then why didn't he let her go when he realized she wasn't me? Why keep her? Why kill her?

She must have recognized her abductor, I realize. I stop typing and reread my notes.

If the intruder was a surviving family member of someone who died early at the Bird Haven, he might have had intimate knowledge of the grounds and how we lived. If he thought the abduction of a young woman would draw a media circus to the Flock and expose the reason for those early deaths—we were slowly being poisoned by toxic shellfish—he was right. But, most likely, he didn't bank on Dom feeling trapped, like he had no choice, as reporters descended.

I need to research all family and close relatives of Felice, Yvette, Ian, Anna, and David. Suddenly, I feel certain that it's all connected: the sickness we suffered, the early deaths, and my father's work.

A thought flutters just out of reach, though.

It's Dom. His paranoia was growing before the damning revelation of Lollie's disappearance broke. After that, most everyone would be dead soon.

Why was he so paranoid? Did he know why we were sick? Did he worry it was only a matter of time before someone figured out what had caused the early deaths?

Did he know about the toxin, and did he exploit its effects to build dependency among his followers?

*   *   *

It's not so much my full bladder that awakens me hours later but my parched mouth. I groggily stumble out of bed and down the hallway to the bathroom, where I guzzle water directly from the faucet. I fish my disposable contacts from my burning eyes and let the bathroom warp into a familiar blur of indistinct shapes. When I sit on the toilet, my head is swimming, and it feels as if the room is tilting. I drank the cheap bottle of white wine faster than anyone should.

I groan and stumble back down the hallway, feeling my way along the outdated wallpaper toward the bedroom. My clothes lie in an abandoned heap on the floor, and pillows are strewn about the room. I stumble as I shrug on a nightgown, the first thing my hand touches in the drawer, and collapse back into the cocoon of the bed.

My thoughts are circling in a drunken loop: theories about Lollie's abduction and our sickness and my father's autopsies clamor for space in my mind, but they're like moths beating at a light. I can't hold on to anything.

The room tilts and I bury my head deeper into the pillow, trying to focus on my breathing. In and out, steady and slow.

It lulls me. I'm drifting from consciousness when I feel Henry's warm body press against mine.

I sink into a comforting memory of lying beside Lollie, the two of us huddled close for warmth even on summer nights when the temperature dropped and reminders of the afternoon sun's heat on my skin seemed unreachable. She'd breathe into my hair, breath tickling my neck, until she fell asleep. Later, of course, it seemed she rarely slept at all.

The memory centers me until the imagined sound of Lollie's breath becomes sharper, shallower. I see the shadow of the intruder in the darkness of the shed. He says my name in his low, flat voice.

Claire.

I open my eyes, hoping to end the memory. The room is shadowy and dark, but it's not the shed at the Bird Haven.

But the short, rapid breaths continue.

I hold my own breath, listening. I'm about to roll over and put my hand on Henry's chest to slow his breathing, calm his nightmare, when it hits me: Henry's not home.

I'm out of bed in an instant. Tripping over my clothes from the day, I stumble from the bedroom and into the hall.

Claire.

He says my name again, and this time I know it's not a dream or a memory.

It's him.

My shoulder knocks into the wall and sends a framed picture crashing to the floor. The blood is pounding in my head so loudly I can't hear if I'm being followed. I stagger into the spare room at the end of the hall and slam the door.

Empty but for a few boxes of Henry's childhood baseball card collection, the room holds no weapons. I cower in the corner farthest from the locked door and try to listen. My blurry vision panics me, so I close my eyes.

At first, I expect a loud eruption as the intruder breaks down the door, but it doesn't come. As the minutes go by, I creep closer to the door, listening for more subtle sounds: the creak of the wood floor in my bedroom, his feet padding on the carpet runner leading down the hall, even the groan of the heavy door that might signal his departure.

The sun comes up, last night's cheap wine clears from my brain, but the jittery terror remains.

It's a stark reminder of the intruder drills Dom staged.

The drills, or night raids, as Dom sometimes called them, were his way of weakening us. In the deepest part of the night, Dom's voice would suddenly ring out, screaming for us to get to safety. We'd huddle together, a sleep-deprived, listless mass, until Dom declared it safe. We didn't know who our enemy was or what they wanted, only that Dom would protect us.

It took years to understand that the drills were just another way Dom controlled us. Disorientation and fear are powerful.

Bare legs cold in my nightgown, I sit shivering for hours. I wish I'd furnished this room with a spare bed like I intended years ago, but Henry argued that it was a waste; soon we'd build a crib and furniture with rounded corners, he reasoned.

But there's no baby. There can never be one, not if Lollie's kidnapper has returned, finally ready to take the right person.

32

Dominic

Then

THE INTRUDER DRILLS were preferrable to this.

I pace my room for hours, locked inside as if I'm a prisoner. I alternate between hot and cold, sweating and shivering, as my body detoxes from medications that have run out.

With the nighttime drills, I was in control. I manipulated the Flock's fear into reliance. But now, in the four days since Lollie's body was found, with bruises ringing her neck indicating she'd been strangled, a media circus has descended on the Bird Haven, and I'm powerless.

It isn't so much the discovery of Lollie's body by Union River that has prompted the spectacle outside but the publication of Cecily's exposé. Claiming to be an "insider" who went undercover as a wannabe Flock member, she was awarded a front-page article in the *Iola Press*. It reads as a day-in-the-life article, including time stamps to detail when we hiked, swam, ate, fucked. It calls out honesty circles as "a manipulative practice used by the false prophet Dominic Bragg to gather blackmail that would make it even more difficult for members of this cult in the wilderness to defect."

Cecily's article was bad enough, but then it unleashed a swarm of new reporters. Representing everything from the tiny local towns all the way up to bigger publications, the media camped out just beyond the locked metal gate and the sign announcing that this is private property.

Yet still the reporters slink through the trees, wade through the water, peep in the windows—anything to catch a look at the Flock. They harass us in the night, knowing I won't call the police for trespassing. Vinny racks the shotgun from the porch, which sends them scurrying, but I also know it adds fodder for their stories.

One reporter, a petite woman with a face so young no one would take her seriously, got ahold of a bullhorn and shouted at us, cycling through the same pedantic questions for hours:

"What do you know about Laurel's killer?"

"Did you kill Laurel?"

"What did you see?"

Thankfully, she's gone now, probably called home to dinner by her mother. Though I can't see the media vans through the trees, I know they're there.

Downstairs, Lido bangs out frantic melodies on the old piano, and in the lulls, the sound of talk radio wafts up to me. They're listening for news about Lollie, her killer, anything that will tell them what to think. I should be there, filling that void for them, but I can't bring myself to go downstairs.

I stay in my room, holed off from the rest of the Flock. My only companion is the wild rabbit Hunter caught grazing in the vegetable garden. Like us, it's not healthy; it leaves a trail of saliva and feces around the room as it hunts for food.

As I watch the rangy rabbit, my mind ricochets between thinking of ways to fight, to silence and intimidate the critics so we can live in peace, and ways to end it all.

I could send the Flock out at night to rattle those who sleep in the news vans. I could leave dead animals lining the road where they park. I could hand-deliver ominous obituaries as a warning to the reporters.

It'd hardly make a difference, though. Our funds are alarmingly low, and the Flock now talks about their looming transcendence with a resigned acceptance. That was my goal, of course: make talk of death so ever present that the Flock assigns otherworldly significance to it while becoming numb to the reality of it.

I try to meditate to clear my mind, but the voices in my head shriek at me. At first, when my medication wore off, the voices were fun to talk to. But then they multiplied, like little lice, burrowing in my mind. I can't keep up with their words. I've taken to sleeping in the closet to keep them away, but it doesn't help.

I fall into crying jags that fade into fitful sleep. I wake, achy and confused, in the closet until the darkness and voices envelop me again. In my lucid moments, I'm furious I've let my rage and the drugs cloud my carefully crafted persona as an enlightened guru. Money, power, people: you can't gain them if you can't control yourself.

Since I researched how to persuade, how to ensure conformity and compliance, there's always been a plan. Once it became clear the Flock wasn't growing enough, I knew I'd need to leave this mess behind and start over as someone new. I was never meant to transcend with the rest of the Flock; my disappearance, the mystery of it all—that's what gives me credibility. If I die here, with the group, I'm not notorious. I'm a pathetic blip in the town paper.

Somewhere out west—Arizona or Colorado, maybe—I could be a new person, build a new following. Elevate myself from this disconnected cabin in the wilderness, surrounded by rank-smelling rejects. No more grassroots efforts to reel in the weak and gullible. I could recruit with the internet, reach people desperate for enlightenment. Trim my hair, dress my lean frame in a slim-fitting, monotone palette, tilt my chin just so—I can become a vessel of fantasy for hungry souls. Think private coaching, subscriptions to spiritual lessons, retreats. There's so much money to be made.

I curl on the closet floor, shaking as the voices hurtle through my mind, and a single thought becomes clear: it's time to leave. I didn't see the way out until the missing piece arrived at the Bird Haven this summer: Claire Hollis. Claire and her connections.

Just as I warned the Flock, I understand through my madness that the end is near.

Only Dominic Bragg's ending is different from theirs.

33

Claire

Now

Flanked by cedars, the shady splendor of City Park is more pronounced than usual when I arrive. The sun won't set for another few hours, but the even the clouds have gathered here to watch the spectacle of Lollie's vigil unfold.

In the ten years since she was taken, strangled, and left by the river, I imagined her killer would have been found, exonerating me in both the public eye and in my mind. Without guilt weighing me down, I'd have the poise, dignity, and wardrobe of a normal thirty-year-old woman.

Either that or I'd have killed myself by now.

Instead, I'm here. My puffy eyelids bear an uneven swipe of eyeliner, evidence of my shaking hand, still trembling from the terror of the intruder last night. I overbrushed my hair until it haloed from my head in a dull nest of frizz. I couldn't decide how much black was appropriate to wear, so I settled on a monotone mix of somber gray layers.

The people of Iola gather below the covered pavilions in the park. At a picnic table, a woman passes out white candlesticks.

I feel an inexplicable wave of disappointment: Lollie would have liked glowing lanterns better.

A group of women passes. They're my age, and I'd probably be friends with them in another life, one where Lollie never existed. Pinned to their jackets are loops of black-and-pink ribbon. "For the loss of a daughter or sister," I hear one woman explain, fingering it as if it were a jewel-studded brooch.

As if on cue, I spot Lollie's mother, younger sister, and stepfather. Diane Tai is stuffed into a double-breasted suit, looking oddly formal in the leafy park. Lollie's little sister looks much older than she did in the photo that hung above our mattress at the Bird Haven. Her hair is shorter than Lollie's, but the slope of her nose and the way she holds her shoulders are the same. I recognize her stepfather from the possessive way he grips Diane's arm. Lollie rarely spoke of him except to say that she was never good enough for him and that he was waiting for anything—like Daisy Shea's revelation that Lollie had joined a cult—to disown her.

Lollie's family shuffles through the matted grass, stopping every few feet to accept condolences from passersby. Even from a distance, I can see Diane's face is hard and hawk-eyed. She's on the alert for trouble after my anonymous call asking her to cancel the vigil.

A hand touches my elbow lightly. I whirl, still shaky from the night before. It's my father, dressed in his weekend-casual chinos and a plaid scarf so crisp I wouldn't be surprised if he ironed it.

"I wondered if you'd come, with all the publicity," he murmurs, nodding his head to the right.

I follow his gaze and see Arlo holding a small microphone, the one that captured my "confession" about the locked door, in front of a rookie police officer. She was probably still toting her dolls on the playground when Lollie died, but I doubt that'll stop her from giving Arlo an interview that casts me in a bad light.

Before I can reply, a shrill voice rises above the murmur of the crowd.

"You!"

My muscles tense. I know the short, pantsuit-clad mother of my dead best friend is approaching before I turn around. I'm surprised to see that her anger is directed at my father.

She's easily a foot shorter than him, but she pokes her finger in the air, pointing at his chest as if getting ready to jab him. "How dare you show your face here?"

My father raises his chin slightly, the epitome of poise in the face of this red-faced woman. "Mrs. Tai, we don't mean any harm . . ."

"Bullshit!" she spews. "Either your daughter's a murderer or she's covering for one. And you're no better, because you concealed any evidence from *my* daughter's autopsy."

A hush falls over the onlookers.

"Claire had nothing to do with the crime against your daughter. And, frankly, I don't appreciate you accusing me of suppressing evidence. We're both very sorry for your loss—"

Mrs. Tai looks at me now. Her eyes glitter with hate. I don't see Lollie in them at all.

"You know who killed my daughter. Tell me," she demands as she takes a step forward. "Tell me."

My father's arm juts between us. He pulls me back and steps between me and Lollie's mother.

Anger thrums from him too. "That's enough." His voice carries a note of no-nonsense, impatient irritation that was so familiar to me as a teenager. "Claire didn't murder your daughter. She doesn't know who did. He was a shadow and a voice to her, nothing more. If she could identify him, she would have. She's been traumatized ever since."

Mrs. Tai steps back. "I knew it," she whispers. "I knew it." Louder this time. She whips her head around, darting her gaze through the crowd of onlookers.

She points to a woman with a phone pointed at us. "Did you get that?"

She spots Arlo. "Are you recording?" She wheels to face me again.

"I knew it," she repeats. "I knew you were lying. You always claimed you slept through Laurel's abduction. You repeated it on the podcast just a few weeks ago. I always knew you were a liar."

I turn on my heel and dodge the onlookers and towering cedars as I run to my car. With shaking hands, I turn the key in the ignition and pray no one's behind me as I reverse, punch down the accelerator, and fling the steering wheel in a squealing turn away from City Park.

It's not until I pass the shuttered Arcadia Cinema, where the row of black birds hung, wings dangling, over Main Street just a week ago, that I realize I'm crying. I turn on Depot Street and pull to a shaky stop on the shoulder of the road. I'll careen off the edge of old 26 and crash into the ridge if I attempt to take on the drive in my unsteady state.

Wiping my eyes, I look around. There's a crop of trees beside a clearing. A sign, battered by the wind and rain, reads *Blair County Speedway*.

Abandoned now, the speedway was a dirt track that closed after a terrible crash that killed four drivers.

Something about the speedway niggles at my mind, so I wait, squinting at the overgrown entrance, until it comes to me:

Just yesterday, as I read Cecily's profiles of the earliest Flock members to pass away, I noticed that Anna and David's son was one of the four who'd died in the fiery crash that closed the speedway. After his death, his parents quit their jobs, sold their home, and moved to the Bird Haven.

What if this is the connection? Anna and David's son, their mysterious health problems, and my father's careless work that never revealed why they died?

I put the car in drive and creep forward into the abandoned speedway.

34

Dominic

Then

"WE PAN OVER the forest, preferably when the leaves start changing color. We splice in images from the lake and the view from the birding platform. Birds flying overhead. People working in the garden, smiling. Stretching in the clearing, also smiling. Let's see, what else?" Jock looks around. Framing his hands, he peers as if looking through a camera lens. "Other wildlife but nothing threatening. Some deer grazing, maybe."

I nod as Jock outlines his vision for a promotional video for the Flock. We walk along the rocky shoreline. It's the first time I've emerged from my room in days.

"I could shoot it with a basic camera," he continues. "We could upload it to YouTube or another social media site. Actually, that gets me thinking: what about not only one video but a whole series?" He waves his arm expansively. "We could interview the Flock for one video. In another, you could give a tour of the Bird Haven. What do you think?"

"I think you have a creative eye, but I'm not interested in mass-marketing the Flock."

"Think of it more like PR, to counteract what's been said in the media," he argues.

He glances over his shoulder, as if he could see the news vans from here.

In the aftermath of Lollie's discovery, the media circus has continued. It's been nearly three weeks since she was taken and our peace was shattered. It's been a siege on not only my mental state but the others' as well. We live in a fearful daze, feeling both hunted and harassed.

"Everyone who's here is someone I've vetted as a higher being who is capable of transcending to the next vibrational plane. Not everyone can be in the Flock."

We step around a downed limb blocking our path. Not far from us, a branch cracks. I strain to hear more, but Jock continues to prattle on about glossy videos to improve our public image.

These woods were a second home to me as a child. A retreat from the bullies and persistent teachers who didn't accept my dyslexia or my hearing impairment and didn't know about the voices that kept me from learning like everyone else. Everywhere I turned, rejection, isolation.

As a teenager, I came here to heal broken birds and preach to the voices in my head atop the birding platform, the only place I felt I had power. I found an article proposing that people with psychosis might just be experiencing a spiritual awakening, and suddenly everything made sense. I read all the social psychology texts I could. I learned how to gain real power, how to use it to my benefit.

College, a menial job: those things were never meant for me. When I decided to move to the Bird Haven and collect other rejects of the community and shower them with as much love and acceptance as they needed, I knew I'd found my calling. A guru, a leader, a messiah—call it what you will. I gave them a home and an ear in exchange for unquestioning loyalty.

Another branch snaps, closer this time. My hearing's not good, but I know animals don't follow humans. My neck swivels and I search the woods.

A moon-round face peers through the brush. Clean-shaven, with a pert nose and a wide forehead, a man steps forward. He wears shiny brown brogues on his feet, a sharp contrast to my bare soles.

He dares to grin as he wields a cell phone in his hand, moving it closer to us.

"Dominic Bragg, Gary Rife for NewsNet. Tell us: Did you kill Laurel Tai?"

"Hey!" Jock shouts, stumbling into the water. Water splashes me, but I don't react. Jock scrambles out of the lake and up the shore toward the reporter. "What the hell do you think you're doing?"

The reporter holds on to a branch to steady himself as he angles his camera phone to capture the scene.

"Do you know who dumped Laurel's body by Union River? Was it someone in the Flock?"

With cherubic cheeks shiny with glee, the reporter turns to me, his phone only inches from my face.

"Why did Laurel die?"

I don't shield my face. I don't lunge for the camera. I don't shriek *No comment!*

No. I straighten, despite Jock clawing at my pants for purchase on the muddy bank. I level my gaze directly into the lens. They'll air this footage on the news tonight. I stand long enough in silence to capture the viewers' attention, to make them glance at their televisions to wonder about the dead air. Finally, I speak.

"You can't die unless you want to."

* * *

Sunny and Helena tack blankets over the windows. The room falls into darkness as I scramble on my knees across the dusty wooden floor. I sit below the blackened window, panting hard.

The reporter's eager eyes flicked from the camera in his hand to me when I spoke. He lowered his phone and didn't bother to tuck it into the pocket of his mud-splattered chinos. He turned and crashed through the woods, no doubt returning to his news van to broadcast the video to the world.

I tried to breathe through it, but my vision tunneled, my hands turned jittery and my neck sweaty with panic as he disappeared from sight. Attacked at my own home.

"Crouch down, everyone. Come on, now. Lay on the floor if you can. They're watching. Speak low or not at all. They're using our words against us. Nothing is safe."

The Flock drops to the ground. Bare legs and arms intersect, and the room reeks of unwashed bodies. Wheezing and breathless, they wait for direction.

"We must close ranks. Don't talk to anyone, not even each other."

One of the twins is mumbling. "The news is looking for clues of abuse. They'll confuse and amuse. We refuse the interviews, but there's no excuse. They'll misconstrue our cues."

"Hey, quiet. They're listening," I hiss. "Make her stop."

"Sorry," her twin says as she covers her sister's mouth with a shaking hand. "She's started talking exclusively in rhyme. Yesterday, she renounced speech altogether. I don't know what's happening."

"What's happening is saddening and maddening. It's baffling how we're abandoning and dismantling—"

"Stop it!" I shriek. I cover my ears. The twins' frantic whispers trigger the voices in my head. The chatter begins.

I smack my head, again and again. Some of the others follow until the only sounds in the room are palms thwacking on skin, the twins' whispered rhymes, and a snotty whimpering coming from Goldie. Thomas breaks his glasses with a blow but continues to smack his head despite a gash on the bridge of his nose.

Eden scrambles to my side to fuss over me, but I push her away. I have to get away from them.

Certain the media is watching through the window despite the blankets the girls hung, I army-crawl across the floor. I grope my way up the stairs. My rabbit's pawing at my bedroom door, making a mewling sound. It yelps when the door bangs into it.

I crawl to my safe space in the closet, but not before I shake my many pill bottles, looking for something, anything, that can quiet the voices in my mind. Below the bed, I locate a rattling bottle. I dry-swallow the contents and let the closet's darkness envelop me.

I sleep. Overtaken by dreams of traitorous doe-eyed monsters and sacrificial baby birds, I sleep fitfully. For an hour or ten minutes, I don't know. I wake in the cramped closet, accustomed now to screaming muscles and disorienting darkness. The refrains of piano music are the only sounds in the house.

It comes back to me: the reporter in the woods, thrusting a camera in my face. Hunting me on my own land. Interrogating me about Lollie, the girl who once enthusiastically recruited pretty wanderers by day and writhed in my bed by night.

But she didn't have the character I thought she had. When did that change? Was it when Daisy left or when Claire arrived?

Claire.

If not for Claire's arrival this summer, would Lollie have dared to bring attention to herself in the Apple Queen pageant?

If Lollie's kidnapping and murder is the catalyst for the Flock's end, how is Claire involved?

I sit up. I've known she's hidden something from me since I found her curled in the shed the morning after Lollie went missing. She lied then, and she's been evasive since. A ghost wandering the grounds, looking for her friend.

She knows something. Something she's dying to keep secret.

How can I find out how she's involved in Lollie's kidnapping and murder?

Then it hits me: I don't have to find out. The thought is like an arrow hurtling through a cloud.

I don't need to know the details. She already thinks I'm clairvoyant. Then I love-bombed her, so she thinks she's special, different. If it's not enough that she wants me to keep her secret, she's ready to fall at my feet anyway.

I crawl to the door and shout downstairs. "Claire! I need Claire!"

Lido's piano playing stops for a merciful moment. Footsteps, then Claire appears at the top of the stairs. She looks as haunted as the voices in my head. In her hand is a worn copy of *1984*.

"Do you want me to read?" she asks.

There's no place in my mind for the dark prophetic tale today. Besides, I've already absorbed its teachings about mind control on the masses. I shake my head and usher her in as the rabbit scurries from my room. At the window, I peer through the curtains, but the trees shield my view of the road.

"Are the reporters still here?"

She nods. "Most have given up on waiting here, but there's one van still parked beyond the gate."

I wonder if it's the same reporter who ambushed me and Jock this morning.

"Do you remember when I said I need your help? It's time. Take a bicycle to town today. Have Thomas check it before you go, but make sure no reporters see you leave. Go the long way, past the mines. Don't let anyone see you," I emphasize, "and be back before dark."

I watch out the window as Claire follows my directions. With hunched shoulders and darting eyes, she wheels an old blue two-speed from the side of the cabin and strains to pedal on the grass as she heads toward an old footpath near the mines.

Not long after, it begins to rain. I sit at the window, peering through a crack in the curtains, for hours. The sky darkens, and there's a brief bout of hail that pelts the roof. The storm clears, but a light patter persists. A swirling wind rocks the chimes hanging from the rafters of the porch.

It's as if all the tension of the last few weeks has become a physical force. Downstairs, it's silent of talk and movement.

It's nightfall when I see a reflector on the bicycle in the distance. With her hair and clothes plastered to her body, Claire returns, pushing the bike through the soggy, puddle-ridden grass.

When I see she's safely back at the Bird Haven, I know tomorrow is the day of reckoning.

35

Claire

Now

THE ABANDONED SPEEDWAY isn't much more than a pit of dirt and a skeleton of open-air bleachers. A few squat buildings are scattered around the grounds: restrooms, concessions, and a lounge for racers.

I remember it from my one and only visit, when I was just a kid. After months of pleading, my father gave in and brought me to a Friday night race, where we managed to get a coveted seat low enough in the grandstand that we were splayed by dirt when the cars raced past. He wore earplugs and sat stiffly, shoulders thrown back, and even as a kid I knew he was counting the minutes until we could leave.

It was loud and dirty and exhilarating then. Now the wind picks up across the open field to form tiny tornadoes of dirt on the old track, and the towering grandstand is in disrepair.

The crash that killed four drivers and shuttered the speedway happened years ago. As my feet crunch on the gravel walkway leading to the track and the wind whips my hair around my neck, I wonder what I expect to find out here.

Somehow I sense that the crash that killed Anna and David's son is related to everything I've been trying to figure out: who killed Lollie, and why did the Flock die?

I'm standing beside the safety fence lining the track, my fingers laced between the chain links, when a car bounces down the road and parks behind mine. I let my hair lash over my eyes without smoothing it away. I watch a man get out of the vehicle and stride purposefully toward the track, toward me.

I know his voice will be low and flat before he speaks.

*　*　*

"Claire."

I knew I'd never forget his voice, after ten years of replaying the breathy way he said my name the night he took Lollie.

And I knew I'd hear his voice again one day. Last night, in my bed, and today, standing before me, his figure shadowy in a windowless room. It's so eerily similar to the night of the abduction that I expect to see Lollie's sleeping form beside me.

But it's just us in the room. I look around. The floor is a concrete slab, and the walls are lined with empty worktables, a large sink, and refrigerated cases that must have held ice cream treats long ago. We're in the building where concessions were once sold.

My head is swimming, and I'm not sure if the man hit me or if I fainted. I feel hot and dizzy. I lift a hand to my head and realize I'm not restrained.

"Do you recognize me?"

Despite my blurry vision, I try to focus on him. His face is boyish, with plump hairless cheeks. His hair is a messy mop of unwashed brown hair. He'd look like any local, rural young man if not for his eyes: the haunting blankness is repellent. He's camouflaged himself in the corners of my life; I know instinctively it's him who's followed me at a distance for years, emerging only now that Arlo's podcast has ignited my desire to find out what happened.

"You killed Lollie."

He rubs a sunburnt cheek. "You still don't know who I am, do you?"

"Anna and David," I croak.

At this, he lifts his chin and exhales. "My parents," he says in his affectless way.

"Your brother died here."

The stiffening of his shoulders tells me he's still sensitive about the crash that ruined his family.

"Your brother died, and your parents couldn't handle normal life anymore," I continue. "They wanted the life Dom offered, and I get it. I did too. With the Flock, we weren't lost and alone anymore. We rewrote our histories. It was simple. It was . . . reassuring."

"It was a cult. Dominic Bragg lured my parents in when they were most vulnerable, took all their money, and let them die."

Slowly, with my back against the wall, I push myself to standing. He's not tall; we're eye to eye. I always thought I'd be scared and submissive when I saw him again, but instead I feel accepting. Strangely empowered. I always knew he meant to kill me. I'm finally facing my fate.

"And then their autopsies didn't give any answers into how or why they died," I say.

"The year they died, the rate of inconclusive autopsy reports in the ME's office jumped from five percent to twenty-eight percent. It was sloppy, reckless work. Your dad was shit at his job, and no one cared. No one cared this crazy cult leader had sick people living in squalor up at the lake either."

The man looks away and sighs. In a flash, my eyes dart around the room, looking for a weapon. Surprising me with an instinct to defend myself. I thought I'd resigned myself to my death in this windowless room.

But he looks back before I can spot anything to help me, let alone move from where I'm pressed against the cinder-block wall.

"I didn't mean to kill the Apple Queen," he says. "I didn't mean to kill anyone. I meant to take you. But I'd seen the girl, Laurel, talking to your dad on campus a few times. I thought she was his daughter. I wanted someone to pay attention. I wanted someone to care that people were sick and dying at the Bird Haven. I thought if I took her, people would look into the conditions there. But she recognized me. She'd seen photos of me from my parents. She fought a lot, and I knew there was no way to get out of it with her alive. And then, of course, everyone killed themselves and that overshadowed everything. Suddenly the media cared about this cult but still didn't care about my parents and why they died. But they also didn't care who killed Laurel anymore. They thought you or Dominic or someone else in the cult killed her, so no one was looking for me."

"But now I know who you are," I say. "So I guess you'll kill me too."

36

Dominic

Then

THE GROUND IS soft under our feet as we gather in the clearing. A fleeting thought crosses my mind—it'd have been nice to build a gazebo here. Thomas could have designed it, while Vinny and Hunter could have taken on the heavy labor. It'd have been the perfect place for honesty circles and adoration bubbles, but it's too late for that now.

The sun shines bright today, as if to make up for yesterday's gloom. It rained through the night, driving even Claire from the shed into the naturalist's cabin for the heaviest part of the storm. That's where she stays now, still sleeping after her late return to the Bird Haven last night.

We link hands to form a circle. Jock's hand is sweaty, while Raina's is cold and clammy. Across from me, Lido looks nervous, but next to him, Sunny is at peace. They don't know why I've gathered them, but they must sense it subconsciously: there's a current of acceptance—resignation?—flowing through the Flock.

"I want you all to know how much I've loved you," I say, raising my voice to be heard above the birds. Even with my poor hearing, I can tell they're louder than usual today. "I've given you a home and an ear, a family and my heart. I've guided you on the path to enlightenment. Despite all I've done, we've been betrayed, and now we're being hunted. We're not going to wait for more violence."

"Yeah!" Vinny cheers.

"We've been terribly betrayed by Lollie," I continue. "Her vanity and her desire for approval led us here, to this day. Now she's dead, and they still won't leave us alone. There's no way the media and the evil outsiders will let us survive. This treasonous behavior, it's put pressure on us. But I believe I've taught you well, and you are all ready to transcend."

"But—what if we leave?" Goldie pipes up. "We could relocate to somewhere the media can't bother us."

Must she challenge me at every turn?

"No, it's too late for that. Once Lollie was found dead, our future on this earth ended. If she hadn't brought attention to herself and our Flock, we might have lived in peace longer."

"What if one of us comes forward to say we did it?" Jock asks. "It'd take the attention off the Flock. Then only one of us would be affected."

I grip his hand harder. "I won't let one person sacrifice themselves for the group. We're a family. We live together, and we die together."

Eden drops Sunny's and Helena's hands to applaud.

"If we can't leave, couldn't we stay and lay low for a while? We shouldn't have to be rushed into our awakening. What if we're not ready?" Goldie presses.

"I'm confident that I've prepared you all to transcend to a higher vibration. I wouldn't have gathered you here today if I didn't know that the bridge to our new journey has formed."

"I just think there's still hope for us to live in peace, here on earth. The media attention for Lollie will die down; it always does," argues Goldie.

"All of our work here—we've been building toward our moment of transcendence. I'm tired of being tormented. I don't want to spend my final days being hunted, harassed. I'm ready for my awakening. You can choose not to join us, Goldie, but the truth is, life will have no meaning for you without me, without the Flock. If you're afraid to transcend, you're not the spiritual warrior I thought you were."

"Goldie, you'll be with me," Hunter says. "Isn't that what we've wanted? To reach pure awakening, together?"

"I just feel like we're letting our enemies defeat us." Goldie's crying now. Tears stream down her cheeks, but she doesn't wipe them away; she maintains the circle, gripping Hunter's and Faith's hands.

"You need to change your perspective, Goldie," Jock says. When he's passionate, his French accent is even stronger. "By transcending, we're winning, not losing."

"Yes, look around," Thomas adds. "I couldn't pick a more beautiful day as my last on earth. Even the birds are trumpeting our arrival to the next spiritual plane."

The group falls silent, as it always does after Thomas speaks.

"It's time. Let go of your burdens, your pain, your disappointments. Release your failures and your sadness," I say, raising my voice. "Today we protest the unfairness of our lives on earth, and look forward to our journey to a higher vibration."

I begin to hum and sway. The Flock joins in. We move as a single being in the clearing, heads tilted to the sky, drinking in the sunlight.

"Hold hands and follow me," I instruct.

Still humming, I lead the Flock to the path. My feet sink into the damp ground. The wind stirs the brush. I stand by the door to the garage. I kiss each Flock member on the forehead as they pass. I tell them not to cry, not to be scared.

Fourteen people file past me into the waiting vans.

CHAPTER

37

Claire

Now

Lollie's killer hasn't threatened me with a gun or a knife, so when he steps forward, instinctively I know his hands will wrap around my neck.

He doesn't lunge. He's slow but forceful. Maybe he senses I've given up already. The intense pressure of his cold, dry hands on my neck is unbearable. I feel as if my head is exploding. A part of me panics and I claw at his wrists, but he's too strong. My arms drop to my sides as weakness takes over. Dizziness steals my vision.

When I close my eyes, I'm floating. I lose touch with reality and swim in emotions. My mother cradles me in her lap. Lollie brushes my hair. Henry holds me in bed. I feel warm and secure.

The pressure around my neck intensifies, my brain screams, and distantly I realize I've lost control of my bladder.

I'm fainting, falling out of consciousness. Was this how Eden felt before she vomited in her curls? Did Goldie and Hunter know they were dying as the carbon monoxide snaked through the window of the van?

Blackness takes over, but I still hear Lollie's killer panting heavily as he grips my neck. Another sound, faint but growing louder, breaks through the slow, buzzing sound in my ears.

The pressure suddenly eases, and I drop to the floor. I gasp for air and try to swallow. I begin to cough but vomit instead. I roll onto my side and, with blurry eyes, see other figures in the building. Someone holds back Lollie's killer while another kneels next to me. My ears are ringing, and I can't hear any words. I throw up again, and my throat burns with pain.

When my eyes begin to focus, I recognize Arlo pacing in the shadows. He's talking to someone, a girl at my side, and I strain to make out the words. *Live stream* and *no internet* break through the ringing.

The girl—she's young, a college student most likely—pulls me into a sitting position and tells me the paramedics are on their way. She's Arlo's intern, she says. I stare at her blankly and raise my eyes as two police offers storm into the building and handcuff Lollie's killer, who's been restrained in the corner by another of Arlo's companions.

Arlo follows them from the building, phone raised high, recording the arrest. A few minutes later, he returns to the dark building. The light let in from the door is fading fast as dusk approaches.

I wipe my mouth with my sleeve and wince as pain courses through my neck with the movement.

"How?" I croak. My throat burns.

Arlo hears me and lowers his phone, fingers still poised above the screen.

"We followed you out of the vigil," he says. "After what your dad said, I finally had proof you've been lying. I knew you knew more than you were letting on. I wanted to know where you'd go. And, honestly, I worried you might hurt yourself after what happened at the park. We followed you and live streamed it on social media. Thousands of people were watching until we lost our internet connection out here. That slowed us down some, but we spotted your car here and wanted to see what you were up to. I didn't think we'd find you seconds away from being strangled to death."

Gingerly, I touch my fingertips to my searing neck and feel my throbbing heartbeat through my skin. I imagine it's raw and red, with bruises already beginning to darken.

"Thank you," I whisper, the effort of it causing pain to shoot through my body.

Arlo pushes his round glasses higher on his nose and snorts. "I should thank you. My subscribers are skyrocketing. I'm up four thousand listeners in the last hour. Everyone wants to hear about you."

*　*　*

The vegetable plants are rotting. Fallen apples from the tree in the backyard harbor maggots. Weeds overpower the wildflowers, and morning glory seeds litter the garden beds.

As September inches into October, the sun loses its warmth. I wear layers as I work in the garden at my father's house. I've neglected my therapy, and it shows.

In the days after the news of Lollie's killer's arrest broke, Sharon offered me my job at the library. She was kind and motherly, but my neck was still tinged with fading purple fingerprints and my ego was bruised too. I told her I wasn't ready.

Instead, I spend my days tending to the garden. I clear weeds and deadhead flowers, winterize and trim woody growth. The plants will mend and grow, unseen, until they bloom again next spring. I won't be here to see them then, but still I lovingly, mindfully, cultivate the life in the garden.

Henry drove from his mother's house in Mission Falls when he heard what had happened to me. He offered the sturdy comfort I needed, but something more too. As he held me and brewed new ideas for our life together—a move to a new house, a new job, a new start—I felt the stirrings of security tinged with adventure. I felt what I'd chased by joining Dom and the Flock: love, acceptance, and answers to my problems.

I felt regret too. I'd failed to see that Henry had offered those things all along; I'd been mired in shame and destructive spirals of guilt for years.

After years of trying to atone for being in the Flock, I feel as if I've used up my apologies. I speak up at the grocery mart when I'm shorted on change, I ask the hairdresser to fix a bad cut, and I inform Henry I don't particularly enjoy cooking dinner. They're small steps, but I start to reclaim an identity, one that voices opinions and stands up for herself.

I've realized that while my father may not have had my best interests in mind when he influenced my therapist and recovery, Henry is not him. He's helped me get set up with online counseling, and now I talk to a therapist as often as I want from the privacy of our breakfast nook. Henry doesn't pry. The relationship is between us alone. We've started exposure therapy to break through the memory barrier so I can begin to heal.

On the couch one evening, while Henry rubs my stockinged feet, expertly kneading my arches, he tells me he understands if I want to hold off on having a baby for now. When I look at him, I see his eyes are focused on the television, where the newscaster reports that the mountain lodge on the lake is now recognized as a dark-sky park. In his trained nonchalance, I recognize, finally, how much a child means to him.

I don't admit to the birth control pills still hidden in the bathroom drawer.

"Let's revisit it after we find a new house," I offer.

For a moment, while the news anchor shifts to a story about a nature conservancy gobbling up acres of forests near the peninsula, I float. Our couch is relocated to a light-filled new build with no history, and a little boy is dropped in Henry's lap. For the first time, I yearn for the future instead of the past.

After the final episode of *Birds of a Feather* aired, I felt different about Iola. The anchor tethering me to this spot on the map lifted, or maybe it just lightened enough for me to start moving again.

To his credit, Arlo explained what had happened to his followers—a ballooning army of thousands of listeners—succinctly and accurately. He described the tactics Dom had used to make us believe, to keep us with him. A scientist shed light on shellfish poisoning, and a psychologist posited that Dom exploited the effects to build dependency among his followers. Lollie's abduction and murder was confirmed to be a case of mistaken identity, and an audio clip from Diane Tai confirmed she'd always known I was to blame for her daughter's death, intentionally or not. Likening the Flock's final days to other famous cults and their demise, Arlo walked his listeners through the media circus that Lollie's death stirred up and the increasing desperation Dom must have felt before he instigated the carbon monoxide poisoning.

Arlo never apologized for calling me a liar, rightly so. But he did clarify that I didn't kill Lollie.

His listeners latched on to my revelation about the locked door, taking to social media to endlessly debate who locked it, when, and why. My name swirls through the comments, invoking both vitriol and pity: a cocktail that reflects anyone who's both a survivor and a victim.

The grief and guilt that settled blackly in my mind years ago haven't dissipated. I'm still to blame for Lollie's death, in more ways than one. We may know who killed her and why the Flock died, but Arlo's podcast didn't answer everything.

Birds of a Feather's followers are left wondering why, out of everyone, I lived, and where is Dominic Bragg?

I'm digging my bare fingers deeper into the dirt, feeling the damp earth envelop me, when I see it in the southernmost corner of the yard. I pick my way through the wilting hostas and daylilies still bearing canary-colored blooms this late in the season. There, atop the dry bed of a birdbath, sits a small metal birdcage. Its door is unlatched and creaks in the light breeze.

My breath catches in my throat as I examine it. With dirt-stained hands, I lift it up and peek at the base. A note is affixed to the bottom. My shaking fingers smear it with filth as I unfold it.

Your sacrifices pale in comparison to the rewards awaiting you. Keep your heart open and womb empty for me. I'll return for you soon.

Arlo's listeners can debate all they want.

Only I know where Dom is now.

EPILOGUE

Claire

Then

M Y FEET SINK into muddy spots pockmarking the clearing. I woke to find the storm last night has moved east, replacing the clouds with clear skies.

In the distance, near the garage, I see movement and hear the staticky sounds of a weak radio signal. Dark hair and a wiry frame tell me it's Dominic. Though the temperature will hover in the high fifties today, he's wearing too many layers. A small battery-powered radio rests in the weedy grass near the garage, blaring a play-by-play of a Tigers game.

With flushed cheeks, he picks a backpack and plastic grocery bag off the ground near the shed as I approach.

"Claire. Thank you for your help yesterday. It's time I leave now."

"Now? Already?"

Dom nods and slides the grocery bag into the crook of his elbow as he winds his long hair into a knot and secures it with the rubber band circling his wrist. On the portable radio, the sportscaster talks impossibly fast as he recounts a double play.

"It's time," he repeats. "You're the only one who knows my new name. When it's time, I'll come back for you."

He runs his knuckles down my cheek slowly, and my head tilts into his touch. I think of the slip of paper I handed him last night on the porch as I dripped from my rainy ride into town. I wonder if he has his new social security number memorized yet, if that paper with my cramped handwriting has been tossed in the lake so no one ever finds it. A dead child's information, swiped from my father's office files, won't be missed.

"I'll be waiting."

Dom picks up the radio and turns up the volume knob until it's ear-achingly loud. I wince, but I know he has hearing problems.

Hands full, he angles his body, jutting a bony hip toward me. "Do me a favor. Lock that door before I go."

I fish the key ring from his pocket. The garage door's closed when I turn the key to lock it.

"Toss the key in the kitchen drawer and leave it there," he says over the noisy baseball game. "And Claire? You look tired. Take a nap, then go for a walk."

I offer a weak smile. It's true: I'm bone-tired. I tuck the keys into my pocket, letting the rabbit's foot dangle.

"Did you hear that? A stolen base." He shakes his head. Over the sound of a ceiling fan in the broadcast booth, the announcer ticks off minutiae on the field.

I pass him on my way back to the cabin. When I'm in the clearing, he begins to stride away, taking the long route through the many acres of the Bird Haven, past the mines. The staticky sound from the radio follows him.

How long until he comes back for me?

I raise my voice and call to his receding figure. "Where are the others?"

Dominic doesn't turn as he passes the giant birdcages, their doors hanging open. Freeing the cages of broken birds. He calls over his shoulder.

"They're gone for now."

ACKNOWLEDGMENTS

Thank you to everyone who helped bring this story from an idea to a published book.

First, I'm grateful to anyone who has braved the storm of a cultlike experience and had the courage to tell their story. While my book is a work of fiction, I hope it captured the complicated, emotional circumstances that can snowball into something beyond one's control.

I'm thankful for the excellent guidance, expert eye, and support of my agent, Amy Moore-Benson.

The insightful feedback from my editor, Terri Bischoff, helped shape this into a more compelling story. Thank you for challenging me to push the characters further.

I'd like to extend my gratitude to the team at Crooked Lane Books, including Thaisheemarie Fantauzzi Pérez, Dulce Botello, Rebecca Nelson, Mia Bertrand, and Mikaela Bender, for bringing this book to life. I'm so grateful for all of your efforts on my behalf.

Thank you to all the readers who picked up a copy of my first novel or joined me at book club events. Your perspectives have been invaluable to me as a writer.

Finally, I owe the biggest thanks to my husband, Darren. I can't tell you how appreciative I am of your support, feedback, and encouragement. Thank you for believing in me.